A voice she could no longer ignore whispered in Jori's head.

He will never settle here. He's from the city and that is where he will return. Jori didn't appreciate that nagging little voice and its cheerless message.

Thing was, she knew it was right.

Dr. Chris Davis was a very handsome man and she enjoyed being with him...more than Jori ever thought possible. But there could be no future for them. She was committed to staying in Mossbank, caring for her father. It was what she'd focused on for months now. And hadn't God directed her home?

"There's nothing out there that I want enough to leave this town," she told Chris. "This is where I belong. It's where I have to be."

"Nothing to make you leave," he murmured, so softly Jori barely caught his words. "I wonder."

Books by Lois Richer

Love Inspired

A Will and a Wedding #8
*Faithfully Yours #15
*A Hopeful Heart #23
*Sweet Charity #32

*Faith, Hope & Charity

LOIS RICHER

credits her love of writing to a childhood spent in a
Sunday school where the King James Version of the
Bible was taught. The majesty and clarity of the language in the Old Testament stories allowed her to create pictures in her own mind while growing up in a tiny
prairie village where everyone strove to make ends
meet. During her school years, she continued to find
great solace in those words and in the church family
that supported her in local speech festivals, Christmas
concerts and little theater productions. Later in college,
her ability with language stood her in good stead as she
majored in linguistics, studied the work of William
Shakespeare and participated in a small drama group.

Today Lois lives in another tiny Canadian town with
her husband, Barry, and two very vocal sons. And still
her belief in a strong, vibrant God who cares more than
we know predominates her life. "My writing," she
says, "allows me to express just a few of the words God
sends bubbling around in my brain. If I convey some of
the wonder and amazement I feel when I think of God
and His love, I've used my words to good effect."

Sweet Charity
Lois Richer

Published by Steeple Hill Books™

STEEPLE HILL BOOKS

Steeple
Hill™

ISBN 0-373-87032-9

SWEET CHARITY

Copyright © 1998 by Lois Richer

Printed in U.S.A.

There is no fear in love; but perfect
love casts out fear.

—*1 John* 4:18

To my sons Cristopher and Joshua

May you always have an abundance of sweet charity with an added helping of patience. You've already got persistence down pat!
Love, Mom

Prologue

Dr. Christopher Davis yanked off his green surgical cap and tossed it onto a nearby chair in his office. "Thanks, Macy," he muttered, taking the cup from the hovering secretary's hand and inhaling the fresh-ground aroma. "Traeger's always did make the best Viennese extradark roast."

"They should," she mumbled. "They charge you an arm and a leg for those beans." She ignored his grin. "You'd better drink it fast. The next one is a toughie."

"You mean the abdominal?" Christopher frowned. "Yes, it's going to be rough."

"Jimmy Jones," Macy reminded him with a frown. "His name is Jimmy."

"Oh, yeah. I forgot." Chris shrugged off the reprimand, knowing she thought him heartless. "I can't help it," he defended himself. "This is the fifth operation this morning. We had to start at five because of the power surge last night. Hey, it's Tuesday, isn't it?"

At Macy's nod he continued, "That means there will be interns watching." His shoulders tightened but he refused to show his discomfort. "They usually like watching these abdominal things."

"They like watching *you* because you explain everything to them," Macy told him, grinning as she thrust a single white sheet under his nose. "By the way, your mother has summoned you to dinner tonight. Seven-thirty sharp!" Macy rolled her eyes. "And this fax came in a short while ago. The cover sheet was marked urgent." Quietly she left, closing the office door softly behind her.

Christopher sank into his leather chair and started reading.

Dear Chris,

Hey, old buddy! I know we haven't heard from each other in a while, although I have heard rave reviews about your work in Boston. Just yesterday I was talking to our old prof and he said you had resigned. Your timing is perfect, Chris, because I really need your help. Jessica's in her third trimester now, but she's having numerous difficulties. We've been advised to get to Loma Linda ASAP.

I'm hoping you'll agree to fill in for me while we are away. I know this place is nothing like the big city, but I'd sure appreciate it if you could take over here for the next little while. With all your experience, I'm sure you could handle everything easily. The only thing is, I have no idea how long we'll be gone.

Please think about it, would you? And let me know immediately. Thanks, pal.

Dan

Chris scanned the letter quickly, noting that a Dr. Green shared the practice. It took several moments of squinting at the notation below to assemble the patterns into something resembling English. Dan, he recalled fondly, had the worst handwriting he'd ever seen. And that was saying something, he mused, even for a GP. Head to one side, he peered at the odd pen scratches once more. He thought it read, "Jori Jessop is my nurse now and if anyone can keep you in line, it's her. Tall, dark and gorgeous. I think you might even enjoy it here!"

Chris snorted. Yeah, right. He'd known a lot of office nurses in his day and he'd never met one that he was remotely interested in.

Still, he mused, it would be a change. He was tired of these hectic days. He'd finally, at age thirty-six, fulfilled his parents' expectations; attained the status they'd always said he would. In fact, Chris mused, he was on top of his game right now.

And bored out of his mind. Wasn't there supposed to be more to life than working day after day in this cold impersonal hospital; more to life than spending endless days and nights in the operating room? Good grief, he couldn't even remember the patients' names anymore! Life had become one long surgical assembly line.

Which was why he'd asked for a leave of absence six weeks ago. Never mind that he hadn't yet had the opportunity to take it. Maybe now was the perfect time.

"Operating Room Four will be ready for you in fifteen minutes, Doctor." Chris's surgical nurse's voice came through the speakerphone.

Life was bound to be pretty slow in—what was it?— Mossbank, North Dakota.

It sounded like just the place to sit and cogitate. Which was probably all there was to do in a farming community that barely appeared on the map.

Clicking on his computer, Chris peered at the letterhead of Dan's office and then faxed a note to his friend via the modem on his desk, grinning all the while.

At least they had faxes in this one-horse town.

"I know you've had a full day, Dan. But could I talk to you? Just for a moment." Nurse Jordanna Jessop stood waiting for her boss to look up from the chart he was reading.

"Of course, Jori. Come on in." He folded the file and laid it aside. "What's up?"

"I need some advice on something and I don't know who else to ask. It's about my future." Jori kept her eyes focused on her hands and tried to stop twisting them. "The thing is, I've sort of been on hold here, these last few years, and now I think it's time for me to make some decisions."

"You're quitting?" Dr. Dan stared. "But I thought you intended to stay here permanently!"

"No, I'm not leaving. I'm settled here now. That's what I want to talk to you about." She took a deep breath and blurted it all out. "I've decided to have a child."

She peered up at him through her lashes, knowing her friend would be shocked. "I was hoping you could advise me on my options."

"Your, er, options? Jori, are you pregnant?" She could see the sad look in his eyes and hastened to correct him.

"No. Of course not. But I'd like to be. Now, as I see it, I have three choices. I can try to adopt, but the government agency I've been corresponding with didn't seem too hopeful about my chances. Especially since I'm single. Still, I'm not giving up yet. Are you listening?"

"Yes, I'm listening." Dan sounded strange, Jori noted, and decided to make this quick.

"There's also something like a five-year wait if I want to adopt a newborn. And a fast, private adoption is very expensive—and risky."

"Oh, Jordanna, I don't think that's what you want." Dan's voice was full of doubt. "Sometimes birth mothers change their minds. I wouldn't want to see you get hurt."

"Yes, I know. There's also the cost. I'd have to deplete what little I have in my savings to pay for a private adoption. That would leave me with almost nothing if something went wrong with the baby."

"Well, as far as I know, that leaves marriage." Dan grinned happily. "Why don't you try that?"

"With whom? There aren't a lot of available men around here," she said, smoothing the skirt on her white uniform. "And I don't want to move because of my father. Besides—" her full lips turned down "—would you want to date Rodney Little or Gary Norton after you'd seen their medical records?"

"I can't say I'd want to date a man at all," Dan teased. "But I do think there's someone you might be interested in. And fortunately for you he's healthy as a horse. Also tall and good-looking."

"You're not going to trot out that replacement doctor that's coming, are you?" Jori groaned with exasperation. "I told you, I don't want to get involved with some pompous, egocentric surgeon who's doing us all a favor just by agreeing to come to little old Mossbank!" She stood in a huff, frustration making her voice rise. "Never mind! I'll deal with this myself. There's got to be some way I can manage."

"Jori." Dan's voice was soft with sympathy. "Jess and I aren't abandoning you. We'll be back. Just keep the faith, honey. Keep waiting on the Lord."

"The Lord helps those who help themselves." And with that, Jori whirled from the room, chagrin wrinkling her forehead.

"There's got to be a way, Lord," she said to herself. "There's just got to be a way."

Chapter One

"Thank you very much, Mrs. Flowerday. Yes, I'm sure the doctor will be thrilled." Swallowing the burble of laughter that threatened her otherwise solemn facade, Jordanna Jessop carefully lifted the plastic container from the older woman's hands.

"It's the least I can do. We're all so happy to have Dr. Dan's friend here. A doctor needs someone to look after him, keeping such busy hours and all." The warm brown eyes were speculative as she looked at Jori. "He's very handsome, isn't he, dear?"

Mrs. Charity Flowerday shivered delicately. "His eyes are the very same color as the Aegean Sea, I'll wager! And when he stands there in that white coat, well!" She twittered. "It's enough to make your heart speed up, isn't it, dear?"

"I hadn't really noticed," Jori murmured, unwilling to discuss the latest addition to the small town. "It's been so busy, you see."

"Yes, I heard your father went into the home. So sad, dear." She patted Jori's hand affectionately. "And on top of that, I imagine it's hard to get used to a new doctor after working with Dr. Dan for this long. And of course, Dr. Chris is from the city and all. Probably needs a good woman to teach him the ropes." She glanced at Jori speculatively.

"Our Dr. Dan knew about country folks, of course. Such a good man," Charity breathed. "And Jessica is the sweetest woman! I've just been praying as hard as I can for that dear baby." A lone tear trickled down her smooth white cheek until she managed to collect herself, the sweet smile curving her lips once more. "Enough chitchat! I'd better be on my way. I'm baking pies today. The church bake sale, you know. I do wish this weather would cool off. Bye!"

As Charity Flowerday hobbled out the door, Jori turned away, shoulders shaking with repressed laughter. If she was any judge of character, and she was, the doctor would be somewhat less than appreciative of this latest goodwill gesture from the town's busiest busybody.

She didn't like the allusion Charity had just made to Dr. Davis's need for a wife. Oh, well! Charity Flowerday, Faith Johnson and Hope Conroy were known for their ability to pair off any single adult who came to the district. That was fine by Jori—as long as they didn't include her in their shenanigans!

With her normally unflappable control in place, Jori strode down the hall to the tiny, dull office that presently housed Christopher Davis, M.D. She tapped gently before entering. "Dr. Davis?"

There wasn't any answer. Instead, the good doctor sat studying a file, totally unaware of her presence. For some reason Jori couldn't explain, she was loath to break his concentration.

She studied her temporary boss and the way his golden blond head was bent over the file, hiding his spectacular velvet blue eyes. Her gaze focused on his tanned features, assessing him the way a photographer had taught her to size up a subject. His face was all angles and hard edges, perfectly sculpted with a wide forehead, jutting cheekbones and beautiful lips.

Yep, Jori decided silently, a real lady-killer. Good thing he wasn't her type. Of course, she had known that the moment Dan introduced them.

Big, bossy and boisterous. Jori had cataloged the newcomer right away. Dr. Christopher Davis was not her kind of man. Not at all.

"Yes, Nurse. What is it?" The interloper's deep gravelly voice demanded her immediate attention.

Jori flushed lightly before thrusting out Charity's plastic-boxed gift. "This is for you," she told him, a smirk tipping up the corners of her pert mouth as he groaned loudly.

"Not another praline cheesecake delight," he begged, holding his rib cage in protest. A tiny smile teased the corner of his mouth. Privately, she decided he would be a whole lot more handsome if he made an effort to smile all the time.

"How many is that now? Eight? Ten?" His eyes twinkled across at her.

It really wasn't any wonder the ladies of Mossbank had been in a flap this past week, Jori decided, almost melting under that blaze of perfectly even white smile.

"I don't know. Entirely too many, that's for sure." For some reason his intense scrutiny made her nervous and Jori fiddled with some papers on his desk, bursting into speech when he got to his feet.

"This one will be delicious, though. Charity Flowerday is an excellent cook. It will also be the richest," she warned. Her eyes skittered away from his and then returned for a closer look. "She loves to double the chocolate in everything."

"Hmm, double chocolate," he teased. "A woman after my own heart. How old is she?" His grin made it obvious he'd overheard at least part of the matchmaking schemes currently going on around town.

She ignored that and continued her silent scrutiny. He was taller than she, which was saying something. At five foot ten, few men ever towered over her. Dr. Davis, on the other hand, was about six foot four and all lean muscle. He had the broad strong shoulders women always swooned over, and a wide chest that could accommodate any female's weary head.

"I don't believe anyone can get too much chocolate," he muttered softly. "But this is definitely way too much cheesecake. Do you think there will be any more?"

"'Fraid so," Jori murmured, shoving aside four other desserts that had arrived earlier that afternoon to make room for the latest addition. "You should never have said Mrs. Belle's was the best praline cheesecake you had ever tasted. It's like you laid down a challenge around here."

"Too bad you couldn't have said something two days ago," Christopher groused, moving to toss one of the less attractive packages into the trash.

"No!" Jori grabbed the thickly muscled forearm, interrupting his attempt at making a basket.

"I wouldn't do that if I were you," she told him seriously, her long fingers tightening as he tried to pull away.

Christopher glanced from her hand on his arm, to her slim body pressed against his desk, to her flushed face.

"Why?" he drawled, obviously curious about her sudden change from quiet, efficient assistant to the disheveled woman who clung to his arm as if her life depended on it.

Jori took the package from him and gently set it on the tabletop once more. "Emery Laser cleans this place every night. His mother is Jasmine Laser." She waited for the light of comprehension, and when it didn't dawn across his frowning countenance, Jori read the tiny card attached to the white carton she had just rescued.

"'To Dr. Davis, for your kind assistance.' Signed," she said, pausing for effect, "'Jasmine Laser.'"

"I take it I would be stepping on toes," he moaned, sinking back into his chair, hands tugging the golden strands of his shining hair into tousled disarray.

"To say the least," Jori told him, glad she'd averted disaster. "Chucking that…mess…would make you an even greater subject of discussion—rather unkind discussion."

"I wish to heck Dan had explained just what I was getting into when he asked for my assistance," Chris snorted, searching for a place to spread out his files.

Dan Gordon had been Mossbank's general practitioner for as long as Jori had been the office nurse. Their working relationship had been a brother-sister one tempered by a lot of friendly bantering. It was something she was beginning to miss with Dr. Christopher Davis. Of course, Dan had been born and raised in a small town and was well used to the unspoken rules that governed the community, unlike his famous, big-city counterpart.

"Look at this place," the new doctor crankily demanded, pointing to the cake boxes of various shapes, sizes and colors scattered on almost every available surface.

"Think of it as proof of your good standing in this community," she told him. "It shows how much you're appreciated. You're lucky they've taken a shine to you."

When a groan of dismay was her only answer, Jori grudgingly picked up three of the earliest arrivals and stuffed them into the vaccine refrigerator that stood in the corner.

"They can't stay there forever, you know," she advised, frowning at his lounging figure. "Sooner or later you're going to have to find a solution to this problem." Jori stared at him curiously, her brown eyes frankly questioning his intent. "What did you do with the rest?"

His blue eyes lit up at that.

"They're safely stored in Dan and Jessica's freezer, just

waiting for the soon-to-be parents to come home." His golden brows drew together in a frown. "Although I'm not sure a new mother should be eating that stuff." His sudden grin made her catch her breath. "I'm not sure anyone should." He chuckled at his own little joke.

"Well, then—" Jori started to suggest that he simply add to his private stash, but his deep voice interrupted her immediately.

"Forget it. It's full."

"Sorry, can't help you then," she told him, moving toward the door.

"Can't or won't?" he asked crankily. His blue eyes widened with a new thought. "Why don't you take one of them home? Surely you and your boyfriend could manage at least one of the blasted things."

Jori turned to stare at him. "I don't have a boyfriend and if I did, the last thing I'd feed him would be Emma Simms's cheesecake. It's like sand."

He squinted at her curiously. "Someone who looks like you doesn't have a boyfriend?" His perfect lips slashed open in a mocking grin. "No dreams of marriage and babies, Nurse Jessop? I thought all women dreamed of Prince Charming and white picket fences."

"Prince Charming was highly overrated," she told him, grimly noting how close he'd come to the mark. "And for your information, I already have a white picket fence. Someday I intend to have a child to share it with." Jori immediately wished she had been able to shut up about that.

One blond eyebrow lifted haughtily.

"A child but no husband. Interesting. And how do you plan on accomplishing that?" he inquired softly.

Jori tilted her head back, her face heating with color. "It's not really your business anyhow. Those cheesecakes *are*." It was rude but she felt compelled to get his focus off her.

He sighed, blinking at the offensive desserts. "Why couldn't they bring roast beef with mashed potatoes and an apple pie?"

Something in the tone of Chris's mournful voice stopped Jori's swift departure. Turning abruptly, her round brown eyes searched his face. "How did you know?"

"Know what?" he asked. His blue eyes surveyed Jori's confusion with a measured glance before she saw enlightenment dawn and berated herself for once more letting her tongue speak too soon. "You are having that tonight, aren't you, Jori?" He inclined his head, his eyes bright as he considered her sulky expression.

"And if there's no boyfriend, there should be lots to share. Am I right?" Bright and eager, his blue eyes dared her to refuse.

Jori exhaled in defeat. There was no point in denying that she'd planned that particular dinner. He would hear about it through the grapevine anyway, since she always made up a tray for Maddy Hopkins. The same local etiquette that demanded he not choose any patient's cooking over another dictated that she invite him for one meal.

Social responsibility. She hated the phrase. With a sigh of frustration Jori accepted her lot. She had orders to be hospitable to Dan's replacement—at least until he returned. She might as well start tonight.

"Six o'clock," she said without preamble and recited her address. "If you're late I'm not waiting."

Turning, Jori strode from the room, frustrated with the situation. She had counted on a quiet evening at home, alone. Time to get her faculties together before she visited her father tomorrow at Sunset Retirement Home. Time to accept that the Alzheimer's had almost taken over and James Jessop would never be the same.

There was no way tonight would be quiet, not with Christopher Davis's loud, booming laugh and even bigger personality. He easily overtook a room, filling it with himself. She had seen it numerous times in the past week. Nobody was immune to his charm, it seemed.

Jori sighed. "I am. I will be."

She had no room in her structured life for anybody like him. If and when she did date, it was always with someone like herself; someone who prized the stable security that life in Mossbank offered. Someone, she told herself, who could see themselves living in the small friendly community in twenty years' time.

Her days of elegant dining and fancy dress were a part of the past and she was glad. She wanted the calm peace that life in her hometown always gave. Acceptance, serenity, tranquility and no surprises.

"There's no way I'm having anything to do with him," she muttered, ignoring her co-worker's amused glance from across the room. Jori snatched the next file up and tossed it into his pickup basket. "Christopher Davis is the exact opposite of what I'm looking for in a husband."

It was highly unlikely that she'd ever get married, Jori assured herself for the third time that week. But if she did, she would opt for a mundane, ordinary trustworthy man who lived in the same small town. They would raise their child in a good, solid home to grow up in and they'd be with James whenever he needed them.

And there wouldn't be any of the disastrous upheavals that had marked her life in the past. She would build a haven, Jori resolved. A place to be who she was without pretense. With her lips set in a determined line, she called out the next patient's name.

No, siree. Dr. Christopher Davis bore just a little too much resemblance to those handsome, pushy, overwhelming men in her past. And look how ugly that had turned out.

It was best to concentrate on building a life for herself here in Mossbank and ignore outsiders. This was her home;

these were her friends. They'd stood by her when no one else would.

Supermodel Jordanna Jessop was no more. But Jori Jessop owed the people of Mossbank a huge debt of gratitude, and she had no intention of reneging on that debt.

"There goes Jori home," Faith Johnson murmured to her friends as she sipped another mouthful of the iced tea she had just made. "Such a beautiful girl, but so withdrawn."

"I don't think she's withdrawn at all," Charity commented, adding another teaspoon of sugar to her glass. "If I'd had to deal with that awful young man—what was his name?" She stopped to think and then shook her head. "Well, anyway, if I suffered through all that terrible publicity because of a man who said he loved me, I would be quiet, too."

"She is very good in the office," Hope murmured thoughtfully. "I think Dr. Davis likes having her there, too. When she's busy with a patient, he's always looking at her."

"I don't know how she can work with a man who looks like that," Charity fluttered her hand in the warm spring air. "He has the looks of that fellow in the movies, what's his name? Tom Hanks?"

"Tom Hanks has dark hair," Hope muttered.

"I know but the clean-cut, handsomely chiseled look is the same, don't you think?" Charity's eyes gleamed with appreciation. "We need a few more good-looking men in this town."

"Jordanna has such lovely hair, don't you think?" Hope tried desperately to steer the subject away from men. "So long and glossy. Why, she can even sit on it!"

"My hair used to be near that color," Charity told them. She frowned when Faith laughed. "Well, it did! But it was so long ago, I expect you've forgotten. I was slim and beautiful, too. Once."

"She's having him over for dinner tonight." Faith's soft voice dropped into the conversation.

"How do you know that?" Charity's eyes widened.

"I happened to hear her tell Dr. Davis to be there at six sharp."

"Oh, my," Charity whispered. "That sounds promising."

"It sounds ridiculous," Hope told her firmly. "Jori's merely being kind. There's nothing *romantic* about it." She sounded scandalized. "They are from two different worlds. He's flamboyant, loud and unruly. She's quiet and reserved. Not at all suited."

Faith chuckled. "You've said that before." She grinned. "And you were just as wrong about me and Arthur as you are about those two." Her head cocked sideways. "I think they'd make a lovely couple. I wonder..." Her voice died away.

"Well, anyway, he's not staying," Hope mused thoughtfully. "Dr. Davis is only here until Dr. Dan and Jessica return with their baby."

"If they return," Faith whispered. "I've been praying so hard for that wee one. Arthur, too. I'm just going to have to let go and trust that God will lay his hand on their lives."

The three ladies sat quietly in the sun pondering the predicament of their beloved doctor and his wife until Christopher Davis roared past in a racy black sports car.

"He'd better slow down," Charity muttered. "This isn't Boston." She glanced at the clouds building in the sky. "I think there's a storm brewing, girls," she murmured at last. "Perhaps we'd better move inside."

"We should have had our tea at my house." Hope chuckled as she lifted the tray of dishes. "Then you two could have listened in to Jori and Dr. Davis while they have dinner next door."

"What a good idea," Charity agreed blithely. "Why

don't you two scurry on over now? It's Arthur's late night at the store and I've got company coming, so you two will be free to eavesdrop all you like.''

Faith frowned. ''I don't eavesdrop,'' she murmured. ''I just try to help out where I...who's coming for dinner, Charity?'' she asked suddenly.

Charity smiled and patted her friend's gray curls.

''Oh, just a friend,'' she told them softly. ''A good friend.''

''But I want to know who it is,'' Faith lamented. ''You've refused to see anyone that Hope and I have lined up for you even though they were all nice men. Take Frank now. He's—''

''You take him,'' Charity blazed in an unusual show of temper. ''I don't want to go out to dinner with Frank Bellows! He's the *undertaker,* for goodness' sake! What would we talk about? My choice in coffins?''

''Charity, there's no need to get so upset,'' Hope said placatingly, her hand cuddling the older woman's arthritic one. ''Your blood pressure is quite high enough. And after all, we're only trying to help.''

''Well, you can help by letting me invite my own men friends for dinner.'' Charity smoothed her skirt in a motion that both her friends recognized meant her feelings were hurt. ''I don't need a man. I'm perfectly happy just the way I am.''

''All right, we won't ask you over to dinner with anyone anymore,'' Hope soothed. ''We'll let her pick her own men friends, won't we, Faith?''

Charity's round face had almost regained its usual sunny gleam when Faith spoke.

''But she never picks any men to be with, Hope. Not ever!'' Faith's voice rose with indignation. ''She's alone in this house all the time. God didn't mean for us to be isolated and alone on this earth.'' She glanced from one to the other, her green eyes finally settling on Charity.

"Don't you want to share your days with someone else? Don't you enjoy having someone to talk to?" Faith's wide smiling mouth was turned down as she studied her friend.

"If I want to talk, I have you two," Charity declared. "And you natter on for so long that a body needs a good rest to recuperate. I like my silence. I like to be peaceful and quiet. It's refreshing."

"Piffle," Faith exclaimed. "It's not normal. God has more in store for us than solitude. You're lonely and you know it."

Ever the peacemaker, Hope stood to her feet gathering her belongings. "Come along, Faith, dear. It's going to rain any moment and I don't want to get my new suit spotted. Thanks for tea, Charity. Enjoy your dinner."

"Whoever it's with," Faith grumbled on her way out the door. She raced back in to grab her purse, her face wreathed in smiles. "Hah! You thought I'd forgotten it, didn't you? Well, I'm far too young for Sunset Retirement Home just yet, Charity Flowerday!" And having gotten the last word in, Faith stumbled down the steps and out into the strong westerly wind.

"I'm sorry, dear," Hope murmured as she watched Charity move awkwardly from the chair. "She doesn't mean to hurt you."

"I know." Charity sighed as she watched Faith throw up her arms and catch the first droplets of rain on her tongue. "Maybe she's right. Maybe I have been hiding out here, missing out on life. Maybe it's time I got involved in what's going on around me."

"What are you going to do?" Hope's blue eyes were full of fear.

"Live," Charity told her matter-of-factly. "Maybe I'll ask Howard to take me out for dinner instead of me cooking." Her brow was furrowed in thought.

"Howard Steele?" Hope gaped. "But he's years younger than you are!"

"I know." Charity preened in the full-length mirror hanging in the hall. "Do you think I should wear my black silk?" She twisted and turned in front of the glass, trying to see herself from all angles.

"Black silk? But...but that's for special occasions," Hope gasped. "Charity, what is going on?"

"I'm freeing myself. I'm going to be more like Faith—open to new experiences." She pushed her waved hair back into a different style. "No, you're right. The black is too old-fashioned. I think I'll go down to Penelope's and see if she has something a little more in style. A nice bright red, maybe."

"You're going to buy a red dress? To wear on a date with Howard Steele?" Hope sounded scandalized. Her face was a picture of dismay as she watched Charity grasp her car keys and purse and walk slowly to the front door.

"Charity," she asked at last, "are you quite all right?"

"I've never felt better in my life." Charity nodded, motioning for Hope to precede her out the door. "A new outfit, a different hairstyle. It's just the change I need."

"But I liked the old you," Hope said with a perplexed frown.

"Don't say that word again," Charity ordered, moving briskly across the lawn. "You are only as old as you feel and today I feel young and hopeful." To herself she hummed the line from a chorus they'd learned in church last week.

"'With God All Things Are Possible'?" Faith looked at Hope. "Why is she singing that?"

"She's going to buy a new dress. And change her hairstyle. She's even going to ask Howard Steele out for dinner."

"Howard Steele?" Faith gasped. "But his wife only just divorced him six years ago. And he's younger than Charity. He's got long hair." She added the last as if that were the final nail in poor Howard's personality coffin.

"I know." Hope started walking briskly down the street, grimacing at the darkened spots of color on her pristine aqua suit as the raindrops plopped onto it in fat round splatters.

"Oh, well," Faith murmured, continuing blithely on with her skipping steps. "At least she's getting out of that house. Since Melanie's marriage, she hardly leaves the place."

"I know," Hope agreed. "But it's Howard Steele she's getting out with!"

"It's not what I had in mind, either," Faith assured her. "But the Lord works in mysterious ways."

"Well, this is certainly very mysterious," Hope agreed grimly. She mounted the steps to her home, griping at the inclement weather as she smoothed her hair. "I just hope she doesn't regret her hasty decision."

Chapter Two

"I love this place, Lord," Jori murmured, a grin tilting the full curve of her lips as she viewed her home with satisfaction, enjoying the riot of flowers that always grew in her rock garden. "Even if Dad can't be here anymore."

She refused to let the sadness ruin her evening. Flop, her cocker spaniel, stood wagging his short, stumpy tail inside the wrought iron gate.

"Hi, boy. Did you have a good day chasing squirrels? You look kind of tired."

The dog always knew when she would be home and his routine never varied. After bestowing an enthusiastic swipe across her face with his pink tongue, Flop padded along behind his mistress as she opened the door and entered the comfortable white bungalow.

"Jori, oh, Jori!" Her neighbor, Hope Conroy, was calling from over the white picket fence that separated their lawns.

"Hi, Hope. How are you?"

"I'm fine, dear, just fine. Am I stopping you from your shower?"

Jori was a little surprised to know that Hope was aware

of her usual custom of showering right after work. She smiled to herself as she realized this was a large part of the reason she'd wanted to move back home. Everyone knew everyone else and cared about them; there was no pretense here.

"Well, I've got time before dinner."

"I hear you're having a guest. Dr. Davis, isn't it?"

Jori didn't bother asking how the woman knew. Nothing was ever a secret in Mossbank. And Hope was Charity Flowerday's best friend. Little wonder!

"Well, yes," she admitted. "He says he's hungry for something other than fast food so I thought I'd share my roast."

"I thought so. You always have roast beef on Thursdays," Hope murmured triumphantly.

"I didn't realize I'd fallen into such a pattern," Jori murmured, disgusted that her life had become an open book.

"Don't worry, dear. I used to do it myself. All single women do. Especially the organized ones and you've always been organized, Jori. I remember you used to have your marbles stored by color and size. So efficient. I imagine you do the same with your bedding, don't you?"

Jori winced at the woman's admiring smile, wondering when she'd become so boring.

"Uh, was there something you wanted to say, Hope?" she asked at last, hoping they could finish their discussion before Mrs. Johnson moseyed over. Jori loved the woman dearly but Faith Johnson had a habit of rearranging a conversation until no one knew exactly what they were discussing. And today was not a day for more confusion.

"Did you ask her yet?" Faith's high clear voice floated over the fence. "Is she really going to do it?"

"Do what?" Jori asked quietly, studying the flush of embarrassment covering Hope's pale cheeks.

"Well, Faith overheard, that is, er, she thought she overheard..." Hope stopped and brushed a wisp of hair out of her eyes. "Oh, this is so embarrassing. I do dislike gossip."

"Just tell me, okay, Hope. I'll try to answer you." Jori patted the perfectly manicured hand gently and watched the even features organize themselves into their usual uncompromising pattern.

"Very well then, I shall." The older woman took a deep breath and then let it all out in one gasp. "Are you really thinking about having a baby, Jordanna? On your own, without benefit of a husband?" Hope sounded shocked and looked scandalized that she'd even said the words.

"I...I..." Jori stopped short as Faith came to lean on the gate that adjoined the two properties.

"See, I told you. Look at her face. She's going to do it," Faith chanted, clapping her hands in excitement. "A new baby! Imagine!"

"Just a minute," Jori protested, trying desperately to get a word in. "I never said I was going to..."

"I overheard you talking with Dr. Davis," Faith admitted and then clapped a hand over her mouth. Her eyes were huge. "He said it was something to do with a test tube." She stared off into the bright green leaves of Jori's maple tree.

Hope shook her silver blond head. "You can't do it, Jordanna. The good Lord meant for children to have two parents to care for them. You of all people should understand how hard it is to have only one parent around when you need help."

For the third time in as many hours, Jori had to hold her tongue so as not to ask these two nosey women to stop discussing her personal life. She drew a deep breath and prayed for help.

"I'm not going to have a baby," she told them clearly, ignoring the relief that swept across Hope's face. "I'm thinking of adopting a child—one that has no home, no parents and no place to go." She bent down to toss Flop's stick across the grass and then straightened.

"I'm twenty-eight, Hope, and I'm not married. I don't think it's likely to happen any time soon, do you? Considering there are so few single men around Mossbank." She loosed the band holding her hair in a braid and threaded her fingers through the long plait.

"Well, I wouldn't exactly say that," Hope murmured flushing coyly. "After all, Faith and I have both been married at a more advanced age than yours."

"God led me back to Mossbank, I believe that. But He hasn't led any men into my path here and I don't intend to go hunting for one," Jori murmured in disgust, grimacing at the thought. "Mossbank is where I belong and where I want to stay. I have everything I need here. If I can help some child who needs a home and a mother, then that's what I'd like to do.

"I'm sorry, but I have to go now. It's almost time for supper. Bye," she called, striding across the lawn and in through her front door.

After her shower, as she pulled on a comfortable pair of ragged blue jeans, Jori told herself her choice of clothing was in deference to the relaxed atmosphere of her home and had nothing to do with the man who was coming for dinner. Her fingers twitched the hem on a frayed and sleeveless chambray shirt as Jori mentally scorned those ladies who worked so hard at dressing up to impress the new doctor.

"Ridiculous," she muttered to herself. "It's not my style at all. Not that I'm interested," she added, glancing down at the decrepit white sandals which left her toes cooling in the summer sun. "I'm quite content with my life alone, except for Dad, of course."

As she combed out her waist-length hair, Jori brooded on her confrontation with Dr. Davis. He was trouble, that was for sure. And why did he make her think of things long forgotten; things she could never have?

Her eyes slid over the plastic-wrapped gowns in her closet. She could still fit into the elegant outfits that had been part of her daily life seven years ago. Not that it mattered. There was little call for haute couture in Mossbank.

"This is the first time I've had a date because someone is interested in my cooking," she told Flop, who woofed his appreciation. "But that's all he's interested in. And don't go fawning over him, either. You're supposed to remain faithful to the one who feeds you."

Flop obviously understood as he licked her hand before picking up his rawhide bone and heading out of the room. Pushing her hair into a clip, Jori bounded down the stairs, Flop padding along behind.

Everything was simmering nicely in the oven. A fresh garden salad would make the meal complete. Leaving the relative cool of her house, Jori slipped off her sandals and walked barefoot into the lush garden. She squeezed her toes in the moist black loam that was her pride and joy.

Sweet peas, fragrant and multicolored had begun blooming and Jori breathed their heady fragrance. Perfect centerpiece, she decided, snipping a handful. She laid these on the bench at the edge of her plot and then moved over to gather some produce. In her pail she carefully placed furled green lettuce leaves, plump red radishes, three tiny cucumbers, a round onion and a wisp of dill. She was about to straighten up when a laughing voice startled her.

"I must say, this is a side of you I have never really seen before," Dr. Davis teased. "Jori Jessop in the dirt."

"You're early," was the best reply Jori could come up with as she blushed profusely and then prayed he wouldn't comment on it.

Dr. Christopher Davis was dressed in a natty white cotton sweater and blue cotton slacks that showed off his blond good looks to perfection.

As if he needed help, she grumbled to herself. Chris Davis was probably the most handsome doctor she had ever seen. That bothered her.

"I hope you didn't dress up just for me," he chuckled, his quick eyes noting her mismatched clothing.

"No, I didn't," she replied brusquely. "We don't dress for dinner in Mossbank."

When he merely laughed, Jori moved skittishly toward the house, pausing only to hose off the soil clinging to her feet. She wanted to get away from his overwhelming presence, but he followed her into the kitchen.

"I'm sorry. I didn't mean to embarrass you, Jori." His lustrous white teeth flashed his wolfish smile at her. "You look very nice, in a down-home kind of way."

"Yeah, right," she murmured, wishing the evening was at an end already.

"Can I help?" he asked, moving his tall, solid body next to hers at the sink.

Somehow, Jori didn't think he meant to soil his well-manicured hands with dirty garden produce so she motioned toward her small dinette set.

"You can set the table if you want." Her voice was less than gracious, but Jori couldn't help it. He made her so nervous.

Christopher worked quickly, loading the plates, cups and silverware into his arms in order to make the least number of trips possible. Jori winced as her favorite china place settings jostled against each other, but at least he was out of her way. For now.

"I like your house," he offered, still in his friendly jovial tone. "Looks like a real home."

Startled, Jori gazed up at him, intrigued by his assessment. He didn't seem the type to value homes. Before she could reply, Flop sauntered in and wriggled over to their visitor, hips swaying in delight.

"Hello, boy," Chris bent over to ruffle the dog's floppy

ears gently, avoiding the dog's wet, pink tongue. "You're a real beauty, aren't you." Surprisingly, the loud voice was soft and gentle as the big man dealt with the enthusiastic dog. "What's his name?" Chris asked, tipping his blond head back to stare up at Jori.

"Flop," she replied brusquely, turning back to her salad. Moments later she felt his big hand on her elbow, turning her to face his shocked look.

"You named a purebred cocker spaniel Flop?" Disbelief flooded his perceptive blue gaze.

"Well, actually his title is Ginger Boy Parkland but I call him Flop. It's what he does best." She giggled, enjoying the look of stupefaction her remark brought.

The dog was obviously perceptive for he chose that moment to drop his plump body onto the floor, his chin resting on his front paws as soulful brown eyes studied them. Seconds later a huge sigh woofed out of him.

"See," she told him in a conspiratorial tone. "It's his trademark."

Christopher shook his head in disbelief. It was clear to Jori that in his exalted opinion, people didn't acquire bloodline animals, have them groomed, teach them dog manners and then bestow a name like Flop.

"Where did you get him?" he asked.

Jori mentally put a guard on her lips. "My dad," she told him shortly, whisking flour into the dark brown beef juices. "He was a homecoming present after I finished nursing school."

She tipped the succulent gravy into an oval bowl and set it on the table with a smack. A platter set to one side bore a small roast of beef, golden brown potatoes and finger-length carrots. She placed the bouquet of sweet peas in the center of the table.

"Everything is ready. Please, have a seat." Her slim hand motioned to the chair opposite hers and she watched as Chris sank into it, licking his lips discreetly.

"I'm really going to enjoy this." He grinned. Those twinkling blue eyes glinted at her. "I appreciate you allowing me to join you tonight, Jori. Thank you."

As if I had a choice, Jori acidly considered replying, but the words stayed inside her head. "I'll just say grace and then we can eat," she murmured.

"Father, bless this food for we are truly grateful for all your blessings. Amen." He murmured an amen, too, and seconds later she watched him tuck into their feast.

It was a small roast. She always had trouble shopping for just herself. Everything came in such large packages and Jori usually got sick of leftovers long before they were gone. Hence the send-out dinners for some of her father's friends.

But, surprisingly, the meal was rapidly diminishing before her eyes. The doctor heaped his large plate full, taking some of everything and then tasting each item thoughtfully, rolling it around on his tongue. When he came to the beef, he closed his eyes in satisfaction, chewing slowly, obviously savoring the rich flavor.

It had been years since she'd watched her father relish her cooking in just that manner and Jori grinned to herself as she tucked into her own well-filled plate, able, for the moment, to dislodge the discomfort she always felt in this man's presence.

"This is so good, a man might even be persuaded to propose," Chris mumbled, his face alight with pleasure as he rolled his eyes.

Jori choked on her water and welcomed his resounding thump on her back to get her breath. Eyes tearing, she stared into his handsome face.

"Isn't that a little extreme?" she gasped, her eyes wide with shock. "Just for a meal?" Surely he wasn't...

Her face flushed with embarrassment as she realized he'd been teasing her and she'd fallen for it. Again. Silently, Jori called herself a fool for letting him get to her. It was just that he unnerved her, she told her jangling nerves. She had known he would be trouble right from the start. Jori tipped her head back to glare at him as he burst out laughing.

Jori flashed him a look of disgust before resuming her meal. Fine, she decided. She simply would not converse with the man if he couldn't behave. With a sniff of disgust, Jori pushed away her plate; everything tasted the same anyway. He'd spoiled even this small pleasure with his vibrant presence across the table. She stared at her water glass, intent on ignoring him. And Jori could have carried off her pretended disinterest if he hadn't continued the tomfoolery.

Suddenly he was kneeling beside her, holding the sweet peas under her nose with one broad hand, while the other clasped hers, his fingers warm and tingling. His voice was soft with controlled laughter and his eyes were bright with glee.

"Please, Ms. Jessop. Say you'll marry me. To be able to eat like this with a cook that looks like you, I'm willing to take everything else on spec." His clear blue eyes lingered on her face. "Please say you will."

"What I will do is douse you with the garden hose if you don't stop this right now," she warned him severely, repressing her laughter with difficulty. Her hand tugged away from his and reached out for his half-full plate as she avoided his all-knowing eyes.

"I guess this means you're finished," she murmured sweetly, turning to put the dinner plate on the floor. Immediately, Flop moved in, slurping up the entire contents in one fell swoop of his pink tongue. Jori turned to gaze innocently at Chris's startled face.

"Ready for dessert?" Her voice was soft as butter.

"I hadn't finished, you know." He wasn't laughing now. "And I'm starved." Dark as velvet, Chris's dark soulful eyes beseeched her for sympathy. "Please, ma'am, could I have some more?"

It was such an exact duplication of a recent television commercial that Jori couldn't help the laughter that bubbled out of her. He looked like a naughty little boy with his clear solemn eyes, rumpled blond hair and company-perfect sweater. His big hand stuck out toward her.

"Truce," he offered, waiting earnestly for her response.

Jori sighed in capitulation and got up to find another plate for him. He was back in his chair, eyes downcast when she returned to the table.

"Here. Help yourself." Her voice was resigned to his silliness.

Dr. Davis accepted the dinner plate eagerly and ladled huge amounts of food onto his dish once more. Jori leaned back in her chair, quietly sipping her coffee as she watched him. Somehow he didn't seem quite as bad as she had first anticipated. She ignored the chiding little voice in the back of her mind. After all, it wasn't *that* terrible, having him for dinner, she argued with herself.

And when the nagging voice murmured, *I told you so,* Jori ignored its taunting. Her eyes were busy absorbing the picture of Christopher Davis, noted surgeon and infamous ladies' man, eating dinner in *her* kitchen. When he finally leaned back in his chair, she was happy to note that very little of the beef remained.

"I have more if you'd like," she murmured, eyeing the remains of the potatoes in the pot. "If you don't eat it, I'll have to reheat it for at least the next week."

"No, thanks! Much as I'd like to, I won't be able to walk if I eat another bite. It was really great though."

Standing, Jori carried away the serving dishes to the sink, poured his coffee and then sat down to sip at her own. Christopher waited expectantly, peering at her from under those disgustingly long lashes. When it was clear that nothing more was forthcoming, he rushed to the heart of the matter.

"Where's the pie?" he asked, glancing around her small kitchen.

"What pie?" Jori was jostled out of her bemused thoughts by his question and she stared at him, uncomprehending. Pie was the last thing on her mind just then. She blushed, remembering exactly what she had been thinking of—that maybe he would kiss her.

Huge blue eyes reproached her sadly. "You mean you lied? You don't have apple pie for dessert?"

Indignation welled up. His nerve was just too much!

"Look, Dr. Davis. You invited yourself here. I didn't say I had apple pie, you just assumed it." She stared at his strong muscular body tipped back precariously on the oak chair that had been her father's favorite. "And sit properly on that," she ordered imperiously before realizing to whom she was speaking.

She was rattled, Jori admitted silently, as little waves of tension skittered up her spine to her neck. And *he* was doing it to her.

"Yes, ma'am!" His big grin split across his laughing face as Chris straightened his chair before reaching out to pat her small hand with his larger one. "It's okay if you don't, you know," he soothed. "The dinner was really great even without that."

"Well, thank you so much. I'm so happy I could be of service," she muttered through clenched teeth.

His good humor was apparently unbreakable. As he sat waiting, the doctor merely kept smiling at her.

The man had gall, Jori mused. There was no doubt about that. And he knew exactly which buttons to push to get her dander up. Jori sighed.

Just another reason why he wasn't her type. Still, he did live alone and if he had been eating his meals at the town's fast-food places, it was no wonder he craved a plain home-cooked meal. Calling herself a soft touch, Jori relented.

"I don't have any apple pie," she said, capitulating at

last. "But if you could manage a piece of chocolate cake, I can accommodate you."

It was a thinly veiled hint at the amount of food he had consumed, but the good doctor ignored her jibe with that gracious good humor. His brilliant blue eyes sparkled at her as he kissed the hand he still held. Jori pulled her hand away and tucked it behind her back.

"I was just saying that I would really enjoy a piece of chocolate cake right now," he teased.

Jori sneaked a look at him over her shoulder as she cut a huge slice of the rich dessert. "What you should be eating is praline cheesecake," she muttered snidely.

He pretended to stick a finger down his throat, blue eyes rolling backward as he faked a gagging sound. Jori burst out laughing. The oh-so-sober, very handsome, very famous doctor looked ridiculous.

She set a huge piece of fluffy chocolate cake with its whipped mocha icing in front of him and watched him gobble it up with gusto.

"How often do you eat?" she demanded curiously, stunned by the amount of food he had put away.

"I didn't have time for breakfast today," he told her, shamefaced. He had the grace to look embarrassed as a light flush colored his tanned skin.

"And you didn't have lunch because Mrs. Andrews delivered her baby just about then," Jori guessed. "Did you have dinner last night?"

The big man shrugged his massive shoulders. Jori had to voice her concerns, not just for him but for his patients.

"Chris," she chastised him, only realizing as she said it that she had used his first name. "This practice is a very busy one and you can be kept going for days. You have to make time to eat regularly, or you'll find yourself burned out before Dan gets back. Then what will everyone do?" It was a question she didn't want him to answer.

"Are you worried about me or them?" Chris inquired

dryly. It was evident he already knew where her allegiance lay.

"I'm concerned for everyone. If you get sick, you'll toddle off to some expensive hospital in the East and they'll treat you immediately. The people in this town haven't got the money to go to fancy city hospitals. If you leave, they will have no one to help them."

Finished with her spiel, Jori got up and began to systematically clear the table, loading the dishwasher carefully. His fingers on her arm startled her, as did the strength with which he forced her to turn toward him. She was surprised to see his genial face tight with suppressed anger. Blue lightning shot out from his sparkling irises.

"I'm not just playing at medicine, you know," he snapped. "I am fully qualified for most anything that a one-horse town like Mossbank can throw at me." He favored her with a dry look, blue eyes gently mocking. "And I'm not going to cave in if I miss a meal or a night's sleep.

"Don't worry, Jori. All your little farmer friends will be well looked after."

Jori's temper surged upward as the week's tensions of working with him rose to the surface. "If you hate small towns, why did you come here? What is it about this town that you dislike so much anyway, Dr. Davis?" These were her friends and he was acting as if they didn't matter.

"What's the matter, Doc?" she derided. "Afraid you won't get the big accolades in a dinky prairie town? Maybe Boston is where you should have stayed, practicing medicine on people you know nothing about, and care about even less."

"Look, *lady*," Chris's voice boomed out, loud and exasperated. "I came here on my own to help out a friend who was going through a tough time. I don't have to answer to you or anybody." He snorted derisively.

"It's not my fault that there's nothing going on around here besides a matchmaking game and some bored housewives who think baking a bunch of cheesecakes is going to solve anything.''

So he had heard the talk! His handsome face was flushed and angry and perversely, Jori was glad about that, even if she had been elected as one of the contestants in Faith's marriage pool. The man was too full of himself. It was refreshing to see him have to shift out of that smugly superior and condescending mode. She would be more than happy to take him down a peg or two.

''You have eyes, Doctor, but you see nothing. Those 'bored housewives' are extremely busy right now. Many of them hold down full-time jobs off the farm and then help their husbands when they finish. And when those two jobs are done, there's still the laundry, housework and kids to look after.''

She glared at him bitterly. ''But they took time out of their schedules to express their welcome by baking *you* a cheesecake. Okay, it got a little out of hand. You're supposed to be so smart,'' she said with a smirk. ''Find a solution.

''There are local fairs to attend, 4-H events, auctions, barbecues, dances, picnics and a ton of other things to see and do around here.'' She waved her hands to indicate the plethora of possibilities. ''I suggest, Doctor, that you get to know your patients, find out what their existence is like, before you pass judgment on their *dull* way of life.''

In high dudgeon, Jori flounced around the kitchen smacking dish upon dish as she prepared to do battle for her town. Every nerve in her body was on full alert as she whirled to face him.

''The people here are independent and proud. Some of them refuse to leave the land their fathers and grandfathers farmed. They've had to start side businesses from their homes to generate enough capital to let them plant another crop after the first one got hailed out or the last swaths got snowed on.

"They raise their own kids without any fancy psychologists or pricey day cares and mostly without the drug scenes you find in cities all over North America." She risked a glance at him and discovered he was frowning.

"They go to church on Sundays, care about each other and spend lots of time and energy helping out their neighbors. And they maintain decent values in a society where no one cares that seniors are abandoned, rape and assault are commonplace and abusing kids is not unusual."

Jori knew her face was red and that she was yelling, but she couldn't help it. The man deserved to be told a few home truths. Fury tossed all caution to the wind as she berated him angrily.

"They create their own fun by being a community who care about each other. If someone loses a barn, everyone pitches in to build another. If a child is lost, we all search until she's found. That's the way it is on the prairies. You stick together to survive." She shoved a plastic-wrapped slice of cake at him.

"Here's your cake." Her huge brown eyes defied him to comment. "I'm sorry, but I have to ask you to leave. There are some things I need to do right now."

Jori stormed to the front door, ignoring the wagging dog at her heels. She wanted the man out of here. Now. Anyone who was so callous about their patients' welfare should not be part of the only medical team available for miles around.

She yanked the door open and stood grimly beside it, waiting for the eminently eligible surgeon to leave her home. She could see two women walking past her house and groaned inwardly. Mrs. Johnson and Mrs. Conroy. She might have known!

Chris's eyes mirrored his stunned disbelief that anyone should talk to him so peremptorily and if she hadn't been so mad, Jori would have grinned at his shock.

"Good night," she challenged, standing tall and stiff.

Slowly Christopher Davis walked toward the door, still

holding his chocolate cake. His blue eyes had softened to a periwinkle tone as he gazed down at her. Then his hand stretched out as his thumb rubbed across her bottom lip. Jori's eyes grew round with surprise and she felt the impact of that light touch right down to her toes.

"You are quite a fierce little thing when you get your dander up, aren't you?" he asked. "Chocolate," he mused, still staring at her.

"What?" Her voice was bemused, disoriented.

"You had chocolate on your lips." With that, Dr. Chris Davis turned to walk through the doorway with that uncaring long-legged grace. He stopped just outside, turned around and fixed her with an amused look.

"Thank you very much for the meal," he offered politely. "I enjoyed it and the company." Bending his lanky form low, Chris rubbed the spaniel's head affectionately. "Bye, Flop." Then he stood tall and straight, his electric blue gaze meeting her dark one head-on.

"Good night, Jordanna Lori Jessop. Dan was right, after all. I am going to enjoy working with you," he added with a grin. And bending down, he placed a very soft, very chaste kiss against her flushed cheek.

Jori barely heard his whispered promise before he disappeared into the dark night.

"I think I might even enjoy getting to know this town of yours."

And there, ogling them from the lawn next door, were two of the town's busiest old ladies. Angrily, Jori slammed the door on his retreating figure. As soon as she came back to earth, that was.

Darn his supercilious attitude anyway. She had returned to Mossbank to live quietly, help out where she could and let her battered world-weary spirit heal. Now, with one kiss, Christopher Davis had threatened all that; rocked her moorings until she wondered if her life really was on the right track.

Shaking her head, Jori went back to the kitchen to clean up the dishes. But the sensation of his lips against her cheek wouldn't be dislodged.

When reason returned Jori berated her foolishly overactive senses. She wished the illustrious blond doctor would have never shown his face in a place so obviously unimportant as Mossbank.

Jori was still frowning when she climbed the stairs to bed.

She closed her eyes tightly, trying desperately to dislodge Faith Johnson's wide grinning smile from her mind.

She wouldn't think about any of it. Not now. She breathed in a few cleansing breaths and then opened her eyes to focus on the moonlit ceiling.

"Lord, you know I don't want any upheaval in my life. I'm not very good at relationships. Besides, I like things just the way they are—calm, unemotional. Please don't send me any more curve balls. I'm not a very good catcher." Satisfied that God would understand her meaning, Jori closed her eyes and drifted off to sleep with a picture of a baseball diamond and a tall, blond pitcher clad in a white lab coat stuck firmly in her mind.

Chapter Three

"**I**'m so sorry for the delay. The doctor has been detained. I'm sure he'll be here soon, Mrs. Andrews."

Outside it was a glorious July afternoon but Jori noticed little of the beauty of the day. Instead her mind whirled with dark thoughts of retribution. She strove to speak smoothly in order to calm the impatience that was running rampant in the waiting room, unwilling to let her friends see how bothered she was by the city doctor's absence.

"Yes, Mrs. Johnson. The doctor will be with you as soon as he can." Jori gritted her teeth in annoyance as she dialed the hospital for the fourth time without success.

Dr. Christopher Davis was late. Very late. And no one seemed to know just where he was. She doubted he would worry about it too much, given his conversation after their meal together mere days ago.

Meanwhile, she had to face a barrage of patients who wanted to be free from the stuffy waiting room to pick saskatoons, or bale hay, or go to the river for a cooling swim.

"I'm sorry. I can't reschedule you. We're full up. You can wait for an opening if you'd like." Jori listened calmly to the third query from Faith Johnson. Inside, a wild mixture of feelings began whirling around, as she heard the sound of the back door opening.

"You're so much like your mother, Jordanna. I remember her quite well. She was tall like you and willowy thin. When you smile you resemble her the most." Faith stared at Jori happily. "Ruth was always smiling at something, even at the end. Life was so full of joy for her."

Privately, Jori wondered if her mother would have found anything to smile about in this situation. A doctor's office functioned on schedules and adherence to them. Christopher Davis was throwing all her carefully made plans out the window.

When he finally came sauntering into his office, all blond boyishness and charm, Jori's tightly held restraint flew out the window.

"Where in the world have you been?" she growled, protected by the thin office walls, as she slapped down the files in front of him. "These people have lives that don't revolve around your Boston time schedule, you know."

"What's the matter?" Big pools of azure stared up at her as Chris blinked in surprise.

His question was bordering on the ridiculous and Jori let him know it. Hands on her hips she surveyed his relaxed happy grin and blasted away with both barrels, ignoring the intriguing scent of his spicy aftershave as it tickled her nose.

"'What's the matter?' you ask. Well, I have twelve people waiting to see a doctor who was supposed to be here over an hour ago. The hospital had no idea where you were. You didn't answer either your cell phone or pager. What do *you* think is the matter?" Jori told him disgustedly, his calm manner only infuriating her more.

"Show the first patient in, please, Nurse." He cooly dismissed her without a word, bending to glance at the first on a stack of files that signaled the afternoon's work.

When she didn't move, Chris's tanned face searched her turbulent eyes. His features were composed, controlled; masking whatever was going on inside those innocent baby blues.

"Jori. The patients." His low tone brooked no nonsense. He was pulling rank, and she knew it, but Jori was too angry to argue.

Turning, she marched from his office, snapping the door shut with venom before retrieving Mr. Hunter and Mrs. Johnson from the lounge and showing them into separate rooms.

And so they progressed through the afternoon. Chris asked her for something only when absolutely necessary and Jori answered, polite but cool. By five-thirty, their obvious feud was a hot topic with the only other person in the office, her co-worker, Glenda McKay.

"What is the matter?" the other woman asked, passing Jori in the hall. "I can almost see the steam coming out of your ears."

"You can't exactly soar with the eagles when you work with a big turkey," Jori told her, grimacing as she heard her name barked in that imperious tone once more.

"You're too intense. Maybe he had a good reason," she cajoled.

"Try to get him in for X rays as soon as possible," Chris said as he entered the room. "Also, I want a full blood workup on Mrs., er—" he checked his notes "—Ainsworth."

He was trying to ignore the dark forbidding looks his very attractive nurse had been tossing his way all afternoon. It wasn't easy; he could hardly miss the daggers those big brown eyes were throwing out.

He hadn't meant to fall asleep; not really. But he wasn't used to these maternity all-nighters. Delivering babies was a somewhat new experience for him.

Chris grinned. Who knew what Jori would do with that

information, never mind if she found out the rest. He felt as if he were on trial with her already. Dead batteries in the cell phone couldn't be attributed to him, could they?

Of course, Chris reflected as he scribbled a notation on another file, he should have known better than to offend Jori. His patients raved about her constantly—how wonderful, how kind, how sweet, how lovely. He could see for himself just how gorgeous she was. That he had chosen to ignore their thinly veiled hints regarding her single status was obviously his loss.

It was clear that anyone who said anything about Jori Jessop said only good. She was a paragon of virtue, she was a great cook, she could handle emergencies with more aplomb than an army sergeant—the list went on seemingly endlessly.

She was very interesting, too. He had seen that for himself last evening—before Jori had gone from friendly hostess to fiery virago in about thirty seconds, and all without losing that dignified inner sense of self she always projected. Jordanna Jessop was a woman who knew exactly what she wanted out of life, Chris decided. And he was pretty sure she wanted very little from him, at the moment. With a sigh, Chris went to check on yet another patient.

After he administered an injection to one person, checked another's swollen tonsils and conferred with Mrs. Sanderson about her new hip, Chris caught sight of Jori's slim figure hurrying down the hall. A frown marred the smooth tanned skin of his forehead. Why did he have this ridiculous feeling he knew that face?

Chris was positive he'd never met Jordanna Jessop before and yet there was something about her profile that twigged his memory. Maybe it was those dark eyes—thickly fringed pools of sable that hid deep secrets. He knew those eyes. From somewhere.

He wondered for a moment if she didn't look like one of those women who advertised for a makeup company, but quickly decided he must be wrong. He knew very little about the stuff, but he did know that Nurse Jordanna Jessop didn't need anything to enhance her beauty.

She had a healthy glow that lit up her clear creamy skin. Probably due to the pure life she led here in Hicksville, Chris decided sourly, remembering her accusations of days before. Always something going on, she had said.

He was hanged if he knew where the townspeople held these wild shindigs because Chris had heard and seen nothing happening in the small town since he'd arrived. But then, he hadn't been very successful at mixing in with the locals thus far. Maybe he should just ask somebody for help.

Twenty minutes later Chris had learned all he ever wanted to know about the upcoming country fair from a loquacious Mrs. Flowerday. He vaguely remembered the name—something to do with chocolate, he thought.

"Just ask Jori to bring you, dear," the white-haired woman had enthused, patting his hand. "She always comes. Why, Jori's one of our best supporters." She leaned forward to whisper conspiratorially in his ear. "If you can get a bite of her wild blueberry pie, you're in for a real treat. Jori's got a flair for pastry that rivals mine and I'm not bad in that department."

The woman's plump lips had smacked at the thought and Chris's mouth watered at the picture of such bliss. He might even put up with a one-horse country fair for a piece of homemade wild blueberry pie.

"You say it's near here?" He listened as she described the area, understanding not one whit about the Logan or the Neufeld farms. "And she always goes to this fair?"

"Of course. Everyone goes. It's an annual event." Mrs. Flowerday was staring at him as if she couldn't believe Chris hadn't heard of it.

"Well, maybe, if I'm off that day, I'll ask her," he mumbled at last in response to the older woman's urging. "She doesn't like me very much, though.'' He grinned at the understatement.

''Nonsense! Jori likes everyone. She's an angel of human kindness. Why, there's not a person in this town who hasn't been blessed by her thoughtfulness!''

Yeah, right, Chris thought. So it was only with him that she gave with one hand and scratched with the other. Well, he'd see how thoughtful Miss Jori Jessop could be, he decided, and winced as Jori snapped the next file into his hand.

But three days later Jori was as unapproachable as ever and Chris still had not asked her to the fair. He needed an in, he decided, jogging past her house early Saturday morning, his first weekend off. A young girl stood just inside Jori's gate with a pail of plump red raspberries in her hand.

''Hi,'' he called merrily, enjoying the run and the feel of the fresh breeze on his overheated body.

But when the girl looked up at him, her eyes were those of a startled doe and Chris grinned to himself. Aha! Just the thing. Report this thief stealing from her garden and Miss Jessop would undoubtedly be grateful enough to agree to his plan.

Wrong.

Jori Jessop was spitting mad when he showed up at her door later that day and she let him know it in no uncertain terms.

''What in heaven's name were you thinking of?'' she demanded, her long slim hands planted on the full curve of her hips. Her eyes were honed chips of onyx. He shuffled his feet on her well-trimmed lawn, less sure of his good deed now that he had started this.

''She's twelve years old, for Pete's sake,'' she griped. ''What did you think she was going to do anyway, shoot someone with raspberries?''

Her scathing tone was enough to break the thin line of

control Chris maintained. He pulled himself up to his full height.

"Now just a blasted minute, here. I tried to do a good deed and all..."

Her face was a picture in astonishment. "A good deed? How, pray tell?"

"Well, how did I know the girl had permission to be there? I thought she was stealing."

Jori pushed the weight of hair off her neck and coiled it around her hand. Chris watched as she closed her big cocoa eyes and counted silently to ten before speaking again.

"At six-thirty in the morning? Get real!" She sighed longsufferingly before enlightening him. "We have a deal. She picks the berries and I pay her. She comes on her own time, when her mother can spare her. She desperately wants a computer and this way she can earn some money."

"Jori." Chris drew in a calming breath as he tried to set her straight. "She wasn't leaving the pail there. She was taking it."

That aggravating woman merely raised her eyes heavenward as she shook her head in frustration. Her eyes scanned around the yard before she hissed at him.

"Shh...Be quiet. My neighbors have very sound hearing." She jerked her head toward the house that Chris knew belonged to Judge Conroy and his wife. "I told her to take the berries. I was giving them to someone. Nobody was supposed to know about it."

Chris was completely lost. "Let's see if I've got this right," he mused. "You *paid* someone to pick the berries in your garden so that you could *give* them away? Oh, I see. It's all clear now. Thanks." He smiled at her slightly, peering down his long nose in disdain. The woman didn't make an ounce of sense.

Jori evidently recognized his confusion for she told him flatly, "Just forget about it, okay." Her big eyes glared at him. "And the next time you see someone in my yard, keep walking!"

Jordanna Jessop reminded him of a lily, Chris decided inconsequentially. Tall and slim, she looked delicate enough to break in the slightest wind.

Looks, however, were deceiving. Jori could hold her own any day of the week. Just now her pointed fingernail was back and demanding an answer as she glared at him.

"What were you doing at my house, anyway?" she fumed, her wide mouth turned downward. Her narrow feet with their bright red toenails wriggled in the grass.

"I, uh, I was coming to ask a favor," he muttered, hoping she might let him down easily, without the acid.

"A favor? What favor?" Jori's tone was less than encouraging, incredulous even.

"It doesn't matter." He chickened out, backing toward the gate. "I'd better go. Sorry if I spoiled things for the girl." He made it through the gate, barely, before her sweetly baiting voice stopped him.

"I've got a blueberry pie just out of the oven." She waited silently, knowingly, like a fisherman with a trout on the line while Chris swallowed again. He turned just enough to catch the shrewd grin on her face and knew he was hooked.

"Look," she offered quietly. "I'm sorry I was so harsh. If you'll accept a piece of pie and a cup of coffee as an apology, I'll try to explain."

"Well, if you put it that way," Chris demurred, his mouth watering. "*I* certainly don't hold grudges."

Cheerfully, he ambled along behind her, prepared to find out everything about this famous blueberry pie. Silken strands of her chestnut hair caught in the morning breeze and blew across his face.

Chris detected the faintest scent of wildflowers before Jori moved away, her hair trailing behind. His palms itched to grasp a gleaming handful. Tamping down the wish, he walked inside Jori's home once more.

"It's so lovely today." Jori waved toward the kitchen. "Why don't we have our coffee on the patio?"

Minutes later Chris had a huge piece of steaming blueberry pie in front of him as well as a fragrant mug of the dark brew she favored.

"I can't believe you bake, too," he murmured, more to himself. But she heard him.

She grinned, patting a wriggling Flop. "Now about the berries." She changed topics like quicksilver and Chris strained to follow, commanding his eyes to stop staring at the slim tanned column of her neck just visible in the vee of her long dress.

"You know Mrs. Selnes?" When his forehead furrowed in thought, Jori reminded him. "Six kids, three under seven." His face didn't automatically clear so she fed him a little more info. "One of them ate part of a swab last week."

"Yeah, I remember," he agreed sourly. And he did. He wished she would let him forget that unruly mob.

"Well, she has a rather difficult time," Jori told him.

"Ha! That's taking understatement to new limits," he drawled, eyes open wide. "Six kids! That'd give anyone a hard time."

"Yes, well, anyway, Jennifer comes and picks the berries for money to buy a computer. Then I phone Mrs. Selnes and offer my extras. She needs everything she can get her hands on to feed those kids. Her husband is rather useless. I like to help her out. Goodness knows she's grateful enough." Jori's clear forehead creased in thought as she stared straight at him.

"The thing is," she continued, unabashed by his scrutiny. "If she knew I had paid to have them picked, she would insist on paying me and I don't want that." Big as saucers, her dark eyes beseeched him. "Just keep it under your hat, okay?"

Chris nodded slowly. "You mean like the dinner you sent out the other night?"

"How do you know about that?" Jori stared in surprise.

"I stopped in to see the old girl the next evening." He grinned. "Believe me the smell of that roast was memorable."

He chuckled in delight at the dark flush staining her creamy skin once more. She looked slim and very beautiful in the sleeveless yellow dress that flowed to her ankles. Jori's innate grace was apparent when she walked and he wondered again why her face was so familiar.

"I'm impressed," she teased, not quite as acidly as before. "A big-city doctor making house calls. Wow!"

"Thank you, Nurse Jessop. I try." He felt as if he'd finally passed an important test.

"So, what's the favor?" she demanded, obviously anxious to change the subject.

"Uh, the favor?" His mind was addled and Chris had a struggle to organize his thoughts. "Oh, the fair. I wondered if you would take me to the fair." It hadn't come out exactly the way he'd intended, but Chris wasn't going to fuss about that.

His deep blue eyes studied her intently as she digested his request. Her eyes were round with surprise and her pink lips formed a perfect *O*.

"You don't mean the Silven Stream Fair?" she blurted out, obviously aghast at the thought.

"Yeah, I think that's the one. It's some kind of a country fair, isn't it, on today and tomorrow?"

She nodded slowly, as the copper glimmers in her hair caught the sun. A fly buzzed near her face but Jori ignored it.

"Yes, it is, but it's hardly the kind of thing you would

be interested in," she advised him. "Very small town, local people sort of thing. Not your stuff at all."

Chris knew he had it coming, but her immediate rebuff still stung, and made him even more determined to figure out just what held her here.

"All the more reason I should attend. I can find out more about this area and its people—what makes them tick." He played his ace where he knew it would do the most good. "That is what you advised, isn't it, Jori? Getting to know the community that I care for?"

He watched her sip a mouthful of coffee that she had laced with cream. Her eyes studied him seriously.

"You really want to go?" Skeptical didn't begin to cover her tone.

He nodded easily. Let her think about it for a moment. He was pretty sure she wouldn't be able to help showing off her prairie town. And if that was the only way he would get to know Miss Jori Jessop a little better, so be it. Besides, if it turned out the fair wasn't everything he'd heard it was going to be, at least he'd get another chance to try her blueberry pie.

"That was excellent," he murmured. "Thank you." Chris scraped his plate clean, swallowing the last bite with relish.

Jori sat silent, peering at him with that probing gaze until he decided to ask the question that had bothered him for days.

"Don't I know you from somewhere?" Her lips curved and Chris read her thoughts with ease. "It's not just a line," he protested, chuckling at her disbelief. "I keep thinking I've met you somewhere, before Mossbank, and yet I'm positive I never have."

"I used to be a model." She burst out giggling at the look of disbelief on his face. "Really. I guess you've probably seen my pictures in some magazines, although I haven't done anything for the last few years."

He studied the fresh oval of her face more clearly and decided that she had the perfect look for a cover girl. He didn't remember specifically, but he was sure now that he had seen her picture somewhere.

"You used to have shorter hair," he muttered, considering the long fall of hair that trailed over her shoulder. Suddenly he stared straight at her, and asked, "Why did you get into modeling?"

Jori didn't try to evade the question. She merely shrugged her shoulders and stated the bare facts.

"My father became ill, he forgot where he was going or what he was doing. Eventually he was diagnosed with Alzheimer's. He needed round-the-clock care. The pay was good, so I took as many assignments as I could to pay for full-time nursing care at home." She glanced up, tears glistening at the corners of her eyes.

"Dad was always less confused when he was at home and so I tried to keep him comfortable there." She stopped for a moment before continuing. Her voice shook. "He got worse in spite of the best nursing I could afford. I was on a shoot, my last one, when they phoned to say he'd hurt himself."

"I'm sorry, Jori. I didn't know." Chris awkwardly stretched out his big hand to cover hers, uncomfortable with her distress.

She smiled through her tears, wiping a hand carelessly across her eyes. "It's all right," she murmured. "He knows the Lord and in his own way he's happy now. Happy and healthy. Even if he's in the nursing home." The assurance in her voice tugged at his heartstrings. "Anyway—" her soft musical voice caught his ear again "—I decided to come home for a while so I could be near him. I finished up my nursing degree, which I had started before Dad got sick, and I've been living contentedly here ever since."

Chris detected the slight hesitation in her words and

knew there was something she wasn't saying. "But...?" he questioned, waiting quietly for her to finish.

"Why do you say that?" she demurred, keeping her eyes averted from his. Her slim hands twisted the napkin lying on the picnic table.

"I came back to help my father. Instead I hurt him." Jori's voice was bitter with remorse. Darkly glowing, her eyes stared off into space until she took a deep breath and launched into her story.

"After I'd been home for a week, my fiancé came for a visit. He came to show me some pictures of me that had been published in the tabloids. I had never authorized them, and I don't know where they came from." Her beautiful face was filled with distress as she half whispered to him.

"Everybody saw them. The whole country was talking about my promiscuous behavior." Her face was strained as she steered her eyes away from his. "They were shots, supposedly of me, nude on a beach." Her voice was filled with pain. Chris could only imagine having his privacy invaded so intensely. "They were pasteups. You know—" she motioned "—my head, someone else's body." Her eyes were sad.

"I couldn't have gone back to modeling the exclusive lines if I'd wanted to then. My contract specifically said no nudity." Jori grimaced at him. "It was a clause I'd insisted on and Gaston's held me to it. They said I'd degraded them." The last words came out on a whisper of shame.

"The tabloids made a lot of money from those photos but they practically ruined my life. I couldn't get work. Everywhere I went people stared at me with a funny little smile. It was awful. So I stayed holed up in Mossbank where everyone was as kind as could be. Someone finally admitted that the pictures were tampered photos that had been released without my permission. I sued and the magazine paid but legal costs ate it." Her chest lifted with the weight of her sigh.

"I found justice, but it was too late. My fiancé decided he'd had enough when I decided to stay here. Trace didn't want a small-town hick for a wife. He was my manager and had always encouraged my modeling, especially when the money started to really come in. Trace liked the high life—traveling, the whole thing." Jori thrust out her chin defiantly, her words bitter and hard.

"He announced our breakup in a national magazine that paid him for the story and then he moved on with a friend of mine. Maybe you've heard of her—Sabrina LeClair?"

Chris nodded, remembering the name from some party or another, he thought. But his mind was busy with Jori's story. He could guess the rest. She had stayed here, safe and secure in her little town, away from the prying eyes of the world. And her trust in people had never returned.

Suddenly, she straightened. He watched as a mask fell over the expressive but sad features as Jori pulled back into her shell and once more became the courteous but reserved woman he recognized from the office.

"So, Doctor, I don't know where you saw me, but I suppose that's why I seem familiar." She picked up their used cups and his empty plate and moved through the patio doors to the kitchen.

"I'll take you to the fair if you promise me that you will try to see these people for who they are. They're kind and good and they'd give you the shirt off their backs. I know a country fair is no big deal to you but for some of them, it's an event that they anxiously wait for. Don't spoil it."

Her soft, melodic voice was hard with censure, but Chris let it go. He knew her emotions were still whirling and she needed distance. He decided to give her some space.

"When do we leave?" he asked, bending to tickle the dog lying at his feet.

"I'm going to see my dad this morning so I'll pick you up at one. If you're not ready, I'll go without you." The pain and sadness had left her face. She was a woman defending her town.

"And bring a jacket," she ordered, walking in front of him to the door. "It will get very cool before we get home."

"Yes, ma'am." he answered cheekily, saluting irreverently. "Anything else?"

"Yes," Jori returned, her eyes coming to life again. "Be prepared."

"I'm always prepared," he said, and bent to brush her cheek lightly with his lips. "Thanks for telling me, Jori. And for what it's worth, I am coming to enjoy Mossbank. And its people."

She didn't look at him, but kept her dark gaze fixed on her hands. Chris flicked her cheek with one long finger before turning to march down the walk and along the driveway. He whistled cheerily as he sauntered home.

How about that, he had a date. And with the most gorgeous woman this side of the Rockies. Chris chuckled. He guessed he hadn't quite lost his touch. He hoped!

"What's got your face glowing like the sun on a hot July afternoon?" an elderly lady asked him as he strode past.

Chris stopped and turned, searching his memory for the name.

"I'll tell you, Mrs. Flowerday," he confessed, knowing he couldn't keep it quiet any longer, "I just got myself a ride to that fair we were talking about the other day and it's with my beautiful office nurse."

"Jordanna agreed to take you? Isn't that wonderful?" The little old granny beamed from ear to ear. "She needs an outing with a nice handsome man. You are nice, aren't you?" she asked severely. "I'll not stand idly by while you play with her like that other scoundrel did. I should have smacked him when I had the opportunity."

"No, ma'am." Chris gulped. He stared at her frowning

face for a moment and then amended. "I mean, yes, ma'am, I think I'm a nice enough guy."

"Jordanna's the salt of the earth, she just doesn't believe in herself anymore. She's been banged up and bruised by life. Needs a little patience and some love, that's all."

Mrs. Flowerday peered up into the sky and Chris allowed himself a grin as he wondered how Jori would feel about being thought of in that way.

"I won't hurt her, ma'am," he assured the old lady softly and felt the power of those warm brown eyes focus on him once more. "She's been very kind to me, made me feel right at home."

Charity Flowerday snorted derisively.

"Don't try to snowball me, young man," she chided, hitching up her purse under her arm and starting off down the street. "I heard the two of you going at it in the office."

"Yes," he admitted crestfallen as he walked along beside her. "I'm afraid she is rather peeved at me most of the time. She thinks I don't appreciate her little town enough. I'm not sure why it's so important to her." He felt the testing pinch on his biceps and wondered why people always thought little old ladies were weak. He'd have a bruise there from those arthritic fingers.

"Well, you're strong! You can take it," Charity sang out over her shoulder as she veered off away from him. "That indignation is a good sign. If Jori didn't speak to you at all, you'd have something to worry about, now wouldn't you?"

As he rubbed his arm all the way home, Chris decided the woman was probably right.

Probably.

"I'm telling you, Hope, he is attracted to her. Very attracted." Charity beamed at her friends. "I was talking to him and he seemed most interested in Jordanna."

"I'm most interested in who you had over to dinner last night, Charity. Why won't you tell us? Is it a secret?"

"A secret? Oh, my!" Faith breathed softly.

"Hope Conroy, you know blamed well that I hate that word. Faith battens on to it as if it's the next thing to heaven and now she won't give me any peace. Honestly!" Charity rolled her eyes, glaring at her best friends.

"Is it a secret man?" Faith whispered, winking at Hope. "Have you got a secret friend, Charity?" She clapped her hands in delight. "I know! It's Frank, isn't it? He's the secret!"

"You see!" Charity glared at Hope angrily, before huffing into her lawn chair. "No, Faith, it isn't Frank. I'd never invite him to dinner."

"Why not?" Faith demanded in an affronted tone. "Arthur says he's a very nice man. They go fishing together all the time."

"Good! Then Arthur can take him out to dinner. I'm not interested!"

"But why not, Charity? He's a perfectly lovely man. So interesting. Harry says…" Hope sank into a thickly padded wicker chair before reaching over to pour out three cups of tea.

"For the fifth time, Hope, I do not care what Harry says!" Charity's voice rose indignantly. "I have no interest in the local undertaker!"

"I just wanted to know why," Hope murmured soothingly. "There must be something that's made you react so negatively."

"You two," Charity sputtered at last. "Why can't you let me alone?" She sat up and straightened her skirt, shifting her swollen ankles onto a nearby rock. "All right, I'll tell you."

The other two visitors leaned in, as if coconspirators in a plan of the utmost secrecy.

"Frank Bellows never says anything."

"Oh, piffle! He's always talking about his life in Australia and the time he spent in Switzerland," Faith cried indignantly. "You can hardly get a word in edgewise when he starts going on about his daughter in Italy."

Charity felt her mouth flop open in surprise.

"He has a daughter? In Italy? Oh." Her face reddened. "Well, I never knew that. He doesn't say a word to me."

"Have you actually talked to him?" Hope demanded, her face drawn into the severe lines she'd used with her students in the past. "Most times I notice you whisk right past him at church. He'd have to hold you down to talk to you."

"That's because I thought, well, that is...I wondered if maybe he wasn't..." Charity felt her face grow redder by the moment as she searched for the right word. "Wasn't a little...you know?"

"*I* don't know," Faith told them loudly. "What does she mean, Hope?"

"I don't know either, Faith. What do you mean, Charity?" There was a hint of cold steel in Hope's sharp blue eyes.

"I thought he was either deaf or a little bit crazy," Charity blurted out at last. "He always stumbles and stammers whenever he says something. I thought maybe he was handicapped!"

"And so you avoided him because of that? Charity Flowerday, I'm amazed at you!" Hope's forehead was furrowed. "I thought we'd all learned our lesson about judging by appearances long ago." She poured another cup of tea for herself and absently added a cube of sugar. "You've probably made him so nervous, he doesn't know what to say," she expostulated.

"He's probably sick to death of being pressured by you two!" Charity glowered angrily at her friends. "I keep telling you, I don't need a man in my life to be happy. I'm perfectly content the way I am. I enjoy solitude. It gives me time to read and think. I'm managing very well!''

''Oh, Charity,'' Faith murmured, patting the gnarled old hand tenderly as her eyes filled with tears. ''Of course you are. And we didn't mean to upset you.'' She swiped away the tears with the back of her hand and sniffed in a way that brought a frown to Hope's clear countenance.

''It's just that we don't want you to be left out. We've been so happy lately, now that we've found Arthur and Harry and we're worried about leaving you alone too much.''

''Besides,'' Hope added dourly. ''Having a man around can make life interesting. And there's always someone to do things with.''

''Right now, all I want is to relax and enjoy the sunshine,'' Charity told them smartly. ''If I want a companion, there are several friends I can ask. Or I'll get a dog. *I do not need a man.*''

''Oh, my.'' Faith giggled. ''I don't think a dog could replace Arthur. Especially when he keeps my feet warm at night.''

Charity glanced heavenward and sighed. ''I already have a hot water bottle,'' she muttered darkly.

Chapter Four

"Hi, Dad. How are you today?" Jori leaned over to press a kiss against her father's weathered cheek and breathed in the spicy scent of his aftershave. The memories it brought back coaxed tears from her eyes and she brushed them away. Now wasn't the time to get maudlin.

"*And He said to them, "Why are you troubled and why do doubts arise in your hearts?" Luke 24:38.*'" James Jessop inclined his salt-and-pepper head toward his daughter, his eyes intent in their scrutiny. "*Fear not.*'" His faded gray eyes studied her intently. "Do I know you?"

"It's Jori, Dad," she murmured softly, clasping his hand in hers. "Do you want to walk in the courtyard? It's nice and warm today."

"All right." Tall and thin, James Jessop ambled to the door, his hand protectively under her elbow. "Mind the step, miss," he murmured.

Jori searched his face, praying that today would be one of his better ones. She needed him; needed to lean on him for a bit.

Her father held out an armchair for her before slouching

down in a lounge next to her and closing his eyes to the bright sunlight.

"I love the feel of the sun," he murmured. "It's like heaven is shining right down on me. When it was sunny, Ruth used to say the windows of heaven were open. I miss Ruth."

Jori smiled at this hint that his memory was still there. Somewhere. "So do I, Dad."

She sat quietly, content to be near him as he dozed in the sunlight. He seemed calmer today and she was thankful for that. Perhaps, at last, her father was really settling in to Sunset.

"Hi, Jori!" Melanie Stewart called out from the doorway. "Your dad's having a good day today. He ate quite a big breakfast." She stopped as soon as James's eyes opened. "Good morning, Mr. Jessop. Had a good nap?"

"I wasn't napping, Melanie." James voice was cooly rational. "I was just resting my eyes. I never sleep during the day. It's a waste of time."

"Of course." Melanie winked at Jori and waved. "I have to get back to work. Have a good visit."

"Jori, dear!" James hugged her tightly. "When did you arrive?"

"Oh, just a few moments ago," she told him. "I just needed to see my dad for a few minutes. How are you?"

"Happy to stare at the beautiful woman my daughter has become," he averred proudly. "And don't frown like that. You are beautiful. Everyone knows it."

"Beauty is only skin deep, Dad. Isn't that what you always used to say?"

"Did I?" James frowned. "Well, I was wrong. I think beauty goes right to the soul in some people and you're one of them, Jori." He hugged her close and then leaned back. "You're not still thinking about that young man, are you?"

"What young man?" Jori pushed the image of Chris's handsomely smiling countenance out of her mind.

"Hmmm. Who makes you blush like that?" James teased, flicking a finger against her cheek. "*I* was talking about that exceptionally dull young man you brought to visit me one time. Travis or something, wasn't it? Who were you thinking about?" His eyes were bright and Jori felt relief that he was still able to connect that much from the past, even if it was terribly hurtful for her.

"It was Trace," she offered quietly. "And no, I wasn't thinking of him at all. We have a new doctor, Dad. I've been working with him for a couple of weeks now."

"Hmmm," James Jessop murmured. "Seems to me I should know that. Who told me? Faith? No, Charity, I think. Somebody told me something about a doctor." The confusion on his dear face was painful to see and Jori patted his hand.

"It doesn't matter. Anyway, his name is Christopher and he's from the big city. He's very famous." Jori wondered why she'd chosen this particular topic.

"Not that famous," a voice murmured from behind them.

Jori whirled around to stare into those bright blue eyes and felt the heat rise in her cheeks at his knowing grin.

"Dad, this is the man I was telling you about, Dr. Christopher Davis. Dr. Davis, this is my father, James Jessop."

"I know him!" James voice was excited. "Plays chess like a pro." He beamed happily up at them.

"Not nearly as well as you, Mr. Jessop." Chris grinned. "I've yet to win a game."

"You see," her father teased, patting Jori's cheek. "I haven't lost all my marbles." He frowned as her face fell. "None of that, my dear. It was a joke. How can you not laugh on such a wonderful day?"

"Oh, Dad," she whispered tearfully. "I love you."

"Come now, dearest." James brushed his hand over her

swath of glistening hair. "I have few enough good days. Let's just enjoy the ones God gives us." His eyes twinkled merrily. "What have you got planned for today?" he asked curiously.

"Actually, Jori's taking me to the fair," Chris said, butting in. "I'd better get moving. She said if I wasn't ready she'd leave me behind." He grinned at the older man. "I think she means it, too."

"Don't pay too much attention to what my daughter says," James advised solemnly. His eyes were serious. "Sometimes she doesn't express her true feelings, but that's because she's been hurt."

Jori could feel Chris's fathomless blue eyes on her, studying her closely. She tried to pretend a nonchalance she didn't feel.

"Oh, Dad." She laughed nervously. "We're not going in to all that old history today, are we?"

But neither her father nor Chris was paying any attention to her. Each studied the other with an intensity that sent little waves of apprehension up her spine. Finally James nodded, as if he'd found what he sought.

"You take care of her," he ordered in a firm no-nonsense voice that Jori hadn't heard since high school. "I don't want my daughter hurt again."

Chris nodded, shaking the other man's hand with a firm grip.

"Don't worry," he murmured. "I won't hurt her." His eyes were speculative as they slipped over Jori's still silent figure, and she felt the old familiar doubts wash over her until his soft words reached her ears. "See you after lunch."

After that, James seemed content to talk sporadically and Jori finally left him in the dining room, ready to sample the barbecue lunch.

"See you tomorrow," she whispered, kissing his cheek. "Take care."

"First Peter 5:7. *'Let Him have all your worries and cares, for He is always thinking about you and watching everything that concerns you,'*" James quoted, smiling at her. "It's a promise, Jori. You can depend on it, you know."

"I know. Thanks, Dad." Jori drove home thinking about those words and trying to apply them to herself. But it made little difference. She still felt the same old apprehensions and qualms assail her. Why didn't she feel the sense of peace that her father did?

"Aren't you there, God?" she prayed at last, as she changed her clothes. "Can't you see how much I need my father right now?" But there was no response from heaven and Jori was left wondering if God cared at all.

"I'm doing this as a favor to him," Jori told herself sternly. "That's all. It's not as if I need a man to complicate my life."

She brought the Jeep to a stop in front of Dr. Dan's house barely two minutes before one. If Chris was ready, they should make good time driving to the fairground. As one of the judges for the children's entries in the exhibits, she liked to arrive early enough to look everything over thoroughly before settling down to reward the best.

It looked as if someone had recently cut the lawn, she mused, glad to see the city doctor was taking good care of their own doctor's home. She wanted everything perfect when Dan and Jessica returned—with their little one, God willing.

When Christopher didn't appear, Jori honked the horn once and then checked the mirror again. Why, she didn't know. What did she care if her hair was mussed or lipstick smeared? Chris Davis's opinion meant absolutely nothing to her, she told herself.

Yeah, right, her heart thumped.

He came strolling out the front door, wearing perfectly

creased designer blue jeans and a thin pale blue cotton shirt with a designer logo on the pocket. The blue only enhanced the sapphire sparkle of his eyes.

He looks gorgeous, she decided and then chided her brain for noticing. Dr. Christopher Davis was not her type, Jori reminded herself. Not at all.

Chris tossed his black bag and jacket onto the back seat before folding himself into the front. Then he stared at her curiously.

"Somehow, this isn't what I had pictured you driving," he said, head tilted to one side as he watched her manipulate the steering wheel of her Jeep.

"I didn't know you pictured me doing anything," Jori returned pertly, pulling expertly away from the curb before shifting gears. Her long dark hair whipped behind her in the breeze and she tucked the strands behind her ear.

"Exactly what did you picture me driving, Doc?" The question was only half-teasing, her brown eyes crinkling at the corners.

"Something more sedate," Chris replied and then added, "and stop calling me that. You know my name."

"Yes, sir," Jori replied, tongue in cheek. "Sedate? Thanks a lot. It just so happens that this was a bonus from one of my contracts." She patted the black console lovingly. "I can tell you, it's come in very handy during some of our blizzards. No matter what, Baby and I can always get through."

"Baby?" His blue eyes twinkled with mirth. "You really have a way with names, Jori." His long lean fingers marked off the names. "Flop. Baby. What's next?" His mouth tipped up.

"Makes me wonder about your children's future." His face was wreathed in smiles.

Jori merely turned off the highway onto a gravel road, refusing to answer him. He was quiet for a few minutes and then began questioning her.

"Where is this fair held, anyway?" He searched the waving fields of grain that stretched out around them. "I can't see a thing but this stuff."

"This *stuff* is what pays the bills, Doc. And don't you forget it." Jori's voice was firm with reproof. No one would get away with disparaging her county. When she noticed his wide startled eyes focused on her in surprise, she relented a little.

"We have to weave in and out here for a bit," she told him. "Then you'll see an old barn on one side and a house on the other, just before we cross the river. It's not far after that."

Jori burst out laughing at the look of shock holding Chris's handsome features immobile.

"People come away out here just for a fair?" He sounded confused by the whole thing. Jori could hardly wait for the look on his face when they arrived.

"Oh, a few do." She smirked. There was no way this smug city doctor could understand just what this event meant for the area without having lived here. She didn't want to spoil the effect Jori knew it would have on him.

"This must be the house and barn," Chris noticed, studying the weathered old buildings standing sturdily by. He peered through the window looking for the river. Evidently, the carved landscape gave him a slight clue, but he continued to peer down.

"Where's the water?" he complained more to himself than to her.

Jori pressed her lips tightly together, refusing to answer. As they crested the hill, she watched his blue eyes widen in amazement. There were vehicles parked everywhere. On the sides of the road, in the ditch, beside a row of poplars. Grouped together on any open area of unused field, they numbered in the hundreds.

"Wow," he breathed.

Jori burst out laughing. She couldn't help it.

"Come on," she said, pulling in beside a muddy half-ton. "I hope you remembered sunscreen," she observed, privately thinking that his darkly tanned skin was less likely to burn than her own.

"Yes, ma'am," Chris teased, swinging out of her vehicle.

The shimmering wave of heat hit him flat-out and Jori watched as he caught his breath.

Chris followed her lithe figure down the narrow trail to what he presumed was the fair entrance. Jori walked with an unconscious grace, her long legs bare in the summer sun. He liked her outfit, he decided.

She wore a denim skirt and matching vest that left slim, lightly tanned arms bare. Jori had twisted her hair into a ponytail that flowed down her back like toffee. On her feet she wore canvas flats that kept out the dust. He suddenly felt overdressed.

She quickly paid the two elderly gentlemen the fare posted on a piece of cardboard.

"No charge for the workers, Jordanna," they told her.

Grinning, she threw the money into the box on the tabletop. "It's a donation then," she called merrily.

Chris felt her hand on his, tugging him along. "Come on, Doctor," she urged. "I'm late, thanks to you. Don't make it a habit, okay?"

"Late for what?" he asked. Unfortunately the answer eluded him as they walked through an arch of maples to a sight Chris was sure came straight out of the 1800s.

The fairground was set in a huge circular area surrounded on all but the west side by towering green poplars. To the left were a few older buildings. One had a sign on it announcing the Welton School 1958-1977. Beside that stood a long, low building with the word *Exhibits* across the entrance. A broad red ribbon prevented anyone from entering.

Directly in front of him was a softball field where Chris noticed a group of people of all ages eagerly cheering on their teams from weathered bleachers placed on the sidelines. He could hear old-time fiddle music coming from the red-and-white-striped tent behind the diamond. And everywhere there was the smell of horses. Sometimes stronger, sometimes fainter, but always there.

Well, he reflected, it wasn't the World's Fair but it was still pretty interesting. Especially the collection of old machinery puffing and grunting across the way. It looked like some type of tractor pull, but then what did he know about farm machinery?

He felt someone yanking on his arm and looked down dazedly. Jori stood there saying something. He shook his head to clear it before looking down at her again.

"What?"

"I have to go to the exhibit hall to judge the children's work. Do you want to come, or would you rather look around?" She was tapping her foot impatiently and Chris made up his mind quickly.

"I'll go with you first. Then maybe I'll look around." He stared at the people milling about the grounds. "Where did they all come from?" he wondered bemusedly.

Jori giggled, and he decided he liked the sound of her laugh.

"From about a thirty-mile radius. Everyone just shows up when they want. Come on," she urged, trying to hurry him.

She pointed out the bathrooms tucked into the far corner of the grounds. Chris had a sneaking suspicion they were outdoor toilets, although he'd never personally had the opportunity to use one before. My, how his narrow life was being enhanced!

"All the ladies' aid groups offer food for sale to raise money for their charities," she told him. "We'll eat later. They have pies of all kinds here." Jori grinned up at him, her white teeth flashing in the hot sun. "You should be able to pig out to your heart's content."

Chris leered at her playfully, before hugging her shoulders to his big body in a burst of happiness, caught up in the festivities. He did notice that she immediately tugged away from him, and filed that information away for future thought.

Inside the building, it was hot; hotter than outside, he decided. He watched carefully as Jori greeted her friends and then introduced him to those he didn't know. He saw the glimmers of speculation in their eyes and wondered if she was aware of it also.

"I'm going to look around, Jori," he told Jori, who was bent over the sheaf of poems and samples of handwriting submitted for a prize. He touched her arm to gain her attention and noticed that she pulled away immediately but only answered, "Mmm-hmm."

"I'll catch up with you later," he whispered in her ear, deliberately brushing his hand over her back. When she didn't flinch, he moved away, smugly satisfied that she hadn't reacted negatively to his touch. He wondered if Jordanna Jessop would ever thaw out enough to let him hold her the way he wanted to.

Christopher surveyed the room dourly. He gave a cursory glance at the huge cabbages that stood out among the produce displayed, but only because everyone else was. He dutifully smelled the flowers, checked out the ladies' handiwork, the coloring contest and the children's crafts, following the example of those in front.

Then he left, but not before a large woman in a huge straw hat talked him into purchasing tickets for a door prize to be drawn for later in the day.

"What do I win?" he asked innocently.

"A kid," the woman told him, beaming happily.

He had to think twice before he realized she didn't mean one of the human variety. Chris paid for the tickets, sincerely hoping he wouldn't win. There was little room in Dan's backyard for a goat!

Outside, the baseball game was in full swing and he watched from the edge of the stands for a few minutes before deciding to take a closer look at the old school. It was dim inside, with that stale, dusty odor all schools seem to retain.

The old-fashioned desks were a curiosity and he wedged himself gingerly into one until someone else came in. There were initials carved here and there throughout the building and he grinned as he thought of those lovesick kids. A tarnished bell stood atop the teacher's desk, waiting to call the next class to order.

Across the top of the blackboard, the alphabet was carefully chalked in. Underneath, someone had drawn a huge heart with an arrow through. *A.J. and D.S.* Chris wondered idly whose initials they were.

At the back of the schoolhouse, an intense game of horseshoes was being waged between several older men. Chris stood to the side watching until a familiar voice caught his attention.

"Hi, Doc. How's it going?" Aubery Olden stood before him, hand outstretched. As he shook the old man's hand, Chris found himself also checking for other signs. Mr. Olden was one of the few patients Dan had asked Chris to particularly watch out for.

"I'm fine, Mr. Olden. It's a gorgeous day for your fair, isn't it?" The old man's color was good, although he was breathing quite heavily.

They bantered back and forth a bit before Aubery offered him some personal advice.

"If you're after Miss Jordanna, Doc, you will have to take your time. She's a lady who has been depending on herself for so long, she doesn't find it easy to lean on anybody else." The old man coughed loudly for a moment and then grinned. His weathered old face creased with happiness as he spoke.

"But you'll never find a lady more worthy of your love,

Doc. She's a fine one, our Miss Jordanna. Looks after everybody without them even asking.'' He cackled a rasping sound Chris thought was meant to be a laugh. ''She ain't too hard on the eyes, either!''

They grinned at each other while Chris's thoughts swirled round and round. As Aubery explained the game, Chris asked himself how the man had known his very personal thoughts. The old gent was cagey in the extreme, but to Chris's certain knowledge, he and Jori had never been together outside of the office, at least not in anyone's sight before. Anyway, the old guy was off the track a bit.

He liked the very gorgeous Miss Jessop, all right. She floated through his thoughts at the oddest moments. He wanted to kiss her, just once. But she backed off every time he even touched her.

Love? Chris wasn't sure he knew what that was. And he was pretty sure that Jordanna Jessop hadn't the least intention of allowing him to get anywhere near that close. He'd seen the flash of interest in her café au lait eyes, of course. But Jori had told him in too many ways to count that her allegiance was with her townsfolk and in her opinion, he didn't fit in. With a sigh, Chris acknowledged that she was right. He was just passing through.

Wandering again, Chris moved over to the children's play area to watch for a few moments. He considered what it would be like to come to a fair like this with your own kids. Surely children these days knew that bigger and better exhibitions could be found most anywhere. Why would they be content to come here?

And yet, as Chris watched, they eagerly participated in the three-legged races and the potato sack races. He watched them follow the one lone clown about the grounds, giggling with delight when Chuckles finally handed them a balloon.

The scene tugged at his subconscious somehow and

Chris was deep in thought when long, cool fingers covered his eyes.

"Having fun?" The voice was low and seductive and Chris knew immediately that Mirabel Matthews was behind him. Ducking away, he turned to smile coolly at her.

"Hello, Mrs. Matthews." Chris deliberately addressed her in this manner in an effort to keep their exchange as formal as possible, while praying fervently for Jori's return.

The town's loneliest widow stood clad in the tightest white pants he had ever seen. She wore a top to match in a plunging bikini style that looked vulgarly out of place in the country setting of cotton and denim. Glittering diamonds winked at her ears, deep in her cleavage and on her long-nailed fingers.

"Doctor," she remonstrated, "how can you be so formal at a country fair? Call me Mirabel."

Her arm snaked through his and Chris found there was little he could do to disentangle himself. She was like a boa constrictor, he decided dismally, waiting to squeeze the life out of him. Desperately, he glanced over her shoulder, surreptitiously searching for Jori among those curious folks who ambled past.

"Does this make you long for your own little ones?" she drawled, oblivious to his discomfort.

"What? Uh, no, uh...I don't have any. Little ones, I mean." He sucked in a breath of air and tried to extricate himself. "That is, I was just looking, Mrs. Matthews, while I wait for Jori. That's who I came with."

Could he get any clearer than that? Chris wondered. He glanced away from her black-rimmed eyes with their false lashes, trying to avoid the abundant cleavage she was flaunting as he lifted the long, slim octopuslike arm from around his neck and stepped backward.

"Oh, there she is. Sorry, Mrs. Matthews, but we promised to..." Chris let the sentence die away as he yanked his arm from her bloodred-tipped manacles and marched over to the woman who stood across the way, grinning merrily from one gold-hooped ear to the other.

"Thanks a lot," he muttered, brushing his shirt down. To his amazement, two of the buttons had come undone. "The least you could have done was help me get away from that barracuda." His voice was accusing but he was quite sure Jori felt no pity.

Instead, her dark eyes beamed up at him.

"Didn't want to interrupt," she said with a giggle. "Seemed to me that you and Mirabel were getting along famously."

"I need something cool," he rasped. "Where did you get that?" He pointed to the orange-colored ice she held in her hand.

"Come on." She tugged on his arm. "I'll show you. After a run-in with Mirabel, I'm surprised that's all you need."

It *wasn't* all that he needed, not nearly. But Chris decided that a triple-decker ice cream might just fill his mouth enough that he wouldn't say anything too stupid. Maybe he'd even be able to carry on a normal conversation.

Jori found a spot in the covered wooden stands where they could sit protected from the sun while they watched the young 4-H riders take each horse through its paces. But even in the shade with a breeze blowing, it was hot.

After they finished their icy treats, the two of them strolled past the booths housing the different ladies' groups who sold their wares to hungry visitors.

A surfboard sat on a bed of air, begging adults and kids alike to try their skills. In the background there was a long, narrow awning under which any who wished to play bingo could sit in the shade and lose money. It was probably the coolest place on the grounds and Chris wondered for a moment if he could learn to play a game he'd never considered even remotely interesting.

Jori, however, was indefatigable. She dragged him past

the air house filled with multicolored balls and insisted on spending precious moments in the hot, hot sun trying to placate the crying child whose mother wouldn't allow yet another turn on a ride that made him dizzy.

"Isn't it great? Hi, Mrs. Flowerday. Wonderful afternoon for the fair, isn't it?" Jori beamed at the elderly woman who sat decked out in red gingham under a striped umbrella clipped to the arm of her plastic chair.

"It's just lovely, dear." The warm brown eyes slid over the two of them, widening appreciatively as Chris guided Jori out of the path of several wild youngsters. "You two have a happy time, now," she directed cheerfully.

"We will." They moved on through the growing numbers, pausing to chat with a hundred different people that Chris was positive he'd never seen around Mossbank and wouldn't remember if they came into the office tomorrow.

He wasn't sure exactly how it happened, but when Jori gleefully coaxed him onto the giant trampolines, he went, jumping and bouncing as she dared him to leap even higher. Which he did—just to prove he could, of course.

Laughing uncontrollably and giggling so hard she lost her footing, Jori fell in a heap of laughter, long legs sprawled across the surface, tangling with his. Chris wondered if his blood temperature, which was already steaming while they untangled themselves, would withstand the rest of the afternoon.

"I think I've had enough of that for a while," he said firmly, pulling her away from the center.

"Okay." She bounded over the side. "But it's so much fun. One of these days I'm going to buy a trampoline just for myself."

Lest she drag him into some other trap, Chris steered her away from the three children's rides to the animal barns.

"This is my least favorite place!" He watched as Jori's nose curled in distaste at the strong smells, but she obediently walked beside him checking the pens of sheep, cows, steers, rabbits and pigs. As they walked, Jori explained the intricacies of judging animals.

"Many of the local people prepare their livestock in order to win a trophy or one of the cash prizes sponsored by the town's businesses. Lots of the contestants are children. Oh, just look at this." She pointed.

Her good-natured laughter burst out again when she read the plaque someone had hung on the end of the barn, donating a cash prize for the biggest *bore* shown in memory of their father.

"I wonder if he was a big *bore,* too," she said, chuckling with glee, brushing Chris's shoulder with her hand as she laughingly drew his attention to the words.

The motion, innocent as it was, spread a trail of fire across his chest. It was the first time she had willingly touched him and he was loath to move. But if he hugged her back, would she push him away?

"This is too rich! A bore, for goodness' sake! Oh, I can't take any more."

"Neither can I," Chris agreed. "I'm too hot." He fanned his hand across his warm cheeks, wishing for a sudden rainstorm.

Suddenly sober and strangely aware of his intense scrutiny, Jori realized that she was hot, too. But she wasn't sure exactly how much was due to the temperature and how much to the man standing next to her. Even with bits of straw sticking out of his mussed blond hair, he looked inordinately handsome.

Chris Davis got to her the way few other men ever had. And that bothered her. A lot. It also raised an immoderate amount of curiosity in her vivid imagination. Jori wondered fleetingly what would happen if he ever broke through the shell of reserve she held tightly around herself.

Here, in the center of the compound, it was hotter than ever. All at once Jori thought of her special hideout.

"I know the perfect place," she told him grinning, the

image floating into her mind like a mirage. Without thinking, she grabbed his arm, urging him past the throng of
people waiting to register for a school reunion.

"Come on," she begged. "There's nothing really happening till after supper anyhow, and we'll be back by
then."

Chris made her stand still long enough to collar two so-
das and a neatly wrapped plate of watermelon from a
nearby refreshment stand.

Jori tugged on his arm, her expressive eyes sparkling in
anticipation. "Hurry," she ordered, matching her strides to
his longer one.

"What's the rush?" he asked, feeling the trickle of sweat
down his backbone. "We'll both die of heatstroke if you
don't slow down."

Jori ignored him and whizzed away for a moment to
speak to one of the men at the gate before he felt her slim,
firm hand digging into his arm again.

"All right, all right," he grumped. "I'm coming."

Chris knew that the Jeep would be a furnace and while
she unlocked and opened the door, he held back. When he
thought he was prepared, he looked inside. Jori was already
in her seat, feet on the pedals, impatiently ready to put the
vehicle in motion.

"Get in." She waved.

Chris leaned back in his seat. He had no idea where they
were going, but his beeper hadn't gone off yet so he would
play along for a while. Groggily, he let his eyelids fall as
he savored the light breeze from the dashboard vent.

Seconds later, a hard pinch on his upper arm brought
reality back with a slam. Jori's big brown eyes were peering
into his, mere inches away. Her face was tight with stress
until he looked at her and then her generous smile cut a
swath across her face.

"Sheesh, I thought you were dead for a minute there."
Her voice was light and airy as she straightened away.

"Come on, I want to show you something," she said, looking like a cat that had just downed the canary. Chris reluctantly stretched himself out of the vehicle, loath to leave the cool confines as a wave of heat smacked him squarely in the chest.

"Leave the car running, I'll just watch from here," he told her. Jori swung the keys on one finger.

"You'll need these then." She grinned, stepping backward. "And I'm going down there."

Chris looked around curiously. They were in some sort of hollow. There were trees all around, creating a kind of hidden alcove. The road they had followed in was not much more than a dirt track. Directly in front of the Jeep was a pool of water fed by a tiny stream.

Jori disappeared behind a bush. A few moments later she emerged clad in a swimsuit. He was half-afraid to look, but curiosity got the better of him and he stared through the overhanging leaves.

He caught his breath as he watched her long lithe figure stride with ease to the edge of the glistening pool. She wore a black swimsuit that wasn't in the least exotic. He could just make out a thin black strap across her back before she plunged into the clear water with a squeal of delight.

Slowly, feeling like the atmosphere was pressing in on him, Chris walked to the edge of the pool. Jori surfaced near him, her dark hair streaming out behind her, her eyes glittering with suppressed excitement.

"Come on in," she coaxed, splashing some water on him. "It's not very cold, but it sure feels great." She dived under the water gracefully, her shiny red toenails the last to disappear. Seconds later she was standing before him again, her chest filling as she gasped for air.

Chris knew Jordanna Jessop was beautiful. She'd been to exotic places, played with world famous celebrities. And yet as this strong vibrant woman with her mane of walnut hair splashed joyfully in the tiny pool, Chris had the impression that he didn't really know her at all. And it was imperative that he find out what lay behind that tough, glossy facade.

He took off his shoes, pausing to stare at her solemnly.

"I can't go in." He sighed. He dipped his toes into the water and then rolled up his pant legs, eager to immerse more of his overheated frame.

"Why not?" Jori stared at him, head tilted to one side. Her long lashes were spiky with droplets of water and they blinked at him innocently. "You look really hot."

He needed her to tell him that! Chris groaned.

"I haven't got a suit." It should have been obvious, he thought. Jori just smirked.

"There's a suit of my dad's in the back of the Jeep. You're welcome to try it if you like. It's a little old-fashioned, but..." Her voice died away as she stared at him standing on the edge of the river as if rooted to the spot. Her eyes opened wide and he saw a flicker of something in their depths before she blinked and shrugged her indifference.

"Suit yourself," she called over her slim shoulders, then dashed deeper into the water once more, her body flashing in the dappled sunlight, hair gleaming like a seal's coat.

Chris sat there for about thirty seconds before his hand went to his perspiring forehead. In for a penny, in for a pound. He could hardly wait to sink himself into that pond and feel that coolness lap against his skin.

Seconds later Jori heard a huge splash. And then Chris's blond head surfaced next to her. "Took him long enough," she whispered to herself.

She wasn't exactly sure why she'd brought him here. Sympathy, she told herself. She'd felt sorry for him at the fair. He'd been hot and dirty and totally ill at ease.

No one would ever expect Jori Jessop to go pond dipping with a man, but Christopher Davis was one man who intrigued her like no one else had. He also made her more aware of her femininity than she had ever been. She wanted to know why. And yet at the same time, she was afraid; scared to open herself up to his intense scrutiny.

"Well, Doc," she teased, whipping a hand through the water to splash him in the face. "Great, isn't it?"

Chris's eyes had darkened to a deep electrifying blue. He strode through the water toward her with a look in his eye that Jori knew meant trouble. She backed up as far as she could, but he kept advancing until Jori was treading water in the deepest part of their private pool.

"I said not to call me that," he growled. "Now you'll have to pay."

"Go ahead," she egged him on. "Duck me. I like it."

His big warm palms closed over her shoulders. Then he tugged, bringing her against him.

"That's not what I had in mind," he warned with gleeful menace. "The payment is this."

Without any warning, Chris's head bent to hers. His lips were soft yet purposeful. It was a kiss that was full of unasked questions and tentative responses.

When he finally pulled away, Jori could only hang on to his broad shoulders as she stared up at him. When she finally pushed back, it was to duck her head under the water and swim away from him, as if his kiss meant nothing.

But she couldn't let it go. Something about him, the safe harbor of his arms, made her ask, "Why did you do that? We barely know each other."

Chris shrugged and paddled circles around her.

"I've wanted to kiss you properly for ages," he told her, glittering blue eyes met hers straight on. "You can't deny there's something between us."

He grinned that wide-open easy smile at her and Jori felt her heart turn cartwheels. He looked so cute, so *trustworthy*, standing there soaking wet with that silly smile. She tamped down her inner doubts. After all, she wasn't a model anymore. It wasn't as if someone as famous as Christopher Davis would need to use her.

"You know," he continued, "This country fair thing of yours is hot work." She saw his gaze shift to her mouth. "Why did you bring *me* here, Jori? Do you bring all your dates to this little oasis?"

"I've never brought anyone..." Jori's voice trailed away in embarrassment.

Why couldn't she learn some self-control? she asked herself. With heart sinking, she watched the light of understanding dawn in his eyes before they turned a deep navy.

"Well, I'm scandalized." His laughing voice drew Jori out of her introspection. "The always perfect Miss Jori Jessop gave way to the moment and brought her boss to her own private swimming pool. What would the townsfolk think of their favorite citizen now, indulging in such abandon?"

Jori's face was burning. Deep in her heart there was an ache that wouldn't go away. This was a side of Chris she hadn't seen before. He was funny and teasing and lighthearted. All the things she had thought she wanted in a man. Frankly, he was hard to resist in this mood.

Jori turned away, treading water as she strove to regain control.

"I don't do things for the townspeople," she said sharply. "I came here because it's cool and we can relax and be comfortable." Jori scrambled to assume her severest schoolteacher look. "I didn't plan this as some secret assignation, you know. I was just trying to help you."

She wasn't defending herself, merely stating the facts. It came as a surprise to hear Chris's low voice in her ear.

"I know. But there's cool, and then there's *cool*." He grinned.

There was only one recourse and she took it, concentrating on her swimming.

When she finally stopped, puffing and gasping air into

her starved lungs, Chris sat perched at the water's edge on a huge boulder, sunning himself dry. She studiously ignored him as she paddled to the grassy edge and sprawled out on her stomach. The feathery green blades caressed her skin with a delicate touch.

There was no way, Jori decided, that she was pulling on her denim skirt while her swimsuit was still soaking wet. Her dip had left her cool and relaxed and she was loath to break the solitude and peace of the afternoon. Closing her eyes, she pretended to relax in the sun, fully aware of the man across from her as he sat munching watermelon.

"You're self-conscious around me." Chris's soft puzzled voice carried on the still afternoon air. "I don't understand that. I thought models would be used to people watching them in various states of dress."

Chris flopped his long lanky body next to hers on the soft grassy carpet. His arm brushed hers as he found a comfortable position. Immediately her armor went up and something inside whispered, "Be careful."

So we say with confidence "The Lord is my helper; I will not be afraid. What can man do to me?" The old memory verse reverberated through her mind and Jori almost grinned in delight. Talk about timing!

"You're not a client or a customer," she prevaricated. "Anyway, it's different here. This is home. And I haven't modeled for quite a while." Jori twisted her head to look into his smooth velvet eyes, noticing the way the flaxen mop fell carelessly across his forehead.

"I never was very comfortable around men," she admitted, waiting for that wry look of disbelief to cross his face. She wasn't disappointed.

"I'm sure."

"Look, it was just a job. I needed the money and so I modeled. Some of those assignments paid me very well." She stared straight into his face, daring him to interrupt. "So well, in fact, that my dad got most of what he needed to keep him happy.'' She gulped down a deep breath and pressed on, needing to get it all out.

''I'm not especially proud of some of what I had to wear, but I did a good job for my clients. Anyway, my father got to spend a few more years happily in his own home. That was the point.''

Jori took a deep, calming breath before sitting up slowly, dragging her knees to her chest.

''After I took over his affairs, I found out that he had stashed some money away for my education. I wish I'd known. I would have spent more time with him and less working.''

''I'm sorry,'' he murmured. ''I have no right to judge.''

Jori stared down at her feet. She'd noticed his large, capable hands soothe a fussing child, or stroke a patient's wringing hands. Now they tipped her chin up to meet his compassionate countenance, strong yet gentle under her chin.

''I think your father is very proud of what his daughter did for him,'' he murmured, his lips very close to hers. ''What man would not have been proud to see the world admiring his beautiful daughter?''

''It wasn't exactly the traditional approach to caring for one's parents,'' she whispered, mesmerized by his compassionate look.

''Unusual circumstances call for unusual solutions,'' he whispered. ''No one's blaming you for being a model, Jori. Least of all me.''

He bent his head slowly and pressed his lips to hers then, and it was unlike anything Jori had experienced before. His mouth was soft and gentle.

Finally Chris pulled his lips away, but continued to touch the silky strands of her hair.

And all the while a tiny voice whispered in Jori's ear. ''He will never settle here. He's from the city and that is where he will return.'' She hated that nagging little voice and its cheerless message.

Thing was, she knew it was right.

Christopher Davis was very good at kissing and he could draw a response that echoed through her body to her toes.

But there was no future for them. She was committed to staying in Mossbank, caring for her father. It was what she'd focused on for months now. And hadn't God directed her home?

So how could she have these feelings for this man? He would leave, move on with his life and then she would be alone. Again. Jori jerked out of his embrace, her cheeks burning as she watched his blue eyes darken.

"Why do you always do that?" he asked, allowing her to slip out of his grasp. "Are you afraid of me? I'm not like your fiancé, Jori. I don't care much about what happened in the past, or your money."

"That's because you have a lot," she told him, her glance downcast. "If you're in this world long enough, you come to realize that there are people who would do anything for money." She glared across at him. "I'm here because I couldn't stand to be around people like that anymore."

He watched her when she plucked a spear of grass and shredded it with her fingernails. The action only made her seem more nervous.

"Like what?" he asked softly. When she frowned, he clarified. "People like what?"

"People who devalue everything that's important. My father taught me to love God and trust him with my life." She laughed harshly. "Believe me, that's not something that you hear much anymore. And I've decided that that was an important heritage. That's why I'm going to stay right here, in this community. This is where I want to live, maybe raise a family, grow old."

"There are lots of communities like Mossbank in this country," he murmured. "Why limit yourself to here?"

"My dad's here," she told him bluntly. "And I have to be nearby in case he needs me."

"But he's in the nursing home! He has someone there all the time. Some days he doesn't even recognize you."

Jori felt the tears well as she swallowed down the lump in her throat with difficulty.

"I know." She hiccupped. "But he has better days and knows who I am. I can't not be there for him."

"Jori, your father has Alzheimer's. He's not going to get better." Chris shrugged. "I'm no expert in that field, but I do know that these patients don't wake up one morning cured. You're talking about a degenerative disease. Surely, as a nurse, you know what that means."

"Of course I know," she returned angrily. "But I have no intention of deserting my only remaining family. There's nothing out there—" she waved her hand in front of her "—that I want enough to leave Mossbank. This is where I belong. It's where I have to be."

"Nothing to make you leave," he murmured, so softly Jori barely caught his words. "I wonder."

"We'd better get going," she muttered, jumping to her feet. She had to move, to do something that would avoid that knowing look. Chris's blue eyes were bright with understanding. She avoided them. She didn't want to hear him call her a chicken.

She found her clothes and put on her skirt and vest, then turned to find her shoes. As she moved, Jori caught sight of Chris, just standing there, staring at her.

"Well?" Jori snapped, unable to control the exasperation that flashed through her at the notion that she could easily be swayed from her life's plan by a mere kiss. All it would take was a little more of that gentle compassion and she'd start dreaming about a future that was impossible. "Do you intend to stay here?"

"I'm not giving up on you, Jori." The words were quietly spoken, blond head tilted to one side. "You and I have something special going on, you can't deny it. But just when things start to get interesting, you duck out." His wide mouth tightened. "I'm not going to hurt you, Jori." He smiled, brushing one hand down the length of her almost dry hair. "You can trust me.

"You only hurt yourself if you don't live your *own* life. I don't believe either God or your father intended that."

Jori was shaken by his perceptiveness and she let that fear translate into anger. She attacked him verbally while her palms stayed clenched at her side.

"Big deal. You kissed me. The great Dr. Davis! So what?" She snickered. "Am I supposed to be grateful for your attention?" She watched his face darken, a dull red suffusing his healthy skin.

"You kissed me back," he taunted. "You felt the same spark that I did, only you won't admit it. Why, Jori? What do you think is going to happen if you admit that you enjoy being with me?"

In three strides he was standing in front of her. "I didn't force you or coerce you to kiss me, Jordanna Jessop, and I'm sure not going to hurt you. I am not your ex-boyfriend."

Her flashing brown eyes met his glittering blue ones. But what she saw in his eyes only made her more uncomfortable.

"You just shut me out," he murmured. "I thought we'd gone beyond that. I don't scare easily, Jori."

Chris turned away after a few moments and retrieved his clothes. Quietly he slipped them on behind a nearby bush without saying another word. There was a pinched tightness around his mouth, but that was the only hint as to his frustration.

He climbed into the Jeep and sat waiting for her without

uttering a word. But Jori could feel his condemnation. She took her time getting into the hot stuffy vehicle.

He was right. She wasn't playing fair. And it was because she wasn't sure what was right or proper anymore. Christopher Davis had mixed up her mind and emotions so badly, she couldn't decide if she liked or hated him more, and she was very much afraid it was far too much of the former.

She sighed. Perhaps she had been too abrupt. They were going to have to work together for the next little while and she owed him at least an apology. Her eyes closed for a moment before she gritted her teeth in determination. She would try again.

"I'm sorry about that," she offered. "I really am just a small-town girl. This is my home and I can't pretend to be somebody else." It didn't come out exactly the way she'd intended so Jori tried again.

"I'm not the sort of person who has a fling with a visiting doctor if the opportunity arises. I'm too old-fashioned, I guess." Jori turned to glance at his stern profile. He still looked mad.

"I want all the things you see in this little town—a family, friends and a neighborhood where you can trust your next-door neighbor." She stopped for a minute and then lest he still didn't get it, blurted out, "The bottom line is, I don't sleep around."

"Who asked you to?" His voice was low and disgruntled. "All I recall doing was kissing you." He turned then to stare straight into her eyes. "Maybe *Trace*—" he laid heavy emphasis on the word "—was the kind of person who expected that, but I'm not him. And why do you immediately assume I'm looking for some kind of a fling? I wish you'd stop treating me as if I have some terminal disease that I'll inflict on this town."

"I don't do that," she gasped in an aggrieved tone.

"Yes, you do," he asserted grimly. "Look, Jori, I like

you. You're smart and funny and I'd like to get to know you better.'' He grinned at her suddenly and Jori let out the lungful of air she held.

''I'm perfectly willing to take it slow while we get to know one another. I want to know things about you like your favorite food, what you eat when you pig out, what countries you modeled in, how you got started.'' Chris reached out and stroked his hand down the long strands of her shiny tresses.

''We'll take it nice and easy. Just don't run away. Trust me, don't be afraid of me.'' His soft voice soothed her jangled nerves.

The problem was, Jori reflected, she didn't trust anyone who got too close. Not anymore. And especially not after Trace's desertion. Besides, if he knew the truth about her, Jori wasn't sure Dr. Christopher Davis would want to spend any more effort on getting to know her.

But as she stared into Chris's solemn blue gaze, Jori wondered if perhaps the man upstairs was telling her that it was time to let someone into at least a tiny part of her life.

''Peaches,'' she told him finally, letting down her guard just the tiniest bit.

Chris looked up from the study he was conducting on her long pink fingernails. ''What?'' Confusion creased his eyes in perplexity.

''My favorite food—peaches.'' She smiled at him. ''Fresh, ripe and so juicy that it drips down your chin when you bite into it. And I love chocolate.''

''Now that wasn't so hard, was it?'' his deep voice chided as he smiled at her.

As she sat smiling with him, Jori decided that she wouldn't let herself get too used to him. For her own good. He was a very successful doctor who was just filling in for a friend. When Dan returned, Chris would be gone like the wind. Small towns were not his style; they couldn't be. His work necessitated a city and she had no intention of leaving Mossbank. Perhaps they both needed to remember that.

Jori moved back into her seat and put the Jeep into gear. She drove away from their tiny oasis with resolution. This crazy attraction...no, infatuation...was only temporary. It would pass, she reassured her doubting voice as they drove toward the fairground. It was just temporary.

Chapter Five

"Faith, have you seen Charity? I've been searching for twenty minutes and there's no sign of her anywhere!" Hope's voice echoed the frustration she felt. She grimaced at the dusty marks on her skirt but no amount of brushing would remove them.

Faith swallowed the last of her double fudge bar and swiped one hand across her mouth in the hopes of removing the traces.

"Charity? Oh, she went off with Aubery. They were going to get an ice-cream cone, I think. One of those triple-decker things." Faith's eyes blazed with happiness. "Don't you just love this fair?"

"Aubery Olden? Oh, no! And why are they eating ice cream at this time of the day?" When Faith began to answer, Hope waved her away. "No, never mind. I don't want to know." She puffed out a breath of air in disgust. "And to think I went to all the trouble of arranging for Frank to join us all for supper."

"Frank Bellows?" Faith shook her head. "You know how she feels about him, Hope. Good heavens, we've tried to get the two of them together often enough, but Charity's dead set against the man.''

''I don't understand why. He's a wonderful man and Charity would enjoy him if she'd let herself. She's so stubborn.''

Faith wisely refrained from commenting on others of her acquaintance who possessed the same trait and applied herself instead to dabbing at the chocolate smears on her favorite pink blouse.

''I saw Mirabel earlier,'' she offered as a red herring, smugly happy when Hope's startled glance flew to hers. ''She's after our new doctor.''

''Mirabel? But she can't be,'' Hope wailed. ''I so wanted Jori to link up with him. She needs someone now that James is in Sunset. She spends far too much time by herself.'' Hope's blond head whirled around as she searched the crowd. ''Where do you suppose Mirabel is now?''

Faith nodded at the refreshment tent on the right. ''Chatting to your husband,'' she murmured softly. ''And she's sitting beside mine!''

''I was just coming over to mention that,'' Charity's voice sputtered from behind them. ''Isn't it time you and your husbands had supper? There's the nicest little spot by that hedge over there and I've got a cloth on the table already.''

''Charity, you scared the daylights out of me!'' Hope pressed a hand to her racing heart before frowning down on the older woman. ''I wanted to talk to you about supper,'' she said. ''I was hoping you'd join us.''

''I might,'' Charity acquiesced.

''Come on, Faith,'' Hope chortled, linking her arm in the other's with a grin. ''Let's go rescue Arthur and Harry.''

Ten minutes later they were all seated around the red-painted picnic table, plates of cold cuts and salads in front of them.

"I hope you don't mind," Charity said, buttering her roll carefully. "I've asked Aubery Olden to join us."

"You haven't," Hope gasped, spying the old gent making his way toward them. She glanced over her shoulder. "But I asked Frank Bellows!"

"Oh, piffle!" They all stared at Faith's unhappy face. "I suppose it was a bad idea to invite Howard Steele over, too?"

In the end, the seating arrangements had to be revised. Judge Conroy was most vocal in his distaste at sitting four on a side and finally announced that he was moving to the next table. Hope followed him with a backward glance at Charity, who sat happily amid the three men.

"Why don't you go with them, Faith?" she heard Charity offer. "You and Arthur are squished up there like sardines in a can."

"Why did you move?" Hope whispered angrily as Faith sank onto the seat beside her. "Now we can't hear a word they're saying." She glanced in dismay at the cherubic smile on Charity's round face and sighed. "I just wish you hadn't asked Howard Steele," she muttered in frustration. "He's too young for her." Her face brightened suddenly.

"Ah, hello, Jordanna. Enjoying the fair?"

"It's wonderful," Jori replied, following Hope's glance to the table next door. "Mrs. Flowerday certainly seems to be enjoying herself."

"Yes," Faith grumbled in an unhappy tone as Charity's bright laugh rang out. "She does, doesn't she?"

"I saw you with Dr. Chris," Faith murmured in a low, conspiratorial tone. "You left for a while and I haven't seen him since. Did he have a call?"

Jori felt her heart sink at the curious look in those faded eyes. She pasted on a smile and answered as best she could. "No, Mrs. Johnson. No call. We just left to get out of the heat for a bit. He's around here somewhere." She glanced over her shoulder, as if she were searching for Chris. "I suppose I'd better go find him. We're supposed to have supper together.'' She waved her hand and moved away before Faith could ask any more questions. ''Bye for now.''

Chris was deep into a discussion about agricultural practices when Jori found him two hours later. She had deliberately wandered around on her own for a while to give them both some space. After their time at the pond, she needed to regroup, gain perspective.

As she listened to his knowledgeable response on the difficulties with anhydrous ammonia, Jori was forced to smile. It seemed the good doctor knew a lot more about farming than she would have given him credit for. And when he glanced up to grin at her, his sparkling blue eyes negated any progress she might have made in slowing up a racing heartbeat.

''Not a bad looker, is he?'' The voice belonged to Amy Grand, Jori's best friend since kindergarten. ''You two have something going?'' The question was not posed as innocently as Amy's wide green eyes seemed to imply.

''Hi, Amy,'' Jori greeted her friend. She grinned at Amy's outfit. Blue jeans and T-shirt, again. ''We're just friends. I thought a trip to this fair might open his eyes a little.''

Amy smirked saucily before she teased, ''Seems to me your eyes are wide-open, too, my girl.'' She swatted Jori lightly. ''It's nice to see, for a change. I thought that heart of yours would be frozen forever!''

Jori wished for the hundredth time that her friend's voice was just a trifle less strident. At this rate, the whole town would be speculating about them.

Jori wished an emergency would set off his beeper and relieve her embarrassment. But she'd never backed down from trouble before and she faced Chris bravely now.

''We've got to be going, Amy,'' she babbled. ''Nice seeing you again. Bring Bob over for coffee tomorrow night. Bye.''

It wasn't a great exit but it was the best she could do with those glittering navy orbs daring her to ignore him. She tried to make small talk as they moved toward the grill.

"Sorry about that," she murmured. "Amy always says what she thinks."

"Does she always say it so loudly?" he growled. Jori could hear the dismay in his voice.

"Amy didn't mean anything." Jori frowned. "After all, you are new to the area and very good-looking, so…" Realizing what she'd said, Jori slapped a hand over her mouth.

She stopped at the end of the lineup, afraid to meet his gaze, fumbling with her keys. A choking sound made her look up finally. Chris stood behind her trying not to laugh out loud.

"What is so funny?" Jori demanded, hands on her hips.

"You are." He gasped the words out between gulps of laughter. "And thanks for the compliment. I think."

Jori watched him for a few moments and then decided she had gotten off lightly. At least he wasn't mad.

They ate their meal surrounded by a swarm of young people who chatted madly back and forth. There was no need for conversation and not much opportunity if they'd wanted one.

After supper the 4-H youth presented a special routine with their horses marching in formation around the dusty track. Jori sat on the crowded bench with her leg brushing Chris's and tried to concentrate on the patterns that had taken hours of practice to perfect.

"What happens next?" he asked.

Jori tried to control the flutter of nervous awareness that noticed the cowlick on the left side of his head and the way his eyes crinkled at the corners when he smiled.

"There's a talent show now," she whispered back. "Local people who are competing for some of those prizes." She indicated a booth across the way. "The kids have really entered this year because there's a CD player there."

"Are you singing, Jori?" Mrs. Hansen leaned across Chris to ask the question in a voice loud enough to cause several heads to turn.

"No. But I'm supposed to be one of the judges." Jori glanced up at Chris. "I have to move down there." She pointed to where several adults stood around a table placed about twenty feet back from the stage.

"You can come if you want, there are extra chairs. Or you can stay here and I'll meet you after." She waited for him to decide.

"I'll go," he said, inclining his head to the left. "I think I'm a little out of place here." Jori followed his gaze and smirked at the dearth of seniors that had congregated around them on the stands.

"That's one of the best things about a country fair. Everybody fits in," she whispered back.

"I'm judging the singing. You can help if you want. Or leave. It's up to you." She moved down a step.

Her face grew warm as his blue eyes studied her.

He grinned, tightening his hold on her fingers. "I always go home with the woman I came with."

"Well, come on then," she said at last, thrown off by the fatuous grin on his handsome face. "They're ready to start."

"I should tell you that I don't know a thing about singing."

"As a matter of fact, you're tone-deaf," Jori added kindly. She grinned and shook her head at his offended look. "I heard you singing to yourself at the office one day. Totally off-key."

"If my voice is so offensive—" he began indignantly, but Jori just grinned and shushed him.

"The first number is about to come on," she explained. "You'll like it. Just relax and enjoy it. The *guest judge* is allowed."

Four minutes later, Jori knew he was enjoying himself

by the way he clapped for the preschool performers. As the tiny sister and brother tucked their fiddles under their arms and took a bow, Chris cheered enthusiastically. Apparently, the crowd agreed for everyone was on their feet.

Once the group had settled down, the next number came on and gave a rousing version of an intricate square dance number that involved full ruffled skirts with stiff crinolines. There was a fourteen-year-old comedian who poked fun at everyone, a ten-year-old piano whiz and two guitar players who harmonized in a Wild West medley that had every toe in the place tapping out the beat.

"These people are all from around here?" Chris leaned over to ask after the fifth entry. When she nodded, he shook his blond head. "There's a lot of hidden talent in Mossbank."

"Didn't I tell you that?" Jori admonished with a reproving grin. Her eyes widened as a young girl with a cropped haircut and tight blue jeans came onto the stage carrying a set of drums. "I was afraid of this," she whispered.

"What's wrong?" Chris stared at her curiously.

Jori grinned and shook her head. "Wait," she commanded with a grin. "Just wait."

There was a two-second interval between the time the announcement was made and the cacophony of thumping, thudding, clanging noise began. Several times Jori glanced over her shoulder, studying the stupefied look on Chris's face before turning back to her notepad and jotting down something in tiny scribbles.

When the silence finally came, it was deafening. The entire assembled throng sat dazed and paralyzed with shock. Jori nudged Chris in the arm and started clapping loudly. Seconds later others joined in until there was a resounding clamor from all around them. The girl calmly picked up her drums and carried them off the stage, her head held high.

"What is the best thing you can think of to say about that performance, guest judge?" Jori hid her smile as she watched his shocked features rearrange themselves in their normal structure.

Chris's eyes were glazed and unfocused as they stared down at her. Finally his mouth opened and whispered something she had to lean closer to hear.

"That it's over!"

Jori nodded and pretended she was writing something, carefully aware of the scrutiny of the townsfolk.

"Just keep that to yourself," she advised softly. "Another small-town rule is that nobody must be offended by these proceedings. Nobody."

"You mean, 'If I can't say something nice, don't say anything at all'?" Those blue eyes were sparkling and clear as they reprimanded her. "I learned that lesson from my nanny a long time ago," he chided her in an aggrieved tone. "It's just as true in the big city, you know, Jordanna."

A young band was announced then and as they crooned a famous country song about young love, Chris's arm slid along the back of her chair. No doubt it was an innocent move. She just happened to be sitting there, next to him. He didn't mean anything by it. Perhaps he just needed to stretch, Jori told herself. But either way, it felt nice to have that strong arm behind her, sort of protecting her.

It was a strange thought. As if she needed protecting, Jori derided her subconscious. She certainly didn't want him to think she couldn't manage alone! But when his arm stayed there through the next three numbers, Jori couldn't ignore the cared-for feeling it transmitted to her weary heart.

It must be nice to have someone to lean on, she thought, staring at the young woman who was arranging her microphone. Somebody to take over the load once in a while.

Reality intruded. Of course, it wasn't likely that any man

would want to take on a woman who was tied to this town. Never mind someone with all the doubts and fears she had.

No, Jori decided. She wasn't the type of woman Chris Davis would normally be interested in. She just happened to be here now. Chris was sure of himself and his path through life. He would never understand the misgivings that gripped her each day when she considered her future.

"This one is really good," Chris murmured in her ear, drawing her out of her self-examination. "She gets my vote."

The young woman with the guitar strummed quietly as she sang, her voice building to a crescendo as she told of her love for a young man who had left to find his fortune, and rejected her because she wouldn't go with him. The words were achingly poignant and Jori couldn't help glancing at Chris, assessing his reaction to the song.

There was thunderous applause when the young woman finished. She bowed and then quietly left the stage with many in the audience still clapping.

"She was good, wasn't she?" Chris's voice was full of enthusiasm. "I'd like to hear her again but with a different song. Something lighter."

"I take it you don't believe in love lost," she teased, only half joking.

His eyes were bright and clear as he stared into hers; his voice firm and direct. "I believe that love is a rare and valuable gift that God gives to humans," he murmured, his hand squeezing her shoulder. "If you find it, and many don't, you need to do everything in your power to nurture it, keep it growing. Nothing should be allowed to come between two people who love each other. Nothing."

Jori tore her gaze away from his only because someone on the other side was saying something to her and she didn't understand what it was. As if in a trance, she agreed with the other judges that the young woman was indeed the best performer and deserved the CD player. They went through the list of contestants and awarded a prize to each of them, including the raucous drum player.

"You're giving a prize for that…that noise?" Chris demanded in a shocked whisper but his eyes were twinkling in the dusk. "You always play fair, don't you, Jori?"

"I try." She smiled. "There are enough prizes, so why not? It might encourage some future musician." There was more she wanted to say but he hugged her against his big wide chest then and the words got stuck in her throat.

"You're a very special woman, J.J." His lips brushed across her forehead before he set her free and Jori could only hope that it was dark enough that no one in the audience would see.

"J.J.?" She stared up at him in confusion.

"It's my new nickname for you." He grinned. "Makes our friendship more…personal, don't you think?"

Jori wondered if things weren't quite personal enough between them, but he gave her no opportunity to comment, wheeling away to speak to one of the youth gathered nearby. Reluctantly, Jori turned away to converse with the other judges, pushing back the longing his words engendered. How close did he want to be?

After the awards were given out, Chris insisted on another piece of pie and Jori gladly accepted the cup of coffee he purchased for her. Many of the younger children had been taken home now and the grounds were quieter as a senior's group played softly onstage. Here and there a few couples swayed to and fro to the old dance tunes of a bygone era.

"I've got to go back to restaurant eating," Chris murmured, licking his lips appreciatively. He patted his flat stomach with a grin. "I didn't eat nearly as much then." He noted the tiny shiver Jori tried to repress. "Are you cold?"

"A little," she admitted ruefully. "I have my sweater in the Jeep but I'm too lazy to go and get it."

"Do you want to leave?"

"We can't go yet!" She stared at him appalled. "The fireworks will be starting soon."

Chris grinned, flicking a finger against the tip of her nose. "Well, we certainly can't miss *that*," he agreed, a roguish look in his eye.

Jori grinned in reproof.

"Stop making fun of me," she ordered. "I happen to like all these small-town traditions. And nothing, *nothing*," she reiterated firmly, "can compare with *these* particular fireworks."

"Nothing?" Chris teased in a slow and easy tone. "Hmmm. That sounds like a challenge. I never could resist a challenge."

She waited, but when nothing more was forthcoming, Jori got up, tossing her cup into a nearby garbage can. "I guess I'd better get my sweater," she murmured. "I'm getting really cold."

They meandered back to the Jeep, meeting people coming and going along the dimly lit path. Chris obligingly pulled on his jacket when she handed it to him and waited with his back turned while Jori slipped into her jeans beneath her skirt, then she removed her skirt. When she'd pulled on her sweater she sighed.

"Mmm, that's better. I was freezing."

"Why didn't you say so?" Chris murmured, inclining his head. He wrapped his arms around her. "I would have warmed you up."

"Oh." There were a thousand things she wanted to say and nothing at all that seemed appropriate, so Jori simply stood there, his arms around her waist, holding still as his mouth lowered to hers.

His gentle kiss made Jori forget all about the country fair and all the people who might see them together like this. His arms were big and solid, yet gentle as they cradled her, and Jori couldn't move. It felt somehow right to be here with him in the dimness of this rustic setting. When he lifted his head, she blinked several times.

"Do you see stars?" she asked in bewilderment. "Blue and red ones with little tails?"

Chris laughed and moved behind her, turning Jori so that she faced the open field. His arms stayed linked around her waist and she relaxed against him when he murmured in her ear.

"Thanks for the compliment, but I think the real fireworks have begun." His lips brushed her hair gently before his chin rested on the top of her head. "And according to a certain nurse I know, they're pretty spectacular."

They watched in silence as the series of explosions rang across the countryside. One after the other, the small puffs of smoke disappeared as yet another blaze of dazzling, glittering bursts lit up the darkening sky. Jori heard his sigh of appreciation as the grand finale, a glistening, wildly colorful waterfall sprayed its sparkling glory across the thin wires that had been rigged earlier.

She hated to leave the comfort of his arms, but streams of people were flowing out from the fairground and Jori could just imagine the speculation if they found her in the arms of the new doctor.

"And that, Dr. Christopher Davis, is the Silven Stream Fair. It's time to call it a night." She eased away from him and dug in her pocket for her keys.

"Yes, I guess it is. Thank you, Jori. I enjoyed it very much. All of it." His eyes were strangely incandescent in the shadows. The gleam in them made Jori nervous. After unlocking the door of the Jeep, she climbed in, conscious of his hand under her arm. When Chris finally got in, Jori couldn't look at him. Instead she drove carefully back over the winding road, ignoring his sudden silence, thinking.

As an instructive experience for a man used to the city, this day had been an unqualified success. But, it seemed that she had learned a few home truths herself. And one of them bothered her. A lot.

She really liked Chris Davis.

"It was nice of you to take me today, Jori." he murmured when they arrived at his home. "I guess I can see why some people want to live here. It must get awfully boring, though. Good thing the city's not too far away."

It wasn't the best thing he could have said and Jori felt that irritating flick of dismay at his cavalier words.

"They stay here because their families, friends and neighbors are here and because they can stop and smell the roses without driving for an hour," she muttered, trying to suppress her frustration.

"But it's so isolated. You have to drive for ages before you can dine out properly. It feels like another world!"

"I suppose you mean because we don't expedite people here like you did in Boston." She emphasized the city sulkily. "In and out without even knowing your patient's name. Well, *Doctor,* in Mossbank, the guy you malign today is the guy you'll have to do business with tomorrow. You won't find the chilly impersonality of the city here." She tried to stop them, but the bitter words flowed out anyway.

"I suppose that's what you liked most about your work in Boston. You did your thing in the operating room, your patients were gone from your life and you didn't have to think about them anymore."

"Jori, I didn't mean to imply…"

"Yes, you did," she sputtered. "You meant that you feel stuck here. Well, it's true in a way. You can't just change things by shifting a case to someone else. There's no way to opt out if you don't like Mrs. Newsom's test results. You've got to treat her tomorrow and the day after that until she dies of some horrible disease that no one can cure."

Jori stared at him, trying to remember all the good things about him, but the pain of his words would not abate.

"You can't run away here, Chris. You have to sit and patiently wait until that mom is ready to give birth and whether or not you're ready has nothing to do with it. When she needs you, you'd better be there." She stared at the road and forced herself to speak calmly when all she wanted to do was cry. For what, she wasn't sure.

"If you stay in the rat race long enough, you never take the time to listen, really listen to what your best friend or your sick patient or God is telling you. You scurry away, pretending this or that is more important. And it's not. Nothing is more important than God's voice and lots of times he uses the people in your life to speak."

She barely heard his chilly answer.

"Maybe. But I think hiding out is exactly what you're doing. And sometimes you have to get away from the people in your life in order to carry on." He lunged out of her Jeep and slammed the door before walking around to her side of the vehicle. "Thanks for the day, Jordanna. Good night."

And then he was gone, leaving her to wonder about his words and the obvious pain behind them. He was hurting, although he tried to hide it behind a mask of self-sufficiency. And Jori felt totally unable to cope with it.

"Father, you know what this is about, I don't. Please draw near to Chris tonight. And let him see that you are able to deal with it all, you never grow weary or faint. And please, God, if this thing between us isn't your will, let me know. I'm so mixed up!"

Chris wasn't sure exactly how it happened.

After all, he hadn't really attended a church regularly in years. Except for the odd wedding and funeral. And certainly never one like this. The churches he had known had always seemed such cold, grim places; and once he'd started working, well, shifts being what they were, going to church had been the last thing he'd thought of.

He tried to ignore the voice in his head that snorted he was only here today because of a woman. And yet, here he sat, dressed in a suit and tie, on a polished oak bench, waiting for the service to begin.

It was her fault, of course. Jori Jessop had invited him rather casually one day last week and he'd brushed off the invitation with as much politeness as he could. Not his scene, he'd told her brusquely when the truth was, he didn't want to get any more involved with these people. But when old man Olden had told him Jordanna was singing this morning, Chris had experienced a rapid change of heart.

"Sweet as a bird, Jori is. Sings like one, too. Gonna hear her this Sunday," the old fellow had teased, clearly trying his hand at matchmaking.

"What does she sing?" Chris asked the question before thinking.

But Aubery Olden was nobody's fool and he knew when a fish was on the line. Chris felt like one of those suckers he'd seen the kids catch in the river and he waited impatiently while the old man reeled him in.

"Oh, most 'bout anything she takes a fancy to. Soul, blues, gospel. Jori tries 'em all out sooner or later." As he'd buttoned his shirt the old man's eyes twinkled up into Chris's. "Church starts at eleven," he'd said softly.

He'd been greeted enthusiastically when he entered, Chris mused. He had also been amazed by the grip of some of the elderly parishioners, particularly Frank Bellows. A surgeon's hands were his most important tool, Chris reflected, flexing his hands carefully and deciding nothing was broken.

"We're glad to have you here with us today," the man had said, a warm smile tilting his straight lips. Frank had the soft empathetic voice one expected of an undertaker and Chris knew he'd be good at comforting the bereaved.

Frank showed him to a seat, and for lack of knowing any different, Chris had taken his place, idly watching the assortment of families that filled the rows in front and be-side.

When a drooling toddler crawled under the pew in front of him to gnaw on his shoelaces, Chris picked him up eas-ily. The child was a friendly one and grinned happily as he dribbled over Chris's navy blazer. One lone tooth stood out proudly and the little boy used it effectively when his tem-porary caregiver foolishly allowed the child to play with his thumb.

The frazzled mother rushed up moments later and smiled her gratitude as she ushered the rest of her children into the bench.

"Thank you so much, Doctor," she whispered. "He just gets away from me so fast these days."

"He's certainly a mover," Chris agreed, noting that the rest of her brood looked happily excited to be at the small church. He felt a pang of envy when the father took his place at the end of the pew beside his wife, completing the family unit.

To the left a group of young adults gathered, chattering madly over the worship music of the organ. He saw no signs of wealth on any of them and yet they smiled and talked freely, obviously content with their world. They be-longed here and they knew it.

Even the elderly ladies behind him were discussing something with great animation. He was astounded to hear his name moments later.

"That's Christopher Davis, the new doctor." He recog-nized the birdlike tones of Mrs. Flowerday.

"Filling in for Dr. Dan and Jessica, isn't he?"

"And working with Jori. Now, wouldn't that be a match made in heaven!"

They twittered and talked among themselves as Chris wriggled uncomfortably at their matchmaking. He disliked being the topic of conversation. He also felt guilty sitting in this holy place and scheming to get another date with the lovely Jori.

Plans for marriage were the last thing on his mind these days, especially since he knew Jori intended to stick it out in good old Mossbank! Anyway, permanent entanglements weren't his style. Not at all.

Chris was flipping through the worn red hymnal when someone slid into the seat beside him. Jori. He felt his heartbeat quicken as his lips twitched involuntarily, unable to stop smiling.

"Good morning," he greeted her, tamping down the rise of excitement he felt.

Jori stared at him for several seconds before replying. He could tell she was surprised. He felt sort of shocked himself. Today Jori Jessop looked like a model. Her waist-length hair was loose and free, cascading down her back like walnut silk washed sparkling clean. She wore a slim fitted suit in some reddish color that gave a lovely glow to her cheeks.

The jacket had short sleeves, baring her slim arms to the summer heat. Tapered in, it ended in a point just below her waist. The straight skirt had a small slit in the front where it stopped demurely just below her knees. She wore gold hoops in her earlobes and a tiny gold locket that dipped into the V-neck of her jacket. The total effect was one of ultra-French chic and totally suited her slim tall figure.

Her big dark eyes, fringed by those incredible lashes, shone brightly back at him. "Good morning, yourself. And welcome here."

Chris was conscious of a peace and serenity that pervaded the service that followed. Even the squall of a baby in the back, or the muffled whisperings of two fidgeting youths up front didn't disturb him as he joined in singing the old familiar hymns.

When Jori was introduced, he watched as she moved with that smooth long-legged grace to the front. A taped background provided her accompaniment, but Chris didn't notice it much as he listened to her voice soaring through the stillness of the morning. He watched, totally rapt, as she poured emotion and feeling into her words, drawing the congregation along with her. And when she was finished, he was tempted to clap.

"That was beautiful," he whispered when she sat down once more. Jori merely smiled at him and brushed a strand of hair off her face.

It was then he noticed her hand was shaking. Gently, he covered it with his, squeezing her fingers just a little. And there it lay during the entire sermon. Somehow it made him feel a part of her group. As if, at last, he belonged.

The sermon was short but pertinent; a well-placed talk that described the benefits of belonging to the family of God. As he bowed his head and repeated the prayer's simple words, Chris felt a tingle of electricity in his heart. In this, at least, he belonged, he told himself. He was a part of the family of God.

After the benediction, everyone surged toward the doors, pausing to greet friends and extend invitations. Chris followed, amazed by the warm welcome everyone gave him. He'd never been in a church where everyone was so friendly.

"How's your wife, Jason?" That was Frank Bellows, softly questioning the young man who stood holding a squalling two-year-old boy and the hand of a frightened-looking blond girl.

"She's feeling down today, Frank. That chemo's really taking it out of her." The voice was discouraged and Chris knew why. Tracy Forbes was undergoing one of the strongest treatments available. It was no wonder she was ill.

"You got your spraying done, Jason?"

Chris could see the undertaker's white hand on Jason's shoulder, sharing his sorrow.

"No. I haven't had time. It's Tracy that's important now."

"Course it is, son. Of course it is. Still, you've got to look after that fine crop of yours. I haven't anything on for tomorrow. Do you think the kids would like to go for a boat ride?"

Jason Forbes's face turned up in a smile for the first time that Chris had seen. Relief washed across his young face as he grinned happily. "I know they'd like it, wouldn't you, kids?"

Forbes's two-year-old son's face turned up in a happy smile as he stared at the older man. "Fishin'?" he asked hopefully. "Jody fish?"

"Sure you can fish, Jody. You and Casey both." Frank glanced up at their father. "I'll pick them up around nine, then?"

"It's not going to be too much for you, is it, Frank? It's been mighty hot and you know what Dr. Dan said about getting too much sun." Jason peered down at the pale white skin. "You don't want to get heatstroke."

"Don't worry so much, Jason. I've been taking care of myself for a good long time now. Besides—" Frank beamed "—I might just enlist myself some help."

Chris saw the undertaker's eyes move to where Charity Flowerday stood talking to a tall portly gentleman. Frank's eyes were soft and full of an emotion Chris was loath to identify.

"If she isn't busy with Adam, that is." Frank's voice had dropped to a whisper but Chris heard the dismay in his voice.

"Well then, thank you very much," Jason agreed, pumping his white hand. "Tracy'd be glad of the rest."

"No problem at all. Say, Doc, I'd like to speak to you for a moment, too."

Chris stood where he was, waiting for Frank to approach.

"I was wondering if you might like to go out for dinner

one evening?'' Frank asked, half-apologetically. ''I often eat on my own and it's nice to have someone to talk to.''

Chris swiveled his head, trying to keep up with Jori's progress. ''I'd like that, Frank. Can I call you?''

''Sure.'' Frank's gaze narrowed as he watched Chris. ''She's beautiful, isn't she?''

''Who?'' Chris asked, and then flushed at the look of understanding on the other man's face. ''Yes, she is. Unfortunately, she's also as quick as lightning and not too fond of doctors from the city.''

Frank laughed and Chris saw his eyes move to Charity once more.

''Yes, I'm familiar with the situation,'' he agreed. ''Somehow they get one picture lodged in their minds and that's all they can see, whether it's reality or not.'' He turned back to Chris with an uncertain smile. ''Maybe we ought to do something about that.''

''Yeah. Maybe. Got any ideas?'' He watched the older man curiously, noting the sparkle that lit up his grey eyes.

''Not yet. But I'm thinking on it.''

''Let me know what you come up with.'' Chris grinned, shaking his hand. ''I'd like to see if it works.'' Meanwhile, he intended to try some ideas of his own.

Chris waited until Jori was finished speaking to the couple behind them. Then he leaned his head closer to hers, and asked, ''Will you have lunch with me, Jori?''

He figured he had given her less opportunity to resist with a crowd of observers around them. He watched as she stared at him, head tipped to one side. When she spoke, it was hesitantly.

''Well, I was going to go for a picnic. You could join me for that, if you like.''

''That would be great,'' Chris replied, thinking about the last time they'd enjoyed nature together.

''There's just one thing you might not like,'' Jori told him.

"Nonsense." He brushed off her hesitation. "It's perfect weather for a picnic. I'll pick up something and then stop off at your house right after I change. We can choose our spot after that. Okay?"

"Chris, I really don't think..." Jori stared at him, her eyes dark with apprehension.

Someone interrupted them and she was tugged away from him in the sudden movement of people. He mouthed the word *later* at her and she nodded, although her forehead was creased in a frown.

An hour later when he arrived at Jori's, Chris found out the reason for her frown. Not only weren't they to be alone, but she planned to bike there. As in bicycle, a two-wheeled vehicle that one pedaled.

"This is Billy Smith. He's in my Sunday school class and today he memorized all the verses for July. So we're going for a picnic." She glanced at Chris's immaculate clothes. "It's okay, you know. If you don't want to bike, we can drive." Her voice was kindly patronizing and Christopher Davis wanted nothing more than to strut his stuff, especially since that freckle-faced kid was ripping off wheelies around him. If he had to prove himself on a bicycle, so be it.

"Hi, Billy. Congratulations." He glanced down at Jori's superior look. "No way, lady. Then you'll be on about my age. If you want to bike, we'll bike." He surveyed the old green model with dismay. "Although, I must confess, I haven't been on a bicycle in twenty or more years, and this one looks like it hasn't been ridden in two decades."

Gingerly, Chris planted himself on the seat and lifted one leg to the pedal. Jori rode around him.

"Come on, Doc," she cheered, giggling merrily. Even Billy joined in, chortling with glee as Chris wobbled and teetered three feet down the drive.

He caught on to the thing, finally. But there was a good chance the tires wouldn't hold him for long and he reminded himself to fall on the grass and not the gravel. Wobbling crazily, he followed her down a rough track of unpaved road behind her house.

As they pedaled along, Billy started singing at the top of his lungs and Jori chimed in. It was clear they were enjoying the day. Chris began to appreciate the benefits of cycling himself, watching Jori ahead of him.

Seconds later he was flat on his back in a patch of weeds alongside the trail. Jori stood over him giggling, her hand outstretched.

"Come on, I'll help you up." Her laughter rang out in the clear afternoon air as the wind whipped the pigtails of hair she had tied up with yellow ribbons. "What happened, Doc?"

Chris took her hand, deciding it was time for a little retribution, especially since Billy had motored on ahead—far ahead. Tugging slightly, Chris was gratified Jori's graceful body landed on the ground beside him. He turned so that he was lying beside her in the weeds.

"I told you not to call me that." He kept his voice low and menacing. "Now you'll have to pay the price."

Jori was still giggling but she stared up at him as she asked carefully, "And what is the price?"

"This," he murmured and gave her startled mouth a gentle kiss.

"There are certain advantages to bike riding," he told her.

Jori's dark chocolate eyes opened wide. "Such as?" Her voice was innocence personified.

Chris shook his head. "This," he replied, kissing one of her eyelids closed. "And this," he added, kissing her cheek. Before he could kiss her lips again, his stomach grumbled.

Jori jumped slightly at the low rumbling. "What's that? Thunder?" She peered around his shoulder, searching the clouds. "It doesn't look like rain."

Chris sat up, brushing his hands through his hair. Shame-faced, he met her eyes bashfully.

Jori stared at him for a moment before she burst out in a new fit of giggles. Gathering herself, she stood gracefully, brushing down her clothes.

"What are you doing lying around here, dallying?" she demanded, hands on her curvy hips. "Let's move, Doc...man." She had changed the latter only after glancing sideways at him.

"You'd better watch your mouth, miss," Chris advised her. "That's what got us off the track in the first place."

Jori looked at him, frowning, lips pursed. "I don't think it was my mouth you were staring at," she lectured him sternly.

He let her get away with it, standing carefully. Gingerly, Chris mounted the bike once more, intent on keeping his eyes on the road ahead.

"Lead on, Macduff," he urged as his stomach emitted a louder plea for sustenance. Jori, he noticed, suffered no problems from their tumble in the grass. In fact she looked even more beautiful with that flush of pink high on her cheekbones. Her usually candid eyes avoided his as she waited at the side of the road.

"Are you okay, Chris?" He forced himself to look up at her.

"Yeah. But parts of me are more okay than others, if you know what I mean." He patted his hip gently.

Giggling, she rode off, pedaling furiously down the road as if monsters pursued her. Chris heaved a huge sigh and placed his feet on the pedals. He wondered tiredly how far their destination was. Jordanna Jessop and this bucolic country scene wore him out faster than Boston and its eight operating rooms ever had.

In a sunny glade just over the hillside, they found Billy flopped on the ground, chewing a blade of grass.

"You guys sure must be outa shape," he muttered, red faced. "I been here for ages."

"We're older," Chris told him coolly. "We don't like to hurry through life."

Jori raised her eyebrows but said nothing as she spread out their lunch and they hungrily dug in.

"This is a terrible way to eat." Jori laughed as she popped another bite of the fried chicken into her mouth. "Way too much fat." Chris watched her lick her fingers. "But I could force myself to like it."

Billy jumped to his feet. "I'm going fishing. I'll see you later," he said, and took off on his bike.

Chris shook his head when she tentatively offered him the remaining coleslaw and then smirked when she ate what was left. Billy had long since bolted his food and dashed off to check out the trickling brook, so even the last of their shared chocolate bar was hers.

"I don't believe your appetite, J.J. How do you stay so slim?"

"Good genes." She beamed, sprawling on the blanket they had so carefully placed on the ground. "I am stuffed." One long slim hand patted her tummy in satisfaction. Her dark eyes turned toward him, studying his as he sat cross-legged, watching her.

"Actually, I walk a lot. I guess that takes care of most of it. When I was modeling, though, I had to watch every little bite." She sat up and grimaced. "Every ounce counts, we used to say. I decided I'd never eat cottage cheese again."

"Didn't you like modeling?" Chris asked.

"I hated it," she told him starkly. "It's all smoke and mirrors. All anyone cares about is what you look like on the outside," she whispered, playing with the twisted fringe on the blanket. "There are a lot of really bad people in that business but no one sees or cares because on the outside everything looks so perfectly lovely. After a while you start to believe in the hype and you forget who you really are.''

Chris watched the sadness swamp her beautiful face. She was lost in past memories. Painful ones, by the look of it.

"What about your fiancé?" he asked softly, not really wanting to know.

"I thought he was special," she told him softly. Her voice ached with sadness. "He turned out to want the same from me that everyone else did. He only wanted what he could see on the surface—the money, the fame. He didn't care about me as a person and because I believed in the lie, I forgot who I was." Jori's eyes met his.

"I let myself trust in those illusory things. I became the person in those pictures. When things altered and my reputation was smeared, I felt as naked as those pictures. As if the real me was exposed and I wasn't anything like the person I'd pretended to be. Trace turned into someone I didn't even know. And then he ran.''

Chris could only sit and wait for the calm beauty of the afternoon to wash away the grief he'd just witnessed.

And while he waited, he experienced a feeling of guilt. He had been doing the same thing, he realized. From the start he'd judged Jori by what she looked like. Reality had proven less simple to define. In a few short weeks he had seen that she was gentle and yet fiercely loyal to her priorities, energetic and confident of her future, independent but also curiously attached to this town and its people.

But most of all, Chris thought he could see insecurity beneath all that confidence. She didn't want him to, of that he was sure. But every so often, when she thought no one noticed, Jordanna Jessop the confident, give-as-good-as-you-got woman turned into Jori, the small-town girl. It was a complicated picture.

"Sorry," she murmured after several minutes, clear skin flushed. "Sometimes I get maudlin. You have my permission to give me a swift kick in the keister." Her wide mouth stretched in a grin. "My Granny Grey used to say that."

Chris watched her dark head tip to one side as she studied him. He knew the questions were coming and he dreaded them. How could she possibly understand him when she'd grown up protected in this small, closely knit community.

"How did you get into medicine?" Her coffee-colored eyes sparkled at him. "Did you decide when you were five that your lifelong ambition was to be a doctor, and then scrimped and saved to make it so?" Jori stared at him as if expecting her fairy-tale dream to come true. How little she knew.

"Hardly," Chris snorted, wondering just how much of reality Jori had sampled. In spite of her worldwide exposure and life in the jaded world of modeling, she projected a childish naïveté that Chris had never really appreciated.

Until now.

"I don't think you're really all that interested in my childhood," he muttered, trying to think of another subject.

"Really, I am." Jori rushed to reassure him, wide eyes sparkling. "Tell me."

Chris stared. She was serious. He'd thought to escape with a smart remark or two but she sat there peering at him, waiting for his answer. He sighed and straightened his shoulders with determination.

"In my family, the eldest son was expected to be a doctor. I grew up knowing that I would become something in medicine. End of story." He'd deliberately cut it short—by about twenty years.

Jori wasn't satisfied. He hadn't expected her to be.

"How large of a family?" Why were her eyes so big and shiny?

"Four children—three girls, one boy." There, perhaps that would satisfy her.

"What did your parents do?"

Apparently not. Sighing he let her have the information.

"My father is a professor of biological sciences at McGill. My mother's a chemist. My sister Anne is with a research institute in Boston, Joan is still working on her physics degree and Jayne has just finished her residency in orthopedics. Should we go?"

"Wow."

It was clearly the only descriptive phrase she could think of. He grimaced. At least it was different from the "That's nice," that women usually offered.

"You must be so proud of them all." Jori's sunny tones brought him back to earth. He scowled.

"Why? I didn't have anything to do with their successes." He was curious about this woman, Chris admitted. She had a strangely odd outlook on life.

"No, but I mean, it must be great to share so much knowledge in one family. Christmastime must be a riot at your house."

Chris figured he might as well let her have it all. No sense sparing her sensibilities. Somehow, he doubted she'd ever understand.

"My family doesn't celebrate Christmas, or any of the other religious holidays." His tone was cool and controlled. "We never have."

He knew what she was thinking. What a bunch of cold fish. And Jori was right, they were. He'd always felt the same way about his family. But that didn't mean he liked other people thinking the same thing.

Jori, on the other hand, probably always celebrated Christmas. He could picture her singing the carols, joyously abandoned as she decorated house and yard. He knew she would always have a tree and stockings no matter where she was. Chris was pretty sure Flop would be decorated with a big red bow in honor of the season.

Jori Jessop was everything he wasn't—and a lot of things he wanted. Chris was beginning to realize just what he was missing in his life: a family that was close and involved in each other's lives. People who yelled and hollered at one another and then forgave and forgot. He wanted to be part of a couple who shared everything—a bathroom and a bed, and children whose futures were not planned out years ahead of time. Parents who celebrated each child's arrival for the miracle it was instead of mapping out careers for their progeny.

Chris thought back on the thousands of operations he'd performed over the years. As always, the Martins came to mind. A couple so bedraggled and quiet, they'd been ignored by almost everyone in the hospital. He'd only seen them because he was checking on a postop gall bladder and Mrs. Martin had passed out in the hallway right in front of him.

It was Christmas Eve, he recalled. Mrs. Martin had been in labor for a number of hours due to the old-fashioned beliefs of a doctor who should have known better. By the time Chris saw her, the woman and child were both in distress.

The cesarean began routinely until she'd begun to hemorrhage. He'd pulled out all the stops to save her. And finally succeeded. Mr. Martin had been overjoyed to see his wife and child alive and relatively healthy. Tears had flowed down his cheeks as he thanked Chris. And when Chris had stopped in to check on the woman Christmas day, they'd invited him to join their celebrations. They had nothing. But they had such love, such joy. They were a family.

"Chris?" The delicate hand was softly tugging at his arm. Chris realized Jori had spoken to him several times.

"What?" His voice came out gruffly and she shrank back. He raked his hand through his hair in frustration, organizing his mind. "Sorry. Did you say something?"

Brown eyes studied him searchingly for several moments. Finally she gave up when he refused to permit her entrance to the dark secrets whirling around inside his head.

"I just wondered if you wanted to leave now."

Chris knew he'd hurt her by refusing to disclose everything. She could probably guess most of it by now anyway. Years of hiding his little-boy wants for a family like the Martins kept him from sharing his pain, however, and he stood immediately.

"Ready when you are." He grinned, forcing a light tone into his voice. Come on, Davis, get with it, he told himself. Get the mask back in place.

She was a good sport, Chris would give her that. She gathered their picnic without a word and stuffed it carelessly into the huge straw bag she carried on the front of her bike. She mounted the old two-wheeler and waited for him.

When he was beside her, she put her hand on his arm, stopping him from going any farther. Her sympathetic eyes met and held his. One hand reached up to push the hair off his forehead.

"If you ever need someone to talk to, someone to listen," she told him quietly, "I'm here." Then Jori called out to Billy and pedaled away down the lane while he stood staring after her.

Chapter Six

"Hi, Dad. How are you?" Jori tugged the thickly padded leather chair a little nearer her father's recliner and patted his hand. "Enjoying the sun?"

James Jessop stared at her, bleary eyed. "Jori?"

She grinned happily, pleased at this evidence that her daily visits were paying off. Her father seemed to recognize her more and more frequently.

"Yes, it's me, Dad. I brought you some pie. Fresh peach." She held out the plate and slipped the plastic wrap off. "Fosters are having their auction today. Do you want to go?"

"Reginald Foster died?" Her father stared at her with disbelief and Jori rushed to correct the error.

"No, Dad. He's moving, remember? Wanted to be nearer Barbra and her girls. In Minneapolis," she added when he continued to stare at her. Maybe it wouldn't be a good idea to remove him from the security of Sunset just yet, Jori considered.

"Oh." James continued to frown for several more minutes before taking the fork Jori offered and cutting off a piece of the pie. "It's good," he said after another mouthful.

"Thanks. I know it's your favorite so I made a couple of them. You let me know and I'll bring some more."

"Apple's my favorite," he told her firmly, pushing the empty plate away. "Always has been. *'A word fitly spoke is like apples of gold in settings of silver.'*"

"But you always said…" Jori stopped, refusing to be drawn. It would only confuse him more.

"Had your snack, have you, James?" Charity Flowerday patted the graying head with a gentle hand. "What was it today?"

But James seemed not to see her. He merely stood and wandered over to the blooming fuchsia plant nearby.

"Oh, dear," Charity murmured, peering down at Jori. "Did I say something wrong? I didn't mean to interrupt, you know."

"Of course you didn't." Jori sighed. "He's just a little confused today."

"Well, we all have those days!" Charity fluffed out the white pleated skirt of her summer dress. "For instance, I thought today was Friday and that I'd meet a friend here."

"It's Thursday," Jori smiled. "And aren't Dad and I friends?"

"Yes, of course, dear." Charity blushed, veering her eyes away from Jori's curious ones. "It's just that I meant a gentleman friend. It's so hard to get any privacy and I thought if we met here we could talk without Faith and Hope butting in."

Jori stared as the elderly woman shuffled her orthopedic shoes back and forth.

"Oh, don't misunderstand me. I love those two girls. We've been through so much together. But I need a little time and space on my own. Without their meddling."

"But you said you were meeting someone," Jori reminded her, frowning. "A man."

If anything, Charity Flowerday's face grew even redder. Her warm brown eyes were shuttered and she looked away from Jori's enquiring gaze.

"I just said that," she admitted at last, her mouth drooping. "I'm so tired of people trying to match me up with someone. Peter was a wonderful husband, but he's gone now and I've accepted that. I don't want anyone else in my life. Not like that. I have more than enough on my plate with Melanie and Mitch expecting." She glanced furtively over her shoulder and then relaxed a little farther into the chair back.

"I know it was silly but I thought if everyone believed I was interested in some mystery man, well…" She blushed again. "You know. They'd leave me alone."

"Yes," Jori whispered softly. "I know. But why didn't you just tell Faith and Hope the truth? I'm sure they'd understand."

Charity snorted. "Have you ever tried to get those two to stop once they've made up their minds?" She shook her head gloomily. "It only makes them determined to fix me up. I don't want that." Her voice was firm.

"It would serve you right if I told them." Jori grinned. "After all the matchmaking stunts you three have pulled on everyone else, it seems only fair."

"I can see how you'd think that," Charity murmured, glancing up warily. "But you're young and beautiful. You have your whole future ahead of you. You should have a husband and children." She stopped, staring off through the windows to the fountain spraying in the courtyard.

"That's all in the past for me. I shared some of the best years of my life with Peter and I wouldn't change that for anything, but that part of my life is over."

"You must have loved him very much," Jori breathed, gazing at the sweet face. "I can understand how it must seem that no one can take his place."

"No one can ever take another person's place," Charity

agreed archly. "Each of us has our own personal part in the lives of those around us. I didn't mean that. I meant that I can't start reliving my life now. It's too late." She lifted her twisted hands toward Jori. "Besides, who'd want a worn-out crotchety old woman like me?"

"You're a beautiful woman, Mrs. Flowerday." Jori tried to keep the tears out of her voice. "You've given so much of your time and energy and love to this community. Why, no one even notices your hands, except to comment on how much you do with them!"

"I notice them." Charity's voice was so low Jori had to lean nearer. "I look at them every day and feel embarrassed to see how bent and misshapen they've become. And look at my feet." She held out her legs covered in the thick support hose.

"I was once voted the girl with the shapeliest legs, did you know that?"

Jori shook her head.

"No one does anymore. They've all forgotten that I used to be young and beautiful."

Jori was stunned by the admission and couldn't think of anything to say that wouldn't make the woman feel as if she were trying to compensate. She was desperately searching for the right words when, from behind them, James's voice boomed out.

"Man looks on the outward appearance, but God looks on the heart." He stared down at them vacantly, his eyes unfocused.

"Thank you, James." Charity smiled, patting the hand that sat on the back of her chair. "I've told myself that a hundred times, but somehow it just isn't the same."

She stood slowly and straightened, gathering up her purse with brisk birdlike movements that belied the wrinkle of tension on her forehead. "I'm getting maudlin," she said self-deprecatingly. "I'd better go home."

"You could come with us." The soft smooth tones came

from behind them and Jori whirled around to see who was there.

Chris Davis stood grinning beside the smaller, more compact frame of Frank Bellows.

"We're going golfing," Chris announced. "Frank's going to teach me the finer points of the game. Want to come along, you two?"

Jori noted the look of longing in the older man's eyes as they moved over Charity's still figure. What could be better to prove to Charity that she was still a desirable woman than to spend the day with two attractive men? The added bonus of time spent in Chris's company couldn't hurt her either, could it?

"We were just saying we needed some fresh air," Jori murmured, linking her arm in Charity's. "I'm going to take Dad to the auction sale this afternoon, but we could go for a round or two until then. You did say you were free Charity," she reminded the older woman.

"Oh, but, I've never been golfing," Charity blustered, a spot of color on each cheek. "It's a long way around the course, isn't it?" She looked doubtfully at them all.

"Yes, it is rather," Frank agreed quietly. "That's why I always take my cart. Don't get so tired then."

Jori recognized the olive branch for what it was—an attempt to make Charity's physical limitation less obvious and realized that Frank really did want to spend time with Charity, whether she knew it or not.

"That would be great, Frank." Jori grinned. "When shall we go?"

"Why, right away!" Frank stared at Charity, obviously a little stunned by his good luck. "May I?" He held out his arm for Charity and that bemused lady slipped hers through it and walked down the hallway without a backward glance.

"Way to go," Chris cheered in Jori's ear. "He's been trying to get a date with her for ages."

"He has?" Jori stared. "How do you know?"

"He told me. Right after he noticed I was trying to get your attention." Chris slipped her arm through his and encouraged her down the hall. "I guess the Lord's looking out for both of us today."

"Oh." It was all she could think of and as she spotted James sipping his coffee and staring out the window, Jori pulled away. "I have to say goodbye to my dad. I'll be back in a minute."

But if James knew she was there, he gave no sign. His eyes were busy watching the flurry of hummingbirds sipping the red nectar from a bottle on the other side of the glass and he didn't respond to either her hug or kiss.

"Everything okay?" Chris's voice was soft with concern as he waited for her down the hall.

"I guess so. I just can't get used to him not noticing me. It's like he's there one minute and gone the next."

"It is the nature of the disease," Chris reminded her. His voice dropped. "And it probably won't get any better."

"I know." She sighed. "I know. Come on. Charity and Frank are probably waiting for us."

The morning passed in an abundance of laughter as Jori and Charity proved they neither knew nor cared about the difference between chipping and putting. Frank's patience was unending but even he shook his head when Jori whacked a ball off the green and far into the trees and shrubs beyond.

"Why don't we just leave it and you can start at the next hole?" Frank offered in his usual quiet tones. "There are wild roses in there and stinging nettles. You'll be a mess."

"No," Jori refused, determined to give the two seniors a few moments together. "I'm not wimping out. You and Charity go on ahead. She's much more adept at this game than I. Doc, you'd better come along. In case I need some medical treatment." Jori opened her eyes wide as she stared at Chris, daring him to back out when she had it all planned.

"Oh! Yeah. Sure." He followed behind her and then squeaked out a protest. "Ow! Jori, put that club down off your shoulder. I have a feeling I'm the one who's going to need the medical help."

Jori turned back just once and that was to wink at Frank Bellows as he stood transfixed on the green.

"Go ahead," she called cheerfully. "We'll catch up."

Frank smiled and nodded and she knew he'd gotten the message.

"Jori, how could you possibly have hit that ball away back here? You must have more strength than I thought."

"More brains, too." She dug around in the undergrowth of ferns and shrubs. "Couldn't you see he wanted to be alone with her? And Frank is exactly what Charity needs right now. Ouch!" She rubbed the sore spot on her brow and found his eyes just inches from her own.

"You sure have a hard head," she muttered, unable to tear her gaze away from his. "I think my skull is cracked."

She stared at the flopped-over lock of hair lying across his forehead, feeling his arms slip around her waist as he leaned a little closer, blue eyes sparkling.

"Can I kiss it and make it better?"

His kiss was like coming home, Jori decided hazily. His arms were like soft clouds of welcome closing around her. There was no threat; she didn't feel pressured as she had with Trace. She felt safe and secure and more alive than she had in weeks. And when at last his mouth moved to her neck she felt cherished.

"What kind of medical treatment was that?" she protested halfheartedly, drawing away as the heat rose in her cheeks.

"It's a specialty of mine," he replied slowly. "I've been doing a bit of research into it lately. What do you think? Is it effective?"

"That depends on what you're trying to cure." Jori chuckled.

"I take my profession very seriously, I'll have you know," he began indignantly. "If I can help relieve the pain and suffering of the masses, I'm going to try."

Jori snorted, appreciating his attempt at humor. Things *had* gotten a little too intense.

"Yeah, right. And the side benefits don't hurt too much either, do they?"

He looked affronted as he picked up the ball and guided her out of the brush.

"Are you implying that I'm somehow in this predicament because of the side benefits? My dear woman, you wound me deeply." He tried to brush the patch of burrs off his pant leg and grimaced when they refused to budge. When Jori burst out laughing, he frowned even harder. "I suppose you think this is funny?"

"I don't know what you mean," she sputtered, walking beside him with a smug air. "I merely came along for a lovely game of golf, out in the fresh air." Her eyes widened when he grasped the club out of her hand with a loud burst of laughter. "What?"

"We're going that way, remember?" He pointed down the fairway in the opposite direction.

"Oh." She peered across the elegant lawns. "Of course," she muttered as if she knew exactly what she was doing.

"Of course," he repeated seriously. But there was an impish glint in those innocent baby blues.

They finally found Charity and Frank on the restaurant patio sipping glasses of iced tea. The two were deep into some heated discussion that stopped short when Jori approached the table. Charity's eyes widened.

"Oh, my word! Jori, dear. Are you all right?" She brushed gently at the twigs and dried leaves caught in Jori's untidy hair. "What happened? Did you have a nice game, dear?"

Jori was about to explain when Chris flopped down beside her, his teeth flashing in the bright sunlight.

"She had a lousy game. She's the worst player I've ever seen," he muttered in frustration. One hand brushed the lock of gleaming blond hair off his forehead. The gesture was totally ineffectual. "I've had easier eighteen-hour days in the operating room," he declared, motioning for a waitress.

"You're the one who insisted on chopping away at that ball." She leaned back in her chair and puffed the bangs off her forehead. "It's really quite a silly game," she announced. "Chasing a stupid little ball around in a circle. I much prefer swimming or baseball."

"You only say that because you don't understand it," Chris counseled. "There is a sequence, a pattern, that you have to follow. You can't just go batting balls around the course willy-nilly. I'm sure some of those you hit belonged to other players."

"Oh, well. They can always find another one. There are hundreds of them in the bush." Jori thought he seemed inordinately worried. She shrugged indifferently.

"Is that where you were, dear?" Charity's voice sounded choked. "You seem to have gotten quite dirty."

"It's filthy out there," Jori told her seriously. "And Chris kept making me change sticks. They're all backward anyway."

"They're not backward," Chris protested vigorously. "How was I supposed to know you're left-handed?"

"Oh, my." Frank sighed. "If I'd only known. I have a set in my garage that has been there for ages. Ever since my daughter left home. She was left-handed."

Jori swallowed her mouthful of tea, shaking her head in disgust. "I don't understand why you need a set," she argued. "One stick works as well as the next to bat with."

How to request your
Free Books and Gift:

1. Peel off FREE GIFT SEAL from the front cover. Place it in space provided at right. This automatically entitles you to receive three free books and a free gift—an elegant heart-shaped jewelry box.

2. Send back the card and you'll get three brand-new *Love Inspired* novels. These books have a cover price of $4.50 each, but they are yours to keep absolutely free.

3. There's no catch. You're under no obligation to buy anything. We charge nothing—ZERO—for your first shipment. And you don't have to make any minimum number of purchases—not even one!

4. The fact is, thousands of readers enjoy receiving our books by mail. They like the convenience of home delivery...they like getting the best new inspirational romances BEFORE they're available in stores...and they love our discount price

5. We hope that after receiving your free books you'll want to remain a subscriber. But the choice is yours—to continue or cancel, any time at all! So why not take us up on our invitation, with no risk of any kind. You'll be glad you did!

6. Don't forget to detach your FREE BOOKMARK. And remember...you'll get three wonderful novels and a gift ABSOLUTELY FREE!

GET A FREE JEWELRY BOX...

How lovely this elegant heart-shaped jewelry box will look on your dresser or night table! It's yours ABSOLUTELY FREE when you accept our NO-RISK offer!

"Oh, so that's what you were doing," Chris groaned, shaking his head in disgust. "Batting!"

"He did that the whole time," Jori told the other two self-righteously. "And then when I got a home run, he was all stuffy and rude."

"A home run?" Charity inquired, a tiny smile flickering at the edge of her mouth.

"She means a hole in one," Chris explained, raising his eyebrows at Jori. "Although if you were batting all morning, I suppose technically it was a home rum."

"I got it on the fifth hole, too," Jori exclaimed, ignoring his sour tone. "One of the guys there told me that he's never seen it done before."

"The fifth?" Frank frowned. "But that's a really tough one. How in the world did you do it?"

"Don't ask," Chris ordered but Jori ignored him and launched into her personal technique, slapping at the dust on her shorts as she did.

"And so the thing just flew down the hole. I didn't realize someone else was making the shot and when I jumped up and down like that, I guess I distracted him. He sure was cranky." She ignored Chris's snort of disgust and glanced at her watch. "Good grief, I've got to get home and change if I'm going to that auction."

"I was thinking of going myself," Frank murmured. He glanced at Charity and then clearly took his courage in both hands. "Would you like to go, too, Charity? We could have a little lunch here before we head over there."

To Jori's surprise, the older woman readily agreed. "I'd love some lunch. They have the loveliest deep-fried shrimp here. You know, all that exercise has made me quite hungry!"

Jori took a quick second look, but when it seemed that Charity was indeed serious about staying, she got up from her chair and shuffled toward the door. "Thanks for the game. See you at the auction."

"Now that went pretty well, I thought." Chris's fingers on her back propelled her forward.

"What?" She peered up at him curiously.

"Those two." He jerked his head to one side, indicating the senior couple now busily engaged in a discussion. "I knew if he could only get her to sit down and talk, she'd like him. Frank's one of the most interesting men I know."

Jori strode down the street beside him. "I hope that Charity thinks so, too. She's really lonely right now and Frank might be just what she needs."

"A single man, you mean," he derided.

"Nope. Somebody to talk to. She won't come out and say it, but I think Charity is really feeling left out now that Faith and Hope are busy with their husbands. Apparently now they've even started trying to find someone for her and Charity feels that no man would want to be seen with her because of her arthritis."

Chris had one comment and he made it just under his breath. Even so, Jori heard him.

"Women!"

"Well, thanks for walking me home," she said when they reached her front gate. "I've got to go and change before I pick up Dad."

"I'll wait."

"You're going, too?" She peered at him through the tangle of hair that had blown across her face. "Why?"

"Because I've never been to an auction before," he blurted out, eyes daring her to comment. "Why are you going?"

"I'm not really fond of auction sales," she told him, opening the front door and inviting him to sit down with a sweep of her hand. "Especially when it's the Fosters'."

She watched him sprawl in her father's recliner and grinned. Chris Davis overshot the thing by a good foot, his legs dangling out beyond the chair.

"What's so terrible about an auction sale—besides all the junk, I mean?" Chris watched her face close up.

"Auction sales are awful because they always mean we've lost another member of the community. Either through death or because they've moved. And I don't want Mossbank to change," she told him passionately. Her face colored and she glanced away, self-consciously twirling the ends of her hair.

"Reginald Foster saved my life," she told him shortly. "Once when I was ten and then again later when I came home. I hate to think of him moving away from Mossbank. He's been a part of my life for so long." Jolting herself out of her thoughts, Jori turned and started up the stairs. "I'll just be a couple of minutes."

Chris stared at her disappearing figure, wondering at her curious words. This Foster man had saved her life? How?

Jori didn't bring up the subject again and Chris couldn't think of a way to introduce it into the conversation so he let it lapse while they drove to the nursing home. James Jessop was dressed and ready to go.

"Don't understand why Reg thinks he has to leave," he grumbled, fastening his seat belt. "He's the only fellow I know who can fix a piece of furniture so it stays fixed."

"I'm going to miss him, too, Dad," Jori murmured. Chris saw the glint of a tear at the corner of her eye but wisely refrained from commenting on it.

They wandered through the various items set out for auction, pausing now and then as James exclaimed over some tool or another.

"Don't you just love Reg's house?" Jori stared up at the stone walls with the creeping ivy. "It's so solid. It always makes me think of God's love—safe, secure. You can trust it to hold up."

"It doesn't need a bit of work, either," James announced prosaically. "The windows have been replaced. And the doors are all new and solid." He slapped a brick planter with one hand and grinned. "It's as strong as a rock." He turned to Chris. "Jori used to play out there on that lawn. Reg's wife, Gena, would bring her tea for her dolls and they'd pick lilacs and daisies and bring home beautiful bouquets."

"Yes." Jori smiled at her dad. "I love this flower garden. I lugged home all the flowers I could to brighten up the house when Mom was sick. We never had enough room for all these hedges and stuff."

As she trailed past the honeysuckle, Chris watched her delicate nose thin while she breathed in the scent. Seconds later she was bent over a huge yellow rose, cradling it tenderly between her palms.

"And the roses. Aren't they fantastic? I can never get enough roses."

James winked at Chris. "There was a time when she thought dandelions were just fine." The older man chuckled "It was a lot cheaper to buy those by the tons, I can tell you."

"It does look a lot like a family home," Chris murmured, running his hand over the redwood picnic table and chairs as he remembered his own childhood home. Stiff and formal, it hadn't beckoned like this one did.

"If you close your eyes, you can almost hear the kids rolling in the grass," Jori whispered, her thoughts meshing with his. "Up there in that maple is the most wonderful tree house. Or it used to be. We slept out here on those hot summer nights. I can still hear the crickets."

"It's the kind of home that needs a family," James interrupted, bringing them back to the present. "No wonder Reg wants to move—he must be lonely without Gena."

"Yes, I miss her every day, James. But time goes on and I want to be near my grandchildren." The two old friends slapped each other on the back, laughing and teasing as if time stood still.

"Come on inside," Reg invited. "I've just made some blackberry tea."

As they went inside, Chris watched Jori's bright eyes move to and fro as if searching for something. Moments later he found out what it was.

"Mags is gone, sweetie," Reg murmured softly, his hand brushing over the soft waterfall of Jori's hair. "She was a terrific dog but she just couldn't take the cold winters anymore, I guess."

"Oh." Chris saw the tears form in her eyes. "I guess it all changes, doesn't it?" she whispered to Reg.

"Yes, everything does," he admitted sadly. Then his face lit up with a huge grin. "Even you," he teased, tweaking her nose. "I can't even see the scar."

"What scar?" Chris took his place at the wrought iron table on the patio and accepted the cup of tea he was passed. Reg and James sat peering at Jori, lost in memories of long ago. "Did you hurt yourself or something?"

"Or something," she admitted breathlessly, jumping up from the table. "I'm going to go look around, Dad. You guys can talk about male stuff." With a grin and a toss of her glossy head, she was through the door.

Chris glanced from one man to the other, trying to assess the situation.

"She's never forgotten what you did for her, Reg." James Jessop's voice was filled with something Chris couldn't define. "I doubt if she ever will. I think she's finding it hard to see you go."

"It was a long time ago, James. I did what anyone would have done. It was nothing."

"It was everything," the older man corrected, leaning forward earnestly. "It was her life, her future."

Reg smiled. "Let's talk about happier times."

As they began to rag each other about the biggest trout ever caught, Chris excused himself and went outside. There was something here he didn't understand. And he thought he needed to if he was to comprehend what made Jordanna Jessop so determined to stay in this little town.

"Do you collect china?" His voice was dryly sardonic as he watched her finger the mismatched teacups and saucers. "Is that why you're so determined to stay here forevermore?"

"I never said forevermore," she muttered, flushing at his intense scrutiny. "And I do owe these people a huge debt. They saved my life."

"How?" Finally he would hear the truth behind her reasons for wanting to bury herself in this little town of nobodies.

"Oh, it was a long time ago. When I was little." When he didn't look away she sighed and continued. "I was ten and my friend and I were playing on her farm. There was a stack of newly cut hay and we would jump off the barn roof and into that stack." Her eyes closed, long lashes dark on her fair skin.

"I can still smell the perfume of that fresh hay," she murmured. "Even after all these years."

Chris stood, waiting for her to continue.

"I was a tomboy, kind of a daredevil, I guess. I went a little farther up the roof each time. The last time I went as far as I could and took a flying leap into the haystack. Unfortunately, I missed the hay."

He sucked in his breath at the thought and clinically searched her limbs for some damage he hadn't previously noted.

"What happened?"

"Oh, I guess I bounced off some bales and onto the edge of the cultivator that was nearby. Apparently I cut my head open. I woke up four days later in Minneapolis with my head shaved. Boy, was I mad."

Chris sighed in relief. A few stitches, that was all. Nothing serious.

"They told me that when I hit my head, I'd injured

something in my brain that required immediate surgery. The doctor who could operate happened to be in Minneapolis at a convention. He agreed to stay there if they'd fly me in immediately.'' She shrugged. ''He operated and I was fine. End of story.''

''I don't think so.'' Chris drew his eyebrows together. ''You haven't said anything about what makes you so indebted to the people of Mossbank.''

She was silent for a long time before she replied.

''Reg set up a fund and got everybody to chip in to pay for the surgery and my hospital stay,'' she told him. ''Reg even donated his own blood. My dad was out of work and my mother was sick and we didn't have any insurance left and he was so helpful.'' Her slim arms squeezed tightly around herself in a defensive gesture learned long ago.

''That's certainly the mark of a good friend,'' he murmured quietly.

''They did the same thing when my mother died. For months these friends—'' her arm waved to the groups of people now browsing the sale area ''—made sure that we had a hot meal every night. They cleaned house, washed my clothes and helped me with my homework until my dad could get back on his feet.'' Her eyes sparkled and shimmered at him, the depths of her feelings obvious.

''I owe them. A lot. It's a debt I can never repay but I intend to try.''

The auction was beginning and everyone was moving toward that area. Chris decided to let her go for now. He'd find out more later, he told himself. A lot more.

Chapter Seven

It was one of those days—those crazy mixed-up days when everything happened at the same time. Jori pushed the damp wispy tendrils that had worked free of her topknot off her overheated face and decided to go with the flow. What else was there to do?

First the air conditioner had given out.

"Stands to reason," she muttered to herself, checking the stack of files laid ready for afternoon clinic. "It is the hottest day of the year, after all."

Grimacing, she plucked the sticky nylon uniform from her stomach. It had to be the nylon one, because her washer had died last night in the middle of a load, leaving black grease spots spattered over everything. Nestled at the bottom was, naturally, her coolest cotton outfit.

Then, of course, there was the chicken pox epidemic. Jori vowed every kid in town had it, and all at the same time. And of course, every mother wanted her child checked when the poor little things only wanted to be home, with as little as possible touching their very itchy skin.

Which, for some reason, made her think of Chris. The problem was that his itches were buried deep inside and he wasn't letting anyone scratch them, least of all her. With a brisk shake of her head, Jori dislodged the fanciful thought and forced herself to concentrate on matters at hand, checking to make sure the kits were ready.

"Let's see, we've got a throat culture, remove a couple of sutures, at least two physicals." Jori checked the list again.

"Talking to yourself."

"Aaagh," Jori jumped, pressing her hand to her throat. "Don't do that," she remonstrated with the grinning blond giant behind her. "I'm getting older daily and my heart isn't what it was."

Doc Davis just grinned. "It's not actually my specialty," he murmured, lifting one eyebrow. "But I can perform certain resuscitation techniques if you want." The sun caught the blond stubble on his determined chin as he leaned a little nearer.

Jori's cheeks flushed a bright pink at the suggestive note in his voice.

"Doctor!" She checked to be sure no one had heard him. Thankfully, Glenda was busy arranging her own afternoon and so paid little attention to them.

Chris burst out laughing at her concern. "I didn't realize you were so circumspect. I'll be more careful in the future."

"What future?" Jori kept her head bent, concentrating on the files. That way he wouldn't see the longing in her eyes for the future they would never have.

But he wouldn't let her get away with it. One strong finger tipped up her chin so her dark gaze met his laughing blue ones. He traced the curve of her chin for a moment, his eyes brimming with mirth.

"Oh, I just meant I'll plan it better so next time I'll be able to catch you in a consultation room, or something," he told her, his eyes flashing. Oddly, his skin had flushed a deep red and Jori forced herself to look away.

"Quit flirting, Doctor." Her voice was primly correct. "We have patients to see." Jori snapped the files upright against the counter.

She turned to collect the first appointment of the day, but Chris's hand on her arm stopped any progress she might have made. Jori's round eyes flew to his in surprise. Chris's face was stern with reproof, although his blue velvet eyes caressed her with a sparkle.

"I've warned you several times, J.J. My name is Chris."

"Yes, Doc...I mean Chris." She shook her head and strode away while Chris's chuckles followed her down the hall. You couldn't win with the man.

It was appropriate that chaos chose that precise moment to arrive. He was three and well used to speaking his mind; today was no different. His name was Jonathan Grand and he was Jori's godchild.

"Happy bird-day, Auntie Jori," he crowed, alerting the whole waiting room to her milestone. "How old are you?" He chirped the little chorus to the snickers of the roomful of grinning patients.

"Thank you, darling." Jori accepted his hug with aplomb. "I'm twenty-eight, sweetie." She ruffled his brown curls before returning him to his mother with raised brows. "I will get you for this," she promised, teeth clenched in a grim smile.

Amy Grand dangled one jean-clad leg for Jonathan to bounce on.

"I know." She grinned. "That's why I came bearing gifts." With a wide smile, she handed Jori an envelope. "I know you've been wanting to do this for ages, so go for it. Happy birthday!"

Inside were two tickets for a riverboat cruise down the beautiful Missouri River just outside of Bismarck, including a sumptuous dinner for two onboard. Jori stared at her friend, eyes glistening, deeply touched by Amy's thoughtfulness.

"Thank you, Amy. I really appreciate this." They hugged to the benevolent smiles of the rest of the room. Then Jori quirked an eyebrow at her friend. "Two tickets?"

Blunt as usual, Amy blurted out, "For you and Dr. Chris, of course."

Jori figured she might have carried it off if she hadn't turned just then to find said doctor beaming at her over the gray filing cabinets. He nodded, grinning like a Cheshire cat.

Jori turned her back on him. Drat Amy! She had been wanting to ride that cruise for ages, but she wasn't thrilled about having her date chosen for her. Maybe…she smiled at Amy kindly.

"Well, thank you for thinking of him, but actually Friday is Dr. Davis's night on call, so I doubt very much that he could…"

"Yes, he can." Chris cut in, beaming fatuously. "It's all arranged. He switched shifts just for your birthday."

Jori groaned inwardly. There was no way out, it seemed, not in front of this crowd. She smiled shakily at the room in general, muttered another thank-you and went back to work.

He was getting too close, and she knew it. She also knew there was no possible future for them together. He would leave Mossbank. And she couldn't. Closing her eyes in frustration, Jori counted to ten. It didn't help.

Neither did the beautiful flowers Granny Jones brought from her garden, or the delicious peach pie Zelda Adams had baked. And it was downright difficult to look at another praline cheesecake from Emma Simms.

But when Aubery Olden arrived with one of the beautiful wooden bowls he had so lovingly created from a burl of cherry tree, Jori was forced to relinquish her bad humor. They were kind and generous people, her friends. How could they know she was highly attracted to someone who would leave in a few weeks? Someone she would probably never see again.

"You're something less than thrilled with this arrangement, right?" Chris's low tones brought her abruptly out of her meandering.

They had been driving for twenty minutes and, other than the perfunctory greetings and a thank-you for the iris bouquet, she had purposely said nothing to him as the miles passed.

"Oh, sorry. I guess I was just thinking," Jori hedged nervously. She plucked at the skirt of her turquoise dress self-consciously.

A lot of thought had gone into her choice of clothes for tonight. Jori had wanted to look special since it was Friday night and the boat would be packed with people celebrating. A tiny voice in her head called her a liar. Sighing, she accepted the fact that she had wanted to knock the socks off of one smugly superior substitute doctor.

And Jori was pretty sure this turquoise chiffon thing did it. He had gulped when his eyes took in her figure swathed in the garment with a cinched waist and matching belt. Yards of filmy sheer fabric billowed out in a full knee-length skirt.

"Have you heard anything from Dan?" His deep voice carried softly above the Bach concerto playing in the background.

Jori turned to look at him, shifting comfortably in the T-bird's low-slung bucket seats. A tendril of hair had escaped her tumbling topknot of curls and she pushed it behind her ear.

"Yes, Jessica sent me a card. Apparently, she's been checked in. If she doesn't deliver within the next few days, they'll do a cesarean. I don't think the baby is doing that well."

Surprisingly, her voice was normal and Jori relaxed a

little deeper into the seat. She prayed daily for her friends and she just had to believe that God wouldn't let them down when it came to the crunch.

"Dan phoned yesterday to ask me if I could stay longer. Apparently a heart repair on the baby is imminent, although I'm not sure Jess realizes that yet." He glanced at her sideways but Jori faced straight ahead, dreading the question she knew she had to ask.

"And can you?"

Chris turned his dark head to stare at her. "What?" he asked, lost for a moment.

"Can you stay longer?" Jori didn't like asking it, but she had to know. In some ways, it would be easier if he left soon. But her heart soared with happiness when he answered.

"Yes, I can stay as long as I'm needed. My time is my own right now." His tone wasn't welcoming but Jori asked anyway.

"Why did you leave Boston when you were doing so well?"

Chris had known the question was coming. He'd expected it because Jori wasn't the type to ignore significant details like that. She'd want to know everything. But he still didn't have his answer ready. And he knew she'd keep at him until he did. He heaved a sigh of capitulation, searching for the right words.

"Aside from helping out Dan, I guess I had my fill of medicine there. It was a huge hospital and the rotations were fairly spread out, but I felt I needed something different. Something more connected to other people. For now."

There—he had spilled his guts. Let her make what she wanted of it. Knowing Jori, he would bet a tidy sum that she would sense the effort it had cost him to open up.

True to form, she nodded understandingly. "Community, sense of belonging. I think everyone feels it sooner or later.'' They stopped and parked the car. She linked her arm with his as they stepped onto the waiting boat.

''Well, Doc, here we are.'' She grinned up at him before moving away to survey the sumptuous dining room with its elegant furnishings.

He tugged her arm gently. ''Let's go for a stroll around this tug.''

The evening was a balmy one with the sun just setting. Stars twinkled here and there while the lights of the city began to glimmer around them. The gentle motion of the boat was calming and Jori found she was enjoying herself.

In the background, a band began to play old movie tunes. Without much thought they moved into each other's arms and began to sway gently to the music.

''I love this song,'' Jori murmured as the group segued into ''Moon River.'' She sang along with them for a few bars.

''You have a beautiful voice, J.J. I enjoyed hearing you sing.'' Chris whispered, the words gently grazing her ear. ''And this dress—I don't know if *awesome* quite describes you tonight.'' He spun her around.

Jori giggled.

''Yeah, I know what you mean.'' She laughed, leaning back to study him. ''You are quite a picture yourself. Especially in that suit.'' Her dark head tipped back as she studied him. ''Yep, sure beats the lab coat.''

And that was no lie. His blond good looks were certainly accentuated by the black suit and crisp white shirt Chris wore so comfortably. It was the perfect foil for the blue striped tie that matched the exact azure color of his eyes.

He bowed to thank her just as the maître d' announced dinner. While they waited for directions to their table, Jori glanced around once more. There were a lot of men in the room but she seriously doubted that one of them could hold a candle to Chris. And when her heart repeated that silly little pitter-patter as his arm moved around her waist, Jori made her decision.

She'd enjoy tonight because she doubted there would be another one. Chris would be gone from her life soon and it wasn't likely that she would ever see him again.

Once she made that decision, it was easy to enjoy, even savor, every moment of their time together. They both chose the chef's special for the evening and while they waited, Chris told silly jokes.

"Why didn't the chicken cross the road?"

Jori groaned but he insisted she guess.

"Because she didn't want to get to the other side."

Chris's mouth stretched in a wide grin. "Wrong."

She sat waiting, but Chris just grinned at her. Jori sighed. He was like a big kid himself.

"Okay, I'll bite. Why didn't the chicken cross the road?" Jori just knew she would regret this.

"Because there was a stop sign." His blue eyes twinkled. "Guess who told me that?"

"Jennifer," Jori guessed, naming a young lady who was a glutton for joke books.

"Tommy Banks." Chris chortled just remembering the young boy. "And when I asked him what his favorite book was, he told me he really enjoyed *Parents* magazine because then he could keep up with what the adults had planned."

Jori giggled at the picture Chris painted of the freckled little boy whose precocious attitude she had experienced more than once.

They had barely set their salad forks down when the ribs arrived, redolent with oregano, garlic and lemon juice. The baby potatoes were cooked to perfection and the broccoli spears steamed a bright fresh green. They were both hungry and tucked into the delicious meal with relish. When she could eat no more, Jori leaned back in her chair, replete with the fine meal they had enjoyed.

"This is so wonderful." She sighed, gazing out the windows as the sun colored everything in a rosy glow. "I'm going to have to thank Amy appropriately for this wonderful gesture." She glanced at Chris suddenly.

"And you, too." She blushed. "It was really kind of you to rearrange your schedule this way."

"This is good, but I think your roast beef dinner was better." He rendered his verdict with a haughty tilt of his arched brow. Then he spoiled it by grinning. "And you are very welcome."

During the meal they chatted about Mossbank and its people. Jori was surprised to hear how much Chris had learned about each of his patients in the short time he had been in the town.

"By the way," she asked slyly, "what did you do with the rest of your cheesecakes. Did you really freeze them all?" Actually the problem had been bothering her for days.

Jori giggled as he groaned in dismay. But when a flush of red coursed over his face, she became concerned. She would not have her friends hurt by his insensitive attitude.

"Oh, no!" she moaned, anticipating the worst. "What did you do? Tell me."

His blue eyes met hers, tiny points of light twinkling deep within.

"I wanted to save something for Dan and Jessica. So, I cut one piece from each one and froze it with the appropriate name attached. Then I phoned that kids camp out at Minotka Beach." He grinned. "When I explained my situation to them, they agreed to take the rest off my hands." He held his hands palm up. "*Et, voilà!* It's gone!"

Jori breathed a sigh of relief. Then a thought crossed her mind. "How long ago was this?" she demanded.

Chris stared at her strangely. "Last week. Why?"

"I wondered why we had so many indigestion cases from them." She teased him, beaming with mirth. "Marta, the director, forgot to tell me about the cheesecake."

Jori burst out laughing at the look of chagrin on his face. It was clear that the good doctor had not connected the arrival of his dubious gift with the stomach cramps and other assorted maladies experienced by several of the campers.

Holding up his hand, Chris licked his forefinger and made a number one in the air.

"One for you," he conceded in a grumpy voice that only made Jori's grin widen.

She sipped her coffee while they waited for the dessert cart. The room seemed very quiet all at once, but perhaps the band was taking a break.

When the familiar notes of "Happy Birthday" were played, however, Jori sat straight in her chair. He wouldn't…he couldn't…could he?

It appeared that he had!

Two waiters carried out a huge cake decorated with fat pink roses. As they moved, the two men sang to the cheerful clapping of the other diners.

Happy Birthday, Jori lay scripted in delicate pink lettering across the glistening white icing. Around the edge glowed a ring of pink-striped candles. Jori would have covered her face but Chris reached out to grasp her hand just then, holding it on top of the table for all the world to see.

The song ended as the cake arrived beside their table. Jori was thankful when the band resumed their musical selections. Her cheeks felt as though they were on fire, but she kept her chin up and met Chris's glance head-on.

"I wish you a very happy birthday, Jori," he said quietly, and then pressed a delicate kiss to the inside of her wrist before allowing her hand to move away.

"Thank you," she murmured, unable to get anything else out. The whole week had been a chain of one surprise after another, but this took the cake, Jori mused. Then laughed. Hah, a pun!

Chris looked at her uncertainly, his eyes narrowed in speculation.

"She overdid it, didn't she?" His voice was quietly sympathetic. Jori stared at him.

"You mean Amy arranged for this?" She motioned toward the monstrous cake. When he nodded, she groaned and laid her forehead on her palm. "I should have known."

"Yes, you should have," Chris's low tones were reproving. "Not my style at all." He stuck out a finger and dipped it into the fluffy white frosting before popping it into his mouth. "Mmm, not bad, though," he told her, grinning.

"What do you mean, not your style?" Jori strove to keep her voice down. "This is exactly like something you would do, Christopher Davis." She had been sure of that once, but now Jori reconsidered.

"Uh-uh. I'm much more subtle."

Jori searched his face. "Yes, you and a steamroller," she mocked. He sat staring at her, perplexed by her attitude. It was clear that the idea had never crossed his mind and Jori felt guilty. "What is your style, then?" she asked, half-afraid of his answer.

His forefinger beckoned her closer. She leaned across to hear his conspiratorial whisper. "I'll show you later."

Dumbfounded, Jori sat wide-eyed and staring until Chris asked for some cake. She cut him a huge piece and a smaller one for herself, going through the motions automatically while she found herself wondering about "later."

They moved outside and Jori sipped her coffee, loath to break into the charming stillness that had fallen. When Chris moved, Jori jerked out of her dreamworld to find him facing her on the narrow bench.

"This is for you," he told her, holding out a beautifully wrapped parcel held together with a tiny bit of silver ribbon. "A very happy birthday, Jori," he offered.

"You didn't need to do this," she murmured, accepting

it. "You've done more than enough tonight." Her dark eyes searched his wide blue ones for answers, but got lost studying the tiny smile that turned up the corner of his mouth.

Oh so slowly, Jori slid off the ribbon and the pretty iridescent paper. Inside, a slim black box nestled in white tissue. Holding her breath, Jori slipped off the lid to find a delicate gold chain with a tiny boat attached snuggled into a puff of white cotton. A card read, "To Jori on her twenty-eighth. Chris."

"It's beautiful," she breathed, lifting the tiny weight in her palm. "So delicate and fine. Thank you very much." As she lifted her head, Jori found Chris's eyes much nearer than she expected. She pressed a kiss to his cheek, mere inches from his mouth.

"You're welcome," he murmured before turning his head to meet her lips with his own. It was a questioning kiss. Slowly, tentatively his lips touched hers as if evaluating her response while he waited for her answer.

When she returned his caress, he drew her closer. Jori raised her arms and wrapped them around his neck, happy to oblige his unspoken request.

"Is he the one, Lord?" she prayed silently.

"Jori?" His hands slowed then stopped their delicate caress. His lips pressed softly against the side of her mouth before he pulled gently back, his big hands cupping her face as he stared into her eyes.

"I think we had better go dance," he muttered, closing his gleaming blue eyes for a moment. They popped open a second later when Jori tugged on his hand.

In her palm she held the tiny necklace.

"First, would you put this on for me?" she asked quietly, turning around.

As Chris fumbled with the clasp, Jori drew the wispy tendrils of hair off her neck to give him free access. It seemed to take forever, but finally he turned her around, strong fingers pressing into her waist.

In a trance Jori moved into his arms and allowed him to lead her effortlessly onto the polished dance floor that occupied the upper deck. She swayed to the dreamy music, lost in the feel of his arms around her. She was falling for him. Hard. And the landing, when he left, would be more painful than anything she'd yet endured.

This was wonderful, Chris decided, breathing in her fragrance. Jori Jessop was like quicksilver—strong and supple, gorgeous and ethereal.

But Jori was not his type, he acknowledged grimly in another part of his mind. She was a small-town girl who liked it that way. Her life revolved around her community and she wasn't the type to turn her back on it all for a thirty-six-year-old doctor who had little to offer in terms of stability and even less when it came to family, home and hearth.

Frustrated, Chris glared at his watch. Suddenly he wished the boat would dock so they could get home before he did something really stupid—like tell her his feelings.

Just then Chris felt Jori burrow closer against him and, ignoring his better judgment, he wrapped his arms more tightly around her.

Best make hay while the sun shines, he smiled, thinking of Aubery Olden. The old coot had a lot of sense under all that grime. Perhaps he should listen up. Chris dropped his chin on the top of Jori's piled-up hair. As the faint whisper of her perfume drifted to his nostrils he decided to have another talk with the old fellow. Possibly, Chris considered, he could learn a little something.

"The band is shutting down." Jori's voice was husky, dreamlike. Chris understood that feeling completely.

"I think we have time for a last cup of coffee before we leave this boat." He grasped her hand in his and tugged her over to a table.

Jori sat across from him, staring off into space. "I love this place," she murmured, looking back over her shoulder to the twinkling lights of Bismarck at night.

"Do you come here often?" Chris asked, trying for a neutral subject.

She tipped her head to one side. It was one of her mannerisms that Chris had noticed early on. When she was thinking of something pleasant from the past, Jori always rested her head on one shoulder and closed her eyes. He waited and sure enough, three seconds later her hand came up to twiddle with a tendril of hair. He grinned knowingly.

"My dad used to bring me to Bismarck each Christmas," she reminisced, a tender smile curving her lips. "We always went to the top floor of Enderby's because they had a huge display of animated Christmas scenes."

Her voice was dreamy with the memories. She blinked her eyes, peering absentmindedly into the night.

"I would plan ahead for weeks, waiting to see the tree displays and hear the carolers that strolled through the store, dressed in English outfits straight from Dickens. And boy, could they sing."

Jori turned toward him eagerly, intent on explaining the wonders she'd seen. Chris found himself fascinated by the animation that flew across her expressive face.

"It was totally dark up there, with tiny fairy lights hanging all around. Each scene had its own lighting." Her eyes opened wide as she remembered.

"There was always a pond with ice-skaters," she explained. "And Santa and the reindeer, of course." Her long fingers formed a tent as she thought. "Oh, and Frosty usually walked around, handing out candy canes." Her voice was breathless with delight.

"There was a beautiful Nativity scene with the animals all around it." There was a tiny break in her voice, but Jori recovered immediately, continuing her account. "I especially remember the horse and cutters with kids crammed inside, so happy. The sleighs and toboggans slid down little snow hills and there was always the sound of children laughing.''

Chris shared her silence for a few minutes and thought how much he had missed. Jori had such wonderful memories, he mused. It would be something for her to pass on to her own children.

She was speaking again, her voice whispery soft with a tinge of sadness. ''I loved the family scene. You know, where everyone gathers round the tree as they open their gifts. I always wished there were more people to share our tree with. Dad and I could have used a family.''

Her round dark eyes sparkled with tears. Surprised and touched by the loneliness that threaded through her voice, Chris reached out and covered her hand with his. They sat quietly together for a few moments before he broke the silence.

''Do you still go there to see all that?'' He liked to think of her now, wandering through the displays, as enchanted as any child there.

''They don't go to that extent with their decorations anymore. But I still think the window displays are fabulous. And on New Year's Eve I go to *The Nutcracker* ballet.''

''Oh.'' His one word spoke volumes and Jori's ready laugh bubbled out.

''I know what you're thinking, but *The Nutcracker* is a very special ballet. Dad and I used to go. We would get all dressed up in our very best, go out for a special dinner and then to the theater. I never fell asleep even though it lasted until well after eleven. And each year Dad would give me a nutcracker doll to remember the year.'' She grinned. ''I have quite a collection now.''

''You have some lovely memories, Jori,'' he told her, half-envious.

'Yes, I do.'' Her voice wobbled a little, but Chris noticed she recovered quickly. ''What sorts of things did your family do together?'' she asked politely. ''It must have been nice to have sisters.'' He heard the wistful note in her voice and almost laughed.

''I'm not sure you would have enjoyed it,'' he told her grimly. ''My parents are academics. They tried to do a fair bit of entertaining at Christmas so they could work without interruption through the rest of the year.'' He grimaced, recalling those stiff occasions.

''There were a lot of very formal, very boring dinners where the discussions were usually scientific.'' Man, he was getting maudlin, Chris decided. He turned his sardonic grin toward Jori.

''Perhaps that's where I began to learn about surgery,'' he said with just a tinge of bitterness. ''Heaven knows I certainly had enough time to dissect anything that crossed my plate.''

It must be the dark, Chris decided. Here he was spilling his guts about the worst times of his life to a woman who had experienced the best. This is not the way to end a romantic evening, Davis, he told himself sourly. Unfortunately, he couldn't think of anything else to say.

After a few minutes Jori changed the subject.

''You know, there's a wonderful folk festival near here. It's held in a park and they have some famous names performing at all different times. It's very informal but it's fun. You should go on your day off.''

She turned to smile at him and Chris felt an ache in his heart. He couldn't deny it any longer. As he drove down the highway, he acknowledged the truth. He wanted to love and be loved by this woman. He wanted to raise a family with her and grow old together without feeling as if he'd failed someone. He wanted all the dull boring routine things he'd scorned for so long.

But most of all he wanted Jori Jessop by his side for the rest of his days.

The idea was so overwhelming that Chris struggled to

concentrate on the last bit of road ahead. He flicked a quick glance at Jori and smiled. She had fallen asleep. Her dark head snuggled against the seat, she had one hand tucked under her cheek. Beauty and innocence, he mused, staring.

"We're home," Chris whispered, his breath blowing the tiny curls away from her face. The night air wafted in the open door and she unconsciously shivered at the chill.

"Jori," he called a little louder, pressing his hand against her shoulder. No response. Shaking his head, Chris lifted her lax body into his arms, carrying her up the walk to the front door. Flop rushed forward to greet them.

"Down, boy," Chris told him quietly. "The lady is sleeping. Let's not wake her."

She was a soft, gentle weight in his arms. If only... Chris held her tightly against his chest.

He opened the front door and let himself in, shaking his head at the unlocked door. Carefully he eased his way through the darkened house, climbing the stairs to her bedroom. A night-light was burning, barely illuminating the frilly white mound of pillows.

Carefully, gently, he laid her on them, sliding her arms slowly from his neck. Chris watched as she shifted her hips to turn sideways, snuggling into the soft cushions. Her hands moved together to fold prayerlike beneath her cheek as she sighed once before resuming that slow, even breathing. Dark and spidery, her lashes fanned out against her soft cheek.

Slowly, knowing he would regret it later, Chris bent and placed a soft, featherlight kiss against her lips. They were soft as velvet against his.

"Happy birthday, Jori," he murmured, watching to see if she wakened. When she didn't, he straightened and with a last look, turned and left the room.

But as he slowly drove home, Chris knew that the image would not be removed. It was pointless to pretend. Jordanna Jessop was the one woman who could cool this burning discontent in his soul and help him move into the future with confidence. Perhaps with her at his side, he could overcome the regrets of his bleak past and the worries that yawned gapingly in the future.

But he had to remind himself that Jordanna Jessop was not a part of his future. She couldn't be. They were worlds apart.

Chapter Eight

"Hope Conroy, I will not entertain that nosy group in my home one more time." Charity glared at the two women standing on her doorstep. "They poked through my china, discussed my 'strange' furniture and felt duty-bound to comment on my choice of flowers. I am not impressed!"

Hope swept in through the door, dodging the older woman with an agility newly found on a tennis court.

"You say that every time they come over, Charity. But the ladies' society has to have somewhere to meet and you know you love to watch them quilt." She sat down on the sofa with a whoosh of relief, swiping one hand across her forehead. "Why don't you tell the truth? What you're really mad about is all the questions they asked about your men friends."

Charity flicked the switch on the air conditioner one notch higher, trying to hide her flushed cheeks.

"So I've had a few friends over for a meal. So what? I'm certainly old enough to entertain whomever I like." Her gnarled hands reluctantly poured out two more cups of tea. It was evident to the other two that she was reluctant to say more.

"A few? There were five men over here on Friday night," Faith gasped, peering across at her friend's flower-festooned buffet. "I suppose those are from your suitors?" Her eyes gaped at the surfeit of roses. "Who brought the yellow ones? I love yellow roses!"

"I don't remember," Charity muttered, flushing an even darker red. "They come as a group and they go as a group; as if they're attached at the hip." A sigh whispered out through her lips as she lifted her aching feet to the leather stool. "It's very trying."

"Trying? How can it be trying to have half a dozen men fawning over you?" Hope shook her head in disgust. "You'd think you'd be happy to have so much attention."

"I do enjoy their company." Charity sounded embarrassed by the admission. "They're all very nice men. But I'm not as young as I once was and sometimes I really enjoy just being alone."

"So? Rest when they're not around. What's the problem?" Hope peered across the dim room, noting the still-closed blinds. At that precise moment the doorbell rang and Hope saw the tiredness that crept over her friend's usually smiling countenance as she shifted awkwardly to her feet.

"The problem, my dear," Charity muttered irritably as she limped toward the door, "is that they're always around. Hello, Harold."

"Oh, Charity!"

"Yes, it's me. I live here, remember?" Charity fidgeted from one foot to the other, glancing over her shoulder to check if her friends were listening. They were. "Did you want something, Harold?" She had to ask it for Harold had apparently forgotten whatever it was he wanted to say.

"Oh. Yes, I did. That is, I was wondering if you're free for dinner tonight. I remembered you had that leftover beef and I thought maybe we could go for a drive after, down by the river. You know, cast a line?"

"I'm sorry, Harold. I'm having some guests over. Two

young friends of mine. They're bringing dinner with them so, I'm sorry, but you can understand that I couldn't possibly invite you. If it was me who was making the meal, you know I'd be happy to have you stay.''

''No, no! I understand, believe me.'' Harold shuffled uncomfortably on the doorstep, his straw hat in his hands. ''I'll find something at the diner. It's just that I was looking forward to your wonderful cooking.'' The hangdog look on his face tugged on Charity's tender heart, but she stood firm.

''Perhaps another time,'' she suggested quietly.

Harold sniffed miserably, nodded and shuffled off down the driveway. It was all Charity could do not to slam the door.

''Of all the nerve,'' she stormed, flopping into her chair.

''He was just asking you out,'' Hope murmured consolingly as she handed her the teacup. ''Don't get so flustered.''

''He was asking to come for dinner,'' Charity snorted, slapping her hand on her thigh as the phone rang. ''And that'll be another one, looking for a free meal or an open ear to listen to another of those long-winded stories about the good old days. Although I'm hanged if I can remember what was so all-fired good about them!'' She glared at the phone malevolently.

''I am not answering that thing.''

''But, Charity,'' Faith blurted, her eyes huge, ''that's your gift. You've always listened to other people when they tell their troubles. And then you make them feel better. That's your ministry.''

''Not anymore.'' Her voice was firm. ''I'm finished listening to other people. They never take my advice anyhow. From now on I'm going to be quiet and listen to myself. And God,'' she added as an afterthought.

''She's tired,'' Hope whispered to Faith. ''She just needs

to rest. I'll get that," she offered when the phone began its shrill peal once more.

Charity leaned back and closed her eyes, shaking her head in despair. How had it come to this? she asked herself. All she'd wanted was a little attention, someone to notice that she wasn't dead yet. And now she had six, count 'em, *six*, suitors all looking for a free meal.

"It was Aubery," Hope told her. "I said you were too tired to see anyone." She grimaced as the phone started again. "I'll deal with this one, too. This place is like a zoo!"

"There's the doorbell!" Faith jumped to her feet. "I'll send whoever it is away, shall I, Charity?" She sounded eager to dispatch whoever was holding the doorbell down.

"Yes, please," Charity called over the noise, shaking her head as she heard Faith's voice reprimanding her visitors. Curious to know who was there, she hid around the corner where she had a good view of her entry.

"Get your shoulder off that doorbell, Hank Dobbins," Faith ordered. "Do you think the whole world is deaf?"

"Eh?" Hank frowned as he stared at her. "Where's Charity? I brung some bread for supper." He thrust a loaf of semiflattened white bread at Faith, trying to edge past her. "You say something?"

"Turn your hearing aid on," Faith bellowed, glaring at him and pointing to his ear. "I don't know why you bought the thing when it's always turned off!"

"So's I could avoid all the caterwauling you women like to do," Hank told her frankly. "And stop yelling. It's turned on."

"Good. And I don't caterwaul so you can just listen to what I have to say, Hank Dobbins, and don't go trying to ignore me."

Faith didn't budge, standing squarely in the door frame. Short of physically moving her, Charity couldn't see how Hank could get in. She smiled at the scene.

"I didn't come to see you," the old gent informed her with some asperity. "I come to see Charity. To have dinner with her."

"Charity asked me to tell you that she's busy tonight. And tomorrow night." Faith handed back the bread. "So you'd better get on home and butter a slice of this for supper."

"It's that sneaky Tim Carruthers, isn't it?" The old man fumed. "I mighta known he'd try to budge in and get another free meal. Well, he can jest think again! Tim Carruthers, you git out here!" His voice rose as he called out a challenge.

"I am out here, Hank," an amused voice announced behind his back. "If you'd get some batteries for that hearing aid, you'd have heard me coming up the path."

"I got lots of batteries, an' I can hear just fine!" Hank wheeled around and held up his fists. "I'm the one who should be havin' dinner with Miz Flowerday t'night," he announced clearly. "You had yer turn t'other night. So git outta here."

"Tonight's my turn, you silly old coot! You were here last night." Tim shook his head in disgust. "Go home and eat the supper Esther Sue left."

"My daughter's a real fine cook but Esther Sue hasn't got a patch on Miz Charity." Hank licked his lips in anticipation.

"I'm afraid you'll both have to go home," Faith announced firmly. "Charity has other plans for this evening."

"No, she doesn't." Tim edged his way past Hank and stepped up beside Faith. "I made a deal with Aubery for tonight. Cost me plenty, too."

"Are you telling me that you paid someone to stay away so that you could have dinner with Charity tonight?" Faith stared. "But that's ridiculous!"

"I just promised him I wouldn't come to the box social on Friday so he could dance with Myrtle Bigelow. And he gets half of my potato crop. I planted way too much anyhow.''

Inside the house, Charity shook her head at Hope's furious gasp of outrage. She placed one finger across her lips and they both listened to Faith's disgusted response.

''Piffle!''

''Eh?'' That was Hank, fiddling with his hearing aid again. ''What did you say, woman?''

''I said *piffle!* On the lot of you. Now get going and leave Charity alone for a while!'' She turned to go inside but Tim Carruthers was standing there. ''Well?''

''But what about dinner? I've been waiting all day to taste one of her special dishes. It wouldn't be fair to make me…''

''Charity is having dinner with someone else tonight. Now away you go—the both of you!'' Faith whirled inside and slammed the door behind her in a snort of disgust.

''That's wood swearing,'' Hope reminded her, glancing at the solid oak door. ''It's just as bad as actually saying the words.''

''Maybe. But it's a lot better than knocking those two gray heads together! Honestly!'' She stormed into the living room and began gathering up the tea things. ''Now what?'' She shot the pealing telephone a most venomous look. ''Who's left, for Pete's sake?''

''It's Jordanna,'' Hope interrupted. ''She wants to know if this is a good time.''

''Yes, it is.'' Charity sank back into her chair with a sigh of relief and closed her eyes. They opened a moment later. ''That leaves Frank Bellows,'' she told Faith wearily. ''Let's hope he's busy with the church board tonight.'' Her ears picked up Hope's soft voice.

''She's really tired, Jori. The phone's been ringing off the hook and the doorbell's been going nonstop. Can you see if Dr. Chris would come? It mightn't hurt for him to have a look at her. You say he's on the way? Oh, thank you, dear. Bye.''

"I don't need a doctor, Hope Conroy." Charity's tone was not friendly. "I need some breathing space."

"Which you will get. I'm sure Jori and the doctor can help you. It's obvious something has to be done." She grasped her purse as the doorbell rang again. "If that's another male suitor of yours, I'm going to set him straight."

"Well, I am a male," Chris said laughing. "And I can always use some good advice. What's the problem, ladies?"

And the three seniors launched into Charity's predicament, one interrupting the other until the whole story was laid out.

"I can't imagine what I can do," he told them. "But I'll give it some thought. Okay?"

"Is what okay?" Jori stood in the doorway frowning. "Do any of you know that there are two red-faced men arguing outside the gate? What is going on around here?"

The fearsome threesome launched into new explanations.

"I don't know just what it is that I could do," Chris told them. "I mean, I'm new here and so far I've stepped on more than my share of toes. I take it that you don't want anyone's feelings hurt too badly?" He glanced from one to the other of them, pulling out his cell phone as it rang.

"Hello? Oh, hi, Frank. Fishing? Tonight? Hmmm." He glanced at each of the curious faces around him and then smiled a wide grin of excitement.

"Fishing's a great idea. In fact, we were just leaving for the park. Want to meet us there?" He ignored Hope's rolling eyes, Faith's "piffle" of disgust and Charity's slumped shoulders to linger on Jori's frowning countenance and the bag from Hamburger Haven that lay on the floor at her feet.

"Good. We've got dinner so don't worry. J.J., Mrs. Flowerday and me. We need to talk to you about something, too, Frank. About this little plan I've got. Okay.'' He clicked the phone closed and smiled at the group, his teeth flashing in that tanned face.

"All right now, ladies. It's all set. Charity will have dinner on the lake with Frank and I. We can all relax and talk this situation over. Are you ready?''

They bustled about, gathering a jacket for Charity, a thermos of coffee and three more cups. In the midst of it all, Jori sidled over to the doctor.

"I don't know what you've got planned,'' she said. "But it better not hurt my friends.''

"Trust me,'' he whispered, his lips brushing her cheek.

She stood back, hands on her hips and glared at him fiercely, except Chris could see the little tick at the corner of her mouth and knew she wasn't mad at all.

"At this point, I haven't got much for alternatives,'' she grumbled before holding open the door. "You'd better pray this works.''

"Oh, I am,'' he murmured, more to himself. "I'm praying that it works in more ways than one.''

Out in the boat in the middle of the lake, life seemed to slow into a wonderfully calm pattern that was completely free of problems and difficulties. Jori watched as Chris turned into the wind, his chiseled face outlined in the waning sun as he explained his plan.

"So if Charity and Frank pretend to be dating and are seen going out together, the others will give up. All her dinners will be promised to Frank and they won't have a chance.'' His eyes watched the older couple as he whispered to Jori, "I think it just might work. And she needs a break. She looks very tired. The arthritis pain saps her energy, I think.''

"I really am sorry about all this, Charity,'' Frank apologized, his hand tenderly squeezing hers. "We had no right to run you ragged like that. And we should have taken you out instead of making you cook all the time. It's no wonder you're feeling a bit exhausted.'' His eyes crinkled at the corners. "Although no one would know it to look at you. You look as young as you did twenty-five years ago.''

"Why, thank you, Frank!'' Charity preened a bit before glancing at the others. "But aging doesn't really give up, no matter how hard you fight it. This Charity is nothing like the one you knew so long ago.''

"Of course she is!'' He sounded amazed, Jori decided, eyeing the two with a tender glance. "Why, you look exactly as you did then! I remember how those big brown eyes flashed when I corrected that child picking sweet peas in your backyard and howling at the moon. What was his name?''

"Evan Schultz,'' Charity breathed, a smile tipping up the corners of her lips. "And he was trying his darndest to get into the kids' choir at church.''

"Yes, but he had the words wrong. I can still hear him. 'Gee the baloney's good'—that's what he sang,'' Frank told Chris, winking at him and Jori as he held Charity's hand on his knee.

"What was the song?'' Chris looked puzzled at the strange words. "I don't remember a church song about baloney. Or any kind of meat.'' He turned the wheel and slowed the engine just a bit.

"It wasn't about meat. The words were 'G, double O, D, good!' It was about God and his faithfulness to his children.'' Charity's laughter rang out over the water. "And Evan couldn't carry a tune in a bucket! That's why I didn't want Frank to hurt his feelings. I knew the child wouldn't get the part.''

"I wasn't going to hurt his feelings!'' Frank pasted on an affronted look but it couldn't hide the glint of merriment in his kindly gray eyes. "I was going to offer to buy him a trumpet if he'd stop making that infernal noise!'' He smirked at Charity.

"But no, you had to assure him he was doing fine and

that he just needed to practice! Agh! Thank goodness he took up sports not long after.''

Charity giggled like a schoolgirl. Jori was amazed at the change in her. Her eyes sparkled in her flushed face. Her shoulders were thrown back and she giggled happily, leaving her hand wrapped in Frank's.

''She still looks after all the kids in the neighborhood.'' Frank's voice was soft and admiring. ''There's never a kid who can't go to Mrs. Flowerday and find some good advice and a slice of double-chocolate cake to make them feel better.''

''You should talk!'' Charity grinned. ''Who offered to take his boat up to that juvenile camp and tow water-skiers around for three weeks last summer, Franklin Bellows? And then got conned into teaching a class on archery?''

''Okay.'' he held up a hand. ''We're both guilty! But I was trying to make the point that you haven't changed. You're still determined to see God's goodness in people, no matter what.''

Jori met Chris's gaze with her own and they both turned away, pretending they weren't listening.

''But I have changed, Frank. This arthritis has crippled me up so badly, I look ugly.'' She held out her knotted fingers for him to see their twisted disfigurement.

''You look beautiful,'' he whispered, brushing a strand of gleaming silver off her forehead. ''Your skin is as smooth and velvety as an eighteen-year-old's and your nose has the same tip-tilted, smart-aleck angle it's always had.'' He'd smiled benignly when she blushed.

''And you haven't lost that same lovely glow I saw twenty years ago. That comes from inside, Charity. Not from your hands. From your heart. That's why everyone wants to be around you.''

Jori let the wind ripple through her hair as it flew around wildly, her fingers curling in Chris's as they watched Charity and Frank have this special time together. She was so engrossed in Frank's words and the wealth of love in them, that she almost missed Chris's excited whisper.

"What?"

"It's working! She's beginning to see Frank in a new and different light. Thank the Lord! He's been crazy about her for ages." He grinned with delight.

"You mean, you've been matchmaking?" Aghast, Jori could only stare. "Of all the people in this town, you, Christopher Davis, should know how chancy that can be."

"Only if it's done for the wrong reasons and with the wrong people. In this case, I think God means for them to be together."

She stared at him.

"You don't have any fears, any worries?" She shook her head. "I admire you, Doc. You don't have any inhibitions. You just jump in and grab whatever it is you want out of life."

"Yeah, sometimes I do. And I hope you remember that," he whispered in her ear, his arm slipping around her waist. "Some things are worth jumping in after."

And for once, Jordanna felt jealous of a little elderly woman who could cause that glint of loving admiration in her old friend's eye. Jori had been so sure that her ex-fiancé was the man for her, would share those same kind of moments with her.

Instead, he'd publicly exposed her to the world's ridicule by breaking off their engagement and taking off with her best friend. Now she so badly wanted to trust again.

But as Chris's blazing blue eyes searched deep into the depths of hers and she remembered the touch of his mouth, Jori wished, for once, that she could believe that someone could love her again. Part of her wanted so badly to be that one special person to someone else; to have them near, to share hopes and dreams with. To raise a family. And part of her was scared to death to open up to that kind of hurt and rejection.

Maybe it was better to just stay free and clear of it, after all. At least you never got hurt.

You never really live, either, a tiny voice whispered.

The scent of lilacs and lavender was thick in the big airy bathroom as Jori laid back even farther into the deep claw-footed tub. It was the old-fashioned kind that let you put in enough water to really sink into and relax. And boy did she need to relax, Jori thought, grinning.

She had spent the entire day whirling through house and garden, trying to forget the effect a tall, blond doctor had on her nervous system. Consequently, not a weed could be found in the flower beds, vegetable garden, along the walk or within the confines of her rather large yard. Jori had mowed the grass even though ten-year-old Bobby Moore was paid to do it for her. In fact, he had been there only two days before.

The house had been put through a rigorous spit-and-polish regime, from top to bottom. Not a speckle of dust marred the gleaming surfaces in any room. She scrubbed the old kitchen floor to within an inch of its worn life and then waxed and buffed it to a shine that hurt the eyes.

And the worst of it was, it was still only three o'clock in the afternoon!

Jori played with a mound of bubbles and considered what the remainder of the day's entertainment should be. An image of Chris grinning from ear to ear flew into her mind. She shoved it away resolutely. Banishing all thoughts of him from her mind, Jori leaned back once more and closed her eyes.

Unfortunately, he would not leave. And neither would the problem of his presence.

"All right," she mumbled to herself in frustration. "Let's discuss this rationally." She straightened up and glared at the faucet of the tub. "Would a perfectly wonderful doctor who makes pots of money cutting people open and sewing them up, who is inundated with adulation from masses of people telling him he's the best thing since fudge brownies, have any desire to remain in a one-horse country town like Mossbank when his self-imposed sabbatical is over?'' Jori snapped the bubbles with her fingers. ''Of course not!''

It wasn't a very satisfactory answer and so she tried to reason it out again.

''No doubt he lives in some elegant condo with a pool, weight room and a bevy of drooling nurses for neighbors.''

No, she frowned. It was worse to think this way. Jori turned the water on with her toes. ''Well, what makes you think he'd hang around Mossbank, then?''

Answer: he wouldn't. Not for any longer than it took Dan and Jessica to get back home and into the groove.

''And you can't leave. You know you can't. Even if he asked you.'' She squeezed her eyes closed and remembered.

''I'll repay you every dime, every dollar that you've scraped together to send me to school,'' she'd promised Reg and the men with him tearfully. ''I won't renege. You can count on that.''

Reg had told her to pay the debt out after her court case had been resolved.

''The town won't hold it against you if you get on with your life somewhere else,'' he'd insisted. ''We never expected you to stay this long.''

''I promised seven years,'' she reminded him. ''And anyway, I wouldn't dream of leaving. This is my home now.''

Chris's searching blue eyes swam into focus and she could hear his words as clearly as the radio playing in the bedroom.

''Trust me,'' he'd said.

''I could trust him, I think,'' she said to herself, trying to wash away the sensation of those arms holding her so gently. ''But there's no future in this relationship so just stop thinking about weddings and babies and all that stuff. It's not for you!''

Luckily, the motion picture running across her brain in vivid Technicolor ended there, due to the loud peal of the telephone. Water slopped over the side of the tub as Jori rose hastily grabbing a towel to wrap around her wet body. She scurried into the bedroom to lift the receiver just as the caller hung up.

''Shoot!'' Jori tugged on an old chenille housecoat before mopping up the trail of puddles marking her newly polished floors. That job was barely complete when the doorbell rang.

''What is this?'' she grouched. ''Grand Central Station?''

She yanked the door open to find Chris standing on her front step. The look on his face would have been comical if Jori had been in a mood to appreciate it.

''Oh, uh, s-sorry,'' he stammered, staring at the gaping V her robe exposed. His eyes flew to her face. Confusion clouded his eyes. ''Were you sleeping?''

''Don't be ridiculous,'' Jori said, horrified that he had to see her in such disarray. ''It's three o'clock in the afternoon.'' She motioned him into the hallway. ''I would prefer that the entire town didn't witness me in this ratty old thing,'' she told him.

Chris seemed amused by her bad temper, which only made it worse. She clenched her teeth at his grin when he spied the ragged bandanna that held up her hair.

''I can go away and come back some other time,'' he told her softly, watching her face closely.

Jori sighed. She should have gone along with the senior bus trip to Minot and spent her day in the craft store, she told herself tiredly. Perhaps then she would have avoided all tall blond male humans, she muttered inwardly. And dogs, she was forced to add at the sight of Flop's huge brown woebegone eyes peering through the screen door.

"I was in the tub when the phone rang," she explained carefully, as he sat in the huge armchair across from her. She curled her legs carefully under her, making sure they remained covered. "Whomever it was had just hung up when you rang the bell." She shoved the wet stringy hair off her face. "I must look a mess."

Chris sat there staring at her until the color rose in her cheeks.

"Well, don't just sit there staring at me! I look terrible."

"No," he murmured softly, "you just look like a little girl getting ready for bed."

Silence yawned between them like a great gaping hole, but Jori couldn't think of a thing to say. His gaze held hers, solemn and probing. She couldn't look away so she stared back, mesmerized by what she saw in the blue depths of his eyes.

The shrill ring of the phone finally broke the spell. Jori picked up the receiver slowly, dazedly.

"Hello, Jori. How was the birthday cruise with the handsome doctor?" Amy's voice bubbled enthusiastically over the line.

It was a little disconcerting to discuss her date with the man in question sitting across from her. Jori decided to skirt the issue.

"Hi, Amy." She cleared the huskiness from her throat and continued brightly. "Thank you very much, I had a lovely time."

Chris coughed just then and she glanced at him from under her lids. He was grinning hugely.

"What you can remember of it, at least," he teased, blue eyes dancing.

"Who's that?" Amy demanded. "I heard a voice."

"I have a guest right now, Amy." Jori frowned at Chris as she spoke. "Can I call you back later?"

"Well, actually, old pal..." Jori knew there was something coming when her friend began that con.

"What do you need, Amy?" She sighed, staring at her carpet. This was turning out to be a strange day.

"Uh, well, it's about Jonathan."

Jori tried to think of something to say but Amy was rushing on.

"I need a sitter for tonight. We're going out for dinner." It came out in a rush of breath. Amy's voice was so hopeful that Jori's soft heart caved like mush. "Mom's taking Brit, but she's too old to take on him, too."

Jori could quite understand. Little Jonathan was a terror and he would be no end of trouble but it was the least she could do for her friend, she pointed out to herself.

"Dinner? Wow! Must be some occasion. What's up?" Jori demanded, knowing her friend seldom splurged on anything for herself.

There was a pregnant pause and then Amy's tearful voice came across the line.

"I passed."

Jori shrieked with joy. She grinned, happily including Chris in the pleasure of the moment.

"Way to go, kid!" She cheerfully congratulated her friend. "Do I call you Madam Certified Public Accountant now?"

They laughed and talked and arranged, and the entire time Jori sat there, uncomfortably aware of the handsome doctor seated on her sofa, unashamedly listening.

A thought suddenly occurred and Jori asked her friend anxiously, "Have you got something special to wear?" There was a murmured response before Jori hooted, "No way. You're not wearing *that*." She stared at Chris searchingly for a moment then nodded as if that settled everything.

"Look, you and I have enough time to scoot over to Mirabel's and get something really special for tonight. It's my treat." When the voice on the other end of the line started speaking, Jori's voice became louder.

"This is my treat and you are not doing me out of the fun. You've come through for me enough times, Amy."

Apparently she had gotten her way, Chris mused, smiling at the grin of satisfaction tipping those full lips. Then he sat upright at the mention of his name.

"Look, Dr. Davis is here. He can watch Jonathan while you and I go shopping. You would like that, wouldn't you?" She pretended to ask Chris, then ignored his wildly gesticulating hands and shaking head. Jori put her hand over the mouthpiece when he told her no, but after a moment she kept right on talking to her friend as if he weren't there.

"He'd love to do this for you on your special day," she said sweetly, glaring fiercely at Chris.

His shoulders slumped. How did she do it? he wondered. She was always conning him into something. And what did he know about little kids? Nothing, that's what! Sure, he could give them a physical, check them over for health problems, or sew them up very neatly. But he doubted that would be much fun for this Jonathan kid.

"What time are you leaving?" He heard Jori arranging everything as if he had agreed wholeheartedly. Chris got up and walked toward the kitchen. He needed a drink of something to keep his hands busy. Otherwise he'd throttle her.

When he returned, Jori had slipped into white slacks and a blue-and-white-striped sweater. She was dialing a number.

"Just a minute, Jori " he demanded. "I can't look after a…"

She help up her hand as someone answered.

"This is Jordanna Jessop. I'd like to speak to Alex, please."

He tried again.

"Jordanna, I *cannot*…"

"Shhh… Hi, Alex, this is Jordanna."

Chris wondered at the sudden animation that lit up her glowing brown eyes. A huge grin curved her mouth.

"Great! Listen, Alex, I need a favor. A friend of mine has a very special celebration tonight. I want that window table that overlooks the river, a bouquet of fresh flowers and anything they order charged to me." She listened for a few minutes.

"Good. Oh, and Alex, when they're finished can you get a cab for them." Jori's face was dancing with glee as she gave him the names. "They're going to the Palace but they don't know it. Can you do it? Thank you, you are a sweetie! Okay, bye."

Chris let her enjoy the moment and then tried again.

"Jori, I need to talk to you. There is no way..."

Once more she held up her hand and began dialing.

Well, if Jordanna Jessop thought she could bulldoze him into this she had another thought coming. He would darn well wait her out.

"Mrs. Rivers, this is Jori. I need you to pack a bag for Amy and Bob. I've got it all arranged, but I don't want them to know. You're keeping Brit, right? Okay. Well, Jonathan will stay here."

Chris thought she'd never get off the phone, but when Jori finally hung up, he breathed a sigh of relief. Now, perhaps, they could clear this up.

Then the doorbell rang.

"Blast it anyway!" He clenched his teeth in vexation.

Jori's wide eyes stared at him.

"You can't say that around Jonathan," she instructed. "He repeats everything he hears. And for goodness' sake, don't give him chocolate." She opened the front door. "Hi, Amy. All set?"

Everything was happening too fast. Chris felt like a passenger on one of those roller coasters at the amusement park. Everything rushed past and he couldn't quite get a grasp on reality.

Jori's friend Amy was speaking to him. Chris tried to pay attention to her, but tiny hands were pulling on his pants, diverting his attention. He hung on to his waistband with one hand, and pulled the sticky hands away with the other.

"He doesn't need to be fed. And don't give him any chocolate." The woman studied him dubiously and Chris straightened his backbone under the survey. "Jonathan will tell you if he needs to use the potty," she said. Her eyes moved uncertainly over the now stained gray slacks.

"Are you sure you want to do this?" Her question was full of doubt and Chris was about to assure her that he certainly did not when Jori broke in.

"Of course he does, don't you, Chris? We had a lovely time on that cruise and this is our way of thanking you. And, after all, it is *just* Jonathan. Her mom's watching Brittany." Jori's eyes were black hard stones now, daring him to refuse.

When he smiled grimly, the two women moved toward the door, giggling excitedly. Neither one paid him any attention. Jonathan headed straight for the china cabinet.

Chris recognized defeat. He would be graceful, he decided. So magnanimously helpful that Jori would not be able to find fault with him. And then he'd leave. He was pretty sure the kid was here for the evening, so he wouldn't be. It was that simple.

Except it wasn't simple at all, he observed an hour later, staggering under the impact of a three-year-old ball of lead against his midsection. Jonathan laughed uproariously. And launched himself at Chris again.

Chris, however, was not a slow learner and he moved. Too quickly, as it happened. The child banged his head against the edge of Jori's solid oak coffee table and let out a wail designed to bring the cops.

It probably only took a few minutes, but when the racket was finally over, Chris concluded surgery was infinitely less tiring than comforting a crying child who was seriously hurting. He decided to take the boy outside. The dog, that was it!

Chris was pleased with himself. Jonathan could play with Flop. Kids like dogs. Dogs like kids. They'd have a great time.

Except that Flop had apparently met little Jonathan before. The cocker spaniel took one look at the three-year-old and barked. Then he sped as fast as his stumpy little legs would carry him, to the thick growth of trees and bushes behind the house.

"Dog," Jonathan said, pointing. "Me go." As he started after the frightened animal, Chris decided diversionary tactics were needed.

He couldn't very well let the tyke get lost in the woods, Chris knew, but he didn't want a recurrence of that blood-curdling screeching, either. Chris searched the yard for something, anything! When his frustrated glance returned to little Johnny, the kid was in the garden carefully picking the flowers off Jori's pea plants.

"Flowers," he told Chris, grinning his toothy smile. "Pitty flowers."

"Yeah, kid," Chris agreed morosely. "It's a pity, all right." Sighing, he bent to take the little boy's hand. "Come on, Jonathan. Let's go see cars. Okay?"

The round cherub face twisted in sorrow first. The fat little hands dropped the crushed white blossoms on the ground sadly.

But the word *car* seemed to have some significance. The shiny black button eyes sparkled at his baby-sitter in delight.

"Car, Car," he sang in a cheerful tone. "Wide in car."

Too late, Chris realized what the word *car* meant to this three-year-old. As they walked out the gate, Chris looked to see if Amy's car, with a *baby seat,* was by the curb.

Unfortunately, only his vintage black T-bird, restored

and refurbished at an exorbitant sum, sat there. Jonathan seemed delighted. He patted the gleaming rear fender lovingly, and crowed, "Pitty car. Wide in car wif man." Fat little hands imprinted themselves on a wax job Chris had painstakingly completed only this morning. He groaned as the child leaned closer to press a slurpy kiss on his shiny chrome bumper.

"Jon wuv car," he told Chris, smiling happily.

They stood in the hot sun for ages while Chris tried to persuade the little boy to walk down the street for a look at the red sports car parked nearby. But the kid wasn't buying. Jonathan clung to the door handle, persistently saying the same thing over and over, his happy face dropping a little more each time.

"Jon go car wide. Dis car."

Chris picked him up, thinking he'd carry the tiny boy inside, but a wail of distress soon stopped him. Several ladies were entering the house across the street and they turned to peer down their noses at him, heads shaking disapprovingly, obviously concerned by his inability to placate the boy. He set the kid down. Immediately, Jonathan ran back to the T-bird.

"She will pay," Chris promised himself grimly, jaw throbbing as he gritted his teeth once more. "I will make her pay for every single moment of this very long afternoon." He opened the door, resignation in the slump of his shoulders.

"Okay, kid. We're just going to sit in the car, now. Just sit."

The boy scooted across the driver's side and nestled into the passenger's seat. Jonathan was very familiar with what happened next, Chris realized, his heart sinking into his shoes. With great dexterity the kid fastened the seat belt around himself like a pro. His dark eyes shone with excitement.

"Wedy," he chirped.

"Well, I'm not." Chris felt like a grumpy old man, talking to an innocent child like that. But he had reason. Darned good reason to be cranky, he figured.

This was not the manner in which he had planned on spending his afternoon. Not at all! Fleeting thoughts of a picnic, at the beach, in the sun, with Jori, ran rampant through his head. Chris turned to face the little boy. Time for a reality check, oh, great doctor, he chided himself in disgust. Scenario's changed!

"Jonathan. We can't go for a car ride today because I don't have a special seat for you." The kid stared at him, beaming that silly smile. Chris tried again.

"In Mommy's car you have a special seat, don't you, Jonathan?"

The child blinked. "Car wide?" he asked innocently.

"No, Jonathan. No car ride." Chris tried to yell above the kid's bawling. "I haven't got a car seat for you."

The child had well-developed lungs for his age, Chris decided, cringing at the shrill bellows. Surely Jori would hear him downtown and get back here, pronto.

When several minutes had passed without any signs of the relief team, Chris took matters into his own hands.

"Okay, kid. You win," he hollered. "We're going, we're going."

The slow motion of the car finally penetrated and Jonathan's crying ceased abruptly. Chris kept it on a sedate fifteen miles per hour and prayed no one would notice he was plodding down the street at a snail's pace, in a racy black Thunderbird whose engine had not been designed for creeping, with a kid next to him who was not belted in according to government specification. Of course, they'd have to be able to see Jonathan first, Chris reasoned, glancing down. This way they'd think he was out by himself. Cruising, no doubt.

"Better and better," he grumbled in revulsion. "Now they'll really be talking!"

Jonathan's happy face beamed satisfaction as he jabbered away.

"Go wide car. Jon like car. Nice car. Pitty." He turned his solemn eyes on Chris, and ordered, "Sing."

Chris ignored him, hoping the child would forget. Fat chance!

"Sing," Jonathan ordered insistently. "Sing."

Chris turned on the radio. There was no way he was going down the street singing. He already had the windows open because he thought air-conditioning would give the kid a chill. Anyway, he couldn't imagine what tune they could possibly share.

As luck would have it, an old country-and-western song was playing. Chris smiled grimly. He'd always suspected that God had a sense of humor, and "coward of the county" described his present condition perfectly.

Jonathan appeared quite happy with the song, though. He crowed away, off-key, as they turned the corner. Chris braked slowly in front of Jori's, noting there was still no sign of Amy's car. He groaned inwardly, but determined not to show it.

"Okay, Jonathan. All finished. Let's go inside, okay," he wheedled.

"Car wide, more." Jonathan was getting angry. Chris could see the little hands curling into angry fists. "Car wide," he shouted.

"Do you want to drive, too?" Chris inquired sourly, raking his hands through his hair.

That was a mistake.

Faster than lightning, the child had released the latch on his belt and landed with a thud on Chris's lap.

"Jon dwive," he agreed cheerfully.

"Uh, I don't think…" The little face scrunched up and Chris caved in. "All right!"

And so Jonathan drove. Chris turned the key and the motor purred quietly while his prize car sat in one place and the kid happily turned the wheel left and right to the accompaniment of *Brrrm* and *Rooom*.

Chris let himself relax for a moment, wondering if he'd need to replace his front tires after this grueling workout. His blue eyes narrowed in thought. And he would send the bill to Jori Jessop, he decided. It was the least she could do after setting him up like this.

Still, he considered, if it got him any further beneath that protective shell she always threw up against him, Chris decided it was worth it. He was definitely interested in the woman, he acknowledged.

And so, as Jonathan drove his car, Chris sat thinking about Jori. And while a low voice on the radio crooned about her dream lover, Chris fantasized about his relationship with his office nurse. He thought of her laughing eyes, that solemn glint they got in them when she spoke of her past, the way she opened up, just a bit, and then hid her thoughts and feelings.

"Why me, Lord?" The question stemmed from his need to know why he'd been presented with a woman who met every one of the traits he'd deemed desirable in a partner for life and yet seemed totally unobtainable. "Why *me,* Lord?"

Suddenly Chris felt the insistent tug on his arm. And the warm wetness soaking through his pants.

He asked the question again, but with totally different intent.

"I haffa go potty," Jonathan advised him solemnly.

"I think you're just a bit late, pal." Chris grimaced sourly as he stepped gingerly out of the car. His brow furrowed when he surveyed the boy's dirty smeared face.

Great! The kid had snitched a chocolate bar Chris had left in the cup holder. Now they were both covered with the gooey brown stuff but Chris wore more of it than Jonathan.

Chris wondered, What next? just as his eyes caught a

glimpse of the dark wet patch creating a highly *visible* circle on the front of his slacks. He shook his head darkly.

"I concede defeat," Chris informed anyone who was listening. "I have no pride left," he muttered in frustration. "None."

Oh, she'd pay, all right! Big-time!

After a trip to the bathroom and a change of clothes which Chris finally found in Jonathan's blue-striped diaper bag tucked discreetly behind the front door, they sat together on the sofa to read one of the books that had been secreted inside said bag. Chris wished he'd noticed it sooner. There were enough toys in there to amuse ten kids.

A few minutes later they were back in the bathroom removing all traces of a regurgitated chocolate bar that should never have been eaten. Fortunately for Jori's sofa, most of it had landed in Chris's lap.

As he surveyed his new pants ruefully, Chris wished he had his own diaper bag. There was a peculiar odor in the air and he was pretty sure he was the source. He dabbed at the expensive fabric as best he could while swallowing thoughts of retribution.

"Vengeance is the Lord's," he quoted self-righteously.

Soon Jonathan's rumpled dark head rested tiredly against his chest as Chris read about Peter Rabbit. No wonder the kid was so smart if he heard this stuff all the time. Beatrix Potter was not one to mince words, Chris decided.

Halfway through the little book, he realized Jonathan had fallen asleep. The child's tiny hand lay on top of his own as the boy snored gently, his chubby body pressed comfortably against Chris.

This is what it would be like to have a son. The words sounded in his brain with a clarity that made his eyes widen. *Here's a demanding little person who depends on you to make his world all right. Someone who needs you to bandage sore knees, read bedtime stories and take for a*

*car ride. Someone who needs you to be there to tuck him
in at night.*

Chris had never thought of himself as a father. Never
wanted the responsibility. But somehow it seemed perfectly
natural to cuddle little Jonathan's body as he lay sleeping.
And a feeling of intense longing coursed through him even
as the sadness brought reality.

"I'm not the father type," he told that resonant voice.
"I haven't got a clue how to raise children except that it
wouldn't be the way my parents raised us." Thoughts of
happy excited voices debating across the table made him
smile. "Mealtimes are fun times," he murmured. "That's
the first rule I'd make. And everyone laughs."

A picture of Jori holding a baby in the rocking chair
across the room flew into his mind. She should have a
family. She was full of warmth and giving and caring. Jori
would know the right words to say. She would have the
understanding a child would need in this world.

But why did he want it to be his child? He wasn't the
type to settle down in a place like Mossbank. He couldn't;
he accepted that inevitability as the sun rises each morning.
His whole professional career was about maximizing the
medical care that he'd been taught to provide. His whole
life had been about fulfilling his parents' dreams. And unless there was exponential growth in the future of the little
town, he wasn't looking at hanging around. Was he?

In the back of his mind, Chris listened tiredly as his
mother's voice droned on.

"You can be the best surgeon in the world, Christopher.
People will come from miles to be operated on by you.
Your fees will entitle you to the best of everything. You
can advance in your field as far as you're willing to go, be
among the top brains in the world. You can have it all."

But did he want it all?

Jori pushed open her front door to the same quiet peace-
fulness that always reigned in her home. How long would

she have to wait to hear the sounds of children laughing as they slid down the bannister or swung in the backyard? Would she ever have a child of her own?

Now, however, a tiny frisson of fear coursed through her veins. It was so silent. Where were they?

Stop it, she told herself sternly. Nothing bad has happened. And if it had, Chris would be well equipped to handle an emergency.

All the same, Jori breathed a sigh of relief when she came upon the two of them lying on her sofa, snoring in unison. Flop raised his nose from his comfy position on top of Chris's feet and Jori had to smile at the picture they made. Wistfully, she wondered how Chris's own child would look.

Would his son have that flaxen blond hair and those sun-bleached eyebrows? Would his eyes sparkle with the same navy blueness when he was amused? Would he be as tall and broad as his father?

The pain that shuddered through her as Jori contemplated these and a host of other questions forced her to realize just how deeply she was falling for him.

She wanted to be the mother of his son. Jori calmly accepted her own desires, painfully realizing that it would never happen. Chris would never be happy living in a small town like Mossbank. And why would he?

But while he was here, Jori decided, she would enjoy his company whenever possible. Nothing could come of it, and she would learn to live with that, but she wasn't going to regret that she had grown to love this man.

"Chris." She shook his shoulder gently. When those wide blue eyes popped open, Jori wasn't prepared for the feelings that struck her heart. It took a minute for her to regain her poise.

"You're back," Chris murmured, brushing his hair from

his forehead. His eyes darkened as he remembered. "You owe me one," he told her. "More than one."

Jori giggled. She put her hands on her hips, and taunted, "Like what?"

"Supper, for one," he informed her. His blue eyes glinted in the sun.

"One meal for you and Jonathan coming right up," she promised, moving toward the kitchen. She turned in the doorway, tossing a saucy look over her shoulder. "Anything else, your majesty?"

"Yes," he told her. His voice lowered to a whisper. "But I'll tell you later."

It was a promise that Jori rolled through her mind a dozen times as she readied the steaks for grilling. When Chris strolled into the kitchen sometime later, she smiled at the mussed blond hair, dirty wrinkled shirt and stained pants.

"You can shower and change before supper if you want," she told him, eyeing his discolored pants with mirth. "Did you have an accident?"

She kept her tones mildly questioning, which was difficult, because inside Jori was aching to laugh. When his blue eyes glared at her, she moved over to pat his cheek.

"Poor baby," she consoled him. "Did you have a bad day?"

Jori was surprised when his long arms reached out to pull her into his arms. She was even more surprised when his lips touched hers.

"Yes," he answered. "I have had a *very* bad day, but it's getting better."

She wrapped her arms around his neck, still holding the salt shaker in one hand. Her senses were caught on a curious smell. Her nose twitched as she stared up at him.

"Chris?"

"What?" His blue eyes looked at her curiously.

"What is that smell?" she asked, wrinkling her nose in

distaste. To her surprise, he backed away immediately. Her hands fell to her sides as she stood staring at him. A flush of red suffused his strong cheekbones. Jori watched the sheepish look cover his face.

Just then, little Jonathan walked into the room. He was mussed and sleepy eyed, clutching his teddy in one grubby hand. As she bent to pick him up, Jori caught the same scent on his clothes. Eyes wide, she turned to stare at Chris.

"It's him, not me!" Chris's voice was defensive. "He stole a chocolate bar, got sick on me and forgot to tell me about going to the bathroom until it was too late." He looked mortally offended, plucking the expensive material away from his thighs. "Unfortunately, he was sitting on me at the time."

It was jumbled, but she got the drift. And she couldn't help herself. Laughter burst from her like a wave in a tidal pool, filling the room with its sound. She laughed until tears ran down her cheeks and then laughed some more. Her stomach ached and quivered with laughter until finally Jori sobered up enough to see the light of battle in his eyes.

"I told you, no chocolate," she reminded him, stifling her glee.

Chris did not look placated. In fact he looked...rumpled, she decided grinning.

"I'm sorry," she bubbled, "but it's just the thought of someone, anyone, let alone a child, ruining the great Dr. Chris Davis's p-p-pants..." Fresh gales of laughter shook her narrow shoulders as she tried to control her mirth.

Chris marched over to stand in front of her. "It is not funny," he complained. "These were my best pants." He stood watching her set the little boy in his high chair. "In fact, they *were* brand-new."

Jori began feeding the child as he spoke. She was ignoring him, Chris realized. It bugged him.

"Jori," he complained, turning her chin to meet his eyes.

"Yes," she answered, staring at him for a minute before

popping another spoonful of food into Jonathan's open mouth. "What did you say?"

"I said, I had plans for tonight. And they didn't include him." His thumb jerked toward the three-year-old safely ensconced in the chair, huge eyes watching them curiously.

"Perhaps next time," Jori advised him, "you should ask me before you make any plans for me." She fixed him with her best office nurse look. "Now, go get changed while I feed Jon. We'll eat when he's asleep."

"Jon not sleepy," the little boy told her seriously. "Jon play wif toys."

"You will be, sweetie. You're going to eat your dinner and after you've had your bath, you are going to bed."

Jori watched from the corner of her eye as Chris lingered in her kitchen for a few minutes, before he strode, muttering, out the back door.

Contrary to his assertions, Jonathan did go to bed and finally to sleep after his dinner and bath, although not without protest.

"Jon not sleepy. No bed."

She had been calm but firm and finally the little tyke had settled down enough to close his eyes and drift off. Jori went downstairs a few moments later, to find Chris had returned and was seated at her kitchen table.

"Whew," she told him seriously. "I was afraid there for a minute that he wouldn't go to sleep and then he would start bawling." She eyed Chris piteously. "You have no idea how loud he is when he starts crying."

Chris surged to his feet. "Yes, I do. I have a very good idea of just how many decibels he reaches with those lungs. When I return to Boston, I am going to have my hearing checked. And I'm sending the bill to you."

"Poor baby!" Jori grinned saucily before she pointed to the array on her counter. "I have seasoned T-bones waiting for grilling. There are new potatoes, fresh green beans, a salad and garlic bread.'' She smirked. ''Will that cover my debt to you?''

''Not nearly! But it is a good start.''

And so the evening progressed with neither able to stop the little touches and telling glances they each threw when the other wasn't looking. It could have been a very relaxing evening, except for little Jonathan's peculiar timing. And not once but several times!

Chris had finally gone home, grumbling all the while. But not before he had made Jori wish he was staying. For good.

Chapter Nine

"I wish to speak with Dr. Christopher Davis, Nurse. Fetch him immediately, please." The tall, elegantly dressed woman on the other side of the desk gave Jori a thorough once-over as she impatiently tapped her fingers.

Jori raised her eyebrows at the woman's supercilious tone. Indeed. She wondered where the woman had come from. Her white linen suit was immaculate on a day when the dust was blowing freely across the prairies. Ash blond hair was pulled severely back off her tense face and coiled into some complicated knot at the back. Her face was a study in patrician features with its long aquiline nose, highly defined cheekbones and intense blue eyes. At the moment her full lips were stretched in a thin line across her perfectly made-up face as she waited for Jori to obey.

"Your name, madam?"

"Dr. Charlotte Davis." The smoothly arrogant tones gave the information haughtily. "I am Dr. Davis's mother."

Jori felt the world shift and tilt and wondered why she hadn't expected this. This woman was here to make sure Chris returned to the city.

Somehow she struggled past all that and remembered that Chris would be tied up for some time counseling the young girl in his office on the merits of abstaining from sex. There was no way she was going to interrupt that.

"If you would have a seat, Dr. Davis, I'm sure Chris will see you as soon as he is free." Jori waved her hand toward a waiting room already jammed with patients before glancing down to the appointment book dismissively.

She had pulled a few more patient files from the bulging cabinets before Jori noticed that the woman had not left. She raised her eyebrow questioningly.

"Was there something else, Dr. Davis?"

"I don't think you understand." Her tone was mildly condescending. Jori bristled at the supercilious words.

"I believe I understand perfectly," she insisted quietly. "But perhaps you don't understand that this is a clinic. These patients have made appointments and they are waiting to see the doctor." Her eyes seared around the room before coming to rest on the aristocratic woman standing at the desk. Jori relented only a bit.

"Dr. Davis is attending a patient right now," she told his mother, keeping her voice low. "When he is free, I'll tell him you are here." Her voice was firm. "Now, please be seated."

Dr. Davis sat. Her back was ramrod straight as she perched on the edge of the worn chair as if fearful it would contaminate her.

Twenty minutes later, Jori eased into Chris's office. She watched him as he pored over the next patient's file. After a moment his blond head tipped up, blue eyes crinkling. "What?" he asked.

"Um, well, you see..." Jori didn't know exactly why she felt the woman's presence was going to disrupt Chris's concentration on his needy patients, but the niggling feeling of impending doom was there. She tried to tell him quickly.

"Your mother is in the waiting room, Doctor. She wants to see you."

The wide grin that had stretched his mouth fell away as he stared at her. His face froze, a chilly look in those gorgeous eyes.

"My mother is here? J.J., she couldn't be. She's working on a top secret project right now." He smiled absurdly. "You must have misunderstood."

"She said her name was Charlotte Davis." She watched the light of recognition dawn. "Ah, I see you believe me now."

He frowned fiercely. "But surely she hasn't come way out here? My father must be working overtime if he's had to recruit her. And I can just imagine what she wants."

Jori stared at him. He said the words to himself, obviously turning it all over in his mind. "But what does she want?"

The comment wasn't directed at her but Jori answered anyway. "I'm sure I don't know. She certainly didn't bother to explain it to me. After all, I'm just the office nurse." Jori shrugged, her eyes carefully studying him. "Shall I show her in here?"

He seemed to pull himself together suddenly, drawing his shoulders up with an inner strength. His eyes were cold as ice when he looked at her, his mouth a thin, straight line.

"No." The word was sharp. "I have a room full of patients. She's the one who always says work comes first." Chris gathered the file together and tapped it against his desk, aligning the papers inside. When he looked at her, Jori could feel the tension crackling around the room.

"You may tell Dr. Davis that I will see her at five." And with that stark statement, Chris left the office to see his next patient as if nothing had happened.

Jori was stunned.

Shrugging, she went to deliver Chris's message, knowing

Dr. Charlotte Davis would not be pleased. And she wasn't, but not for the reasons Jori had presumed.

"But, I'm afraid you don't understand, Miss..." The words trailed away as the woman stared down her nose.

"Jessop, Nurse Jordanna Jessop," Jori told her, disliking the woman's patronizing tone.

"Very well, Miss Jessop. Apparently what Christopher doesn't understand is that I have very little time at my disposal right now and it is imperative that I see him at once." She issued the edict disdainfully, obviously expecting Jori to race off immediately.

"I'm sorry. Chris did ask me to tell you that he could see you here in the office at five, if you wish." Jori knew that every ear and eye in the waiting room was focused on them. She tried to control the anger raging inside her as the woman addressed her once more.

"*Dr. Davis,* you mean, don't you, Nurse?" It was a very thinly veiled hint which Jori chose to ignore, turning back to her work at the desk.

She was conscious of the woman leaving moments later, but she kept her head bent, filling out the lab forms for one of Chris's most worrisome cancer patients. Just the same, her mind whirled with questions. And with fury.

How dare that woman treat her like some peon!

It was a busy day with a number of drop-ins. Jori flew about, hoping to get the last few letters and notes sent out in the weekend mail. Mondays always presented enough problems. Leftovers from the previous Friday threw everything out of sync.

When Chris's mother returned at five, she ushered the woman into one of the consulting rooms and then crossed the hall to tell Chris. She found him seated, staring vacantly out the tiny window at the sheets of rain that were now falling.

"She's here." It wasn't a question.

Jori nodded. "Room six. Do you want me to arrange

dinner for you both?'' she asked in a rush, feeling sorry for that lost look on his face.

His blue eyes swiveled over to assess her intently. ''I doubt very much if she's staying,'' he told her without expression. A crooked smile tugged at the corner of his mouth. ''But I will be happy to come over for dinner after I do rounds,'' he teased halfheartedly.

Jori smiled at him, letting him know she knew what he was doing. ''Fine,'' she murmured. ''I'm cooking liver. Feel free to bring your mother.''

Chris's tongue stuck out at her. ''Yuk, that's gross. I hate liver. And Charlotte isn't exactly your typical motherly type.'' He glared at her. ''You might have noticed that for yourself, J.J. I don't think a nice cozy dinner at your place is going to make her ease off.''

''Well, what does she want?''

''That's what I'm going to find out.'' He got up and came around the desk, taking her hands in his.

Jori knew it was stupid and she told herself a thousand times that she was being a fool. She even whispered a prayer that God would make her immune to Chris's laughing good looks. But when Dr. Christopher Davis looked at her like that, she totally lost it, wanting only to wrap her arms around him and keep him away from the woman on the other side of the door.

Chris kissed her nose.

''Now, can't you please make something I like?'' he begged piteously, sounding very much like a bratty little boy.

Jori giggled at his downcast expression. ''You're a doctor—you should know that liver is very healthy,'' she lectured.

''It's also full of cholesterol and I can't afford to pile up on that.'' The light bantering had partially restored his natural effervescence.

Jori gave in gracefully. ''Okay. I'll make something

else." She blew out a long-suffering sigh. "I think doctors are very spoiled," she noted for his benefit.

"Not all of them, Miss Jessop. Most are far too busy to play silly games." The voice was cool and very controlled. Dr. Davis had apparently given up waiting for Chris and decided to find him for herself. She stood in the doorway glaring at them both.

"I don't think anyone is playing games here, Charlotte. Least of all J.J. and I." Chris's voice was tight with barely concealed anger. His eyes bored into the other woman, who had the grace to flush. "The question is, what are you doing here? And why now? What's so urgent?"

"You are my son, Christopher. Don't you think I should be concerned about you?" Her voice had lightened considerably, Jori noticed, and she now wore a most beguiling smile.

"It's just unusual, that's all. You were never that concerned about me when I was in Boston. I would hardly think you'd have time to even think about me with your new project." Chris turned to wink at Jori, who immediately felt her heart beat a little faster.

"Yes, well, I do wish your staff had not forgotten me in the room like that," the older woman complained. "I've been sitting there for seventeen minutes. I have to be back at the airport as soon as possible. I'm doing an important experiment tomorrow afternoon." She glared at Jori. "Nurses never understand how important a doctor's time is."

Jori blushed and turned to leave. The woman was a stickler for punctuality, she decided grimly. Seventeen minutes indeed.

"Excuse me," she asked the older woman, hoping to leave unscathed.

"Certainly," Dr. Davis moved deliberately in front of Jori. Her ice-cold eyes fixed on Jori's and she gave her orders. "Christopher and I have a lot to discuss. Please see that we are not disturbed."

Jori said nothing. She refused to start an argument with the woman. She wasn't one to be ordered about but there was nothing to be gained by indulging in a power struggle. For once she put a clamp on her lips, moving past silently to go about her usual routine, locking the office doors when the last patient had finally finished dressing. She left at last, tugging her light poplin jacket around her shoulders.

The heavens chose that precise moment to open again and by the time Jori reached her home, she was soaked to the skin from top to bottom. Even Flop refused to do more than wag his tail and bark a little greeting, standing well back so his golden coat absorbed none of the droplets her coat scattered across the braided rug.

"Fair-weather friend," she grumbled at him. He woofed in agreement and went to lie on the hearth rug.

Jori showered quickly before tugging on a fleece jogging suit in a periwinkle shade that she loved. Her hair twisted easily into an intricate coil of interlocking braids and she pinned the ends under so that the effect was one of neatness. Any remnant of makeup had long since washed away and Jori didn't bother to refresh it.

Minutes later she was in front of the freezer, surveying the possibilities for supper. Nothing but hamburger would thaw properly in the short time she had left, so Jori opted for lasagna with the oven-ready noodles. Before long she had it baking in the oven, a small loaf of garlic bread ready to heat and freshly grated coleslaw to accompany everything.

"I don't know what this is about, Father," she murmured, setting the table, "but work it out to your will." She placed the last item on the table and then quickly shut her eyes once more.

"Only, please, please, if he isn't the one for me, make him leave before I get in too deep. I don't know if I can deal with another heartbreak.'' Embarrassed by the admission, Jori acknowledged inwardly that Dr. Christopher Davis now had in his hands the power to hurt her very badly. And after today, she doubted he had any intention of staying in Mossbank.

The ringing doorbell startled her out of her thoughts. As she yanked open the door, teasing words flew out of her mouth.

''Well, Dr. Davis, it's about time. If you must beg supper the least you could...'' Dead silence greeted her.

Charlotte Davis stood on the doorstep with Chris's tall figure behind. Neither one looked particularly pleased to be there.

''Jori, I hope you don't mind, but Charlotte said she would join us.'' His blue eyes begged her indulgence.

As Jori stared at him, she noticed tiny lines of strain radiating from his eyes and around his pursed lips. His shoulders drooped dejectedly. Chris's whole manner was rigidly tense, as if his plans had been rearranged and there was nothing he could do about it. She was about to answer when Dr. Davis broke in.

''Don't be ridiculous, Chris. Of course your little nurse doesn't mind feeding another person.'' And without batting an eyelash, the woman pushed her way past Jori into the hallway, slipping off her coat as she entered.

Jori straightened her spine. When dealing with rudeness, she decided, one had to face it head-on.

''Oh, please, Dr. Davis, do come in,'' she invited softly. ''And please take off your coat. My home is yours.''

The woman had the grace to flush a dull red. Jori picked up the navy trench coat slung over her father's antique oak table and dabbed up the droplets. She opened the closet and stuffed the coat onto a hanger as she spoke. Her voice mellowed considerably when she spoke to Chris.

''Come on, Doc. Hang your coat up, then we'll eat. Your mother is more than welcome to share our feast.'' She arched an eyebrow at his relieved look. "Does she like liver?"

When his startled gaze met her limpid brown one, Jori could have crowed with laughter. His mouth dropped in surprise before it turned down in a reprimand. But to his credit, Chris said not a word.

Charlotte, however, had already made her way into the living room and was trying to retain her stiff-backed pose in an overstuffed chair that had been Jori's dad's favorite. Worn and tired, its springs no longer firm, it finally engulfed the slim form in a most unladylike way.

"Excuse me a moment," Jori muttered, trying to stifle the bubble of laughter in her throat. All that pompous stuffiness fell around the woman like ashes as she struggled to liberate her rigidly elegant self from the enveloping folds. "I'll be right back."

In the kitchen Jori gave way to the guffaws of laughter that could only be silenced inside the pantry's thick walls where no one could hear. She was surprised to find Chris pushing his way in moments later.

"Thank you," he breathed pressing a kiss to her forehead.

"You're welcome," Jori answered automatically. Her dark eyebrows flew upward. "For what?"

"For not taking Charlotte up on the gauntlet she tossed at your feet." His blue eyes swept in quick assessment over her. "I like your hair better when it's free," he told her softly, brushing his hand over the coil around her head. "But either way, you're still gorgeous."

"Supper," she murmured at last. "I have to get your supper."

Reluctantly, Chris eased away from her. "You always make all calm and rational thoughts leave my mind," he told her. "I just have to get near you and my mind turns to mush."

"Pretty good stuff, that mush." She chuckled. Her finger

pointed to the table. "Dinner's almost ready," she said. "You'd better set another place."

When they finally sat down to dinner, Charlotte Davis looked more severe than ever, watching Chris as he enjoyed the noodles with a gusto that was somehow satisfying to Jori.

"Do you usually eat in the kitchen?" Dr. Davis asked, glancing around. "I suppose one must fit in with the local farm customs."

"Well, yes, there is that," Jori agreed, tamping down her anger. "But generally speaking, I find the kitchen to be more homey."

"What in heaven possessed you to come to this backwater town?" the woman demanded of her son, totally ignoring her hostess.

"I came to help out a friend." Jori listened as Chris quickly told her about Dan and Jessica and their baby. "It's not permanent, Mother," he told her placatingly.

Jori felt her heart drop. She had always known it, of course, but when Chris said it out loud, those words were so much more destructive. She struggled to retain her aplomb as the woman turned toward her.

"Have you always lived here, Miss Jessop?" It wasn't really a question, it was a demand, but Jori forced herself to answer civilly.

"Please, call me Jori," she invited, smiling. "No, not always. I returned a few years ago."

"How can you stand living in such primitive conditions?" The words cut deeply into Jori's pride.

"It's a small town, yes," Jori agreed, "but the city is only a bit away." Her defiant chin went up as she told the woman, "I love it here. I know just about everyone and they know me. We're rather like a large extended family." Jori kept her words crisp and devoid of emotion.

"But my dear, surely you don't intend to stay here, to raise children in this, this Mossbank place? Anyplace less suitable I simply can't imagine. Don't you want them to know the world they will be living in?''

The scorn was evident in her tone and Jori could feel Chris shuffling in his chair. She made a fist under the table and smiled serenely, facing his mother.

''I don't have any children yet,'' she said firmly. ''But if I did, this is exactly where I'd want to raise them. Many of the people who live in rural farming areas are not sophisticated. But they are good people who work hard and care for one another. If the world had more people like them, perhaps there wouldn't be so many problems.''

Jori took a sip of her water. But it was clear that Chris's mother was not finished.

''But my dear,'' she advised in a patronizing tone. ''You miss out on so much of the finer things in life here in the—'' she stopped at the warning glance from Chris, but went blithely on seconds later ''—in this area.''

''People always think that anyone who lives in a small town is limited,'' Jori countered. ''But everything is a trade-off, isn't it?'' Her hand pointed to the table. ''You probably have access to some wonderful wines, but we have pure water from wells that are uncontaminated. And while you can go to the theater or the opera whenever you choose, we *rural* folks can watch a beautiful sunset without obstructions, or listen to the birds twittering in wild areas behind our homes.''

Jori stopped to draw a deep breath. Her fuming brown eyes fell on Chris, who was sitting with his face glued to his plate. She thought his shoulders were shaking. She kicked him. Jori was sick of being laughed at by Chris Davis and his mother.

''Just because I live in this area, doesn't mean I'm not interested in what's happening in other parts of the world. I just choose not to live there anymore. More lasagna?''

At the negative shake of Dr. Davis's perfectly groomed head, Jori swept up the empty plates and returned to the table with slices of angel food cake smothered in garden fresh raspberries and thick whipped farm cream. Those distributed, she returned with the coffeepot and poured some for everyone, before plunking the pot angrily onto a cork mat.

The remainder of their meal was silent except for Chris's attempts at lightening the atmosphere. He tried repeatedly to engage his mother in conversation with only limited success. Dr. Davis described the current social scene he was missing out on. She went into long detailed descriptions of her projects that had Jori's eyes glazing over. Charlotte even name-dropped once or twice about local debutantes who had missed him. And through it all, Chris merely sat silent, shifting uncomfortably in his seat.

Jori was disgusted with the haughty woman who sat across from her. At the same time, she remembered her father remonstrating that a guest was still a guest, no matter how ignorant.

Finally, amid the tense, strained mood of the evening, Dr. Davis and her son finished their dessert. Jori could hardly wait to draw a deep relaxing breath and try to ease the strain from her shoulder muscles.

"Please, take your coffee into the living room," she told them both, tired of everything. "You need time to talk and I have a few things to do out here."

"But, Jori, we can't just leave you with all this," Chris protested. He picked up a few dishes and began stacking them in the dishwasher. Jori scooped the remainder from his hands.

"Thank you, but I think it would be best if you and your mother talked in the other room," she said firmly, refusing to give way.

Dark blue eyes searched hers for a long moment. Finally Chris nodded in agreement. He escorted his mother out, but stopped in the doorway.

"It was a delicious meal, Jori. Thank you very much."

His big hand brushed over the coil of hair around her head. "I'm sorry Mother upset you."

Once he had gone Jori took out her frustrations on her dishes, leaving two chipped plates and one broken cup. She couldn't help it after the remarks she heard coming from the other room.

"Your training is wasted here," Dr. Davis informed her son. "A GP could serve this community just as well with a third of the training and much less expense than you've caused us."

"Mother, you don't understand. Mossbank gives me back so much."

She'd cut him off, obviously furious.

"Mossbank." She spat the word out. "What is there in this backwater town that has you so impressed? It looks nothing like heaven to me. More like the back forty with those dreadful roads." Jori had grinned but kept her ear near the door. "You'll lose your position, Christopher. They won't hold on forever and then everything you've gained will be lost."

"What 'everything,' Mother?" he'd asked quietly, his voice dull.

"The money, the prestige, the importance of your work. The opportunity to advance—make a name for yourself. Maybe even teach someday. That was always your dream, as I recall." Jori heard the squeak of her father's chair. "Don't you care about those things anymore? Don't you want to be a contributor to society where it matters?"

Jori had wanted to yell that it mattered here in Mossbank. To a whole town and the surrounding community, Chris Davis, M.D. mattered a lot. And to her he mattered more than anyone she'd ever known. But of course, it was none of her business and she highly doubted that he would thank her for interfering.

"Can you imagine what people are saying?" Dr. Davis's voice was low and filled with disgust. "Our son, a surgeon just beginning to make a name for himself, suddenly abandons his life's work to move out here—Nowhereville!'' Her voice lowered and Jori had to strain to hear the next part.

"If it's that girl that has you so entranced, there are hundreds of them in Boston that are far better educated and much more suited as your escort."

"How can you say that after Jori invited you here, opened her home and fed you a wonderful meal?"

"Fine, she can cook. So what?" Charlotte Davis had an edge to her voice that brooked no discussion. "The kind of woman you need has to be able to host a dinner for the medical society. She has to be able to hold her own among the rich and elite of Boston, to encourage them to support your rise through the ranks." The contempt was evident in her voice. "That little office nurse would be totally out of her depth."

There was more—a lot more, Jori figured. But she just couldn't listen anymore. She could see all her hopes and dreams driving out of town and her heart sank. Disgusted with herself for eavesdropping, she pulled on an old anorak hanging on the back door, slipped on a pair of duck shoes and went for a walk.

Outside, the cool moist evening air caressed her hot cheeks, dissipating some of the irritation nagging at her. Jori talked to Flop as they walked down the sidewalk. She tried to sort out the variety of emotions that whirled through her mind.

"She's really a piece of work, isn't she, boy? All that haughty posturing. She's certainly pouring on the guilt to try to talk him into going back to the high, muck-a-muck life in the city." She frowned. "I don't want him to go," she told the dog. "I want him to stay here." Flop woofed his agreement.

They walked across the small park that stood kitty-corner to Jori's property. She had played there many times as a child. Cried there, too, when her mother had died, when she had scraped her knees, and when, at eight years old, Douglas Morris had kissed her on the lips. A tiny grin whisked across her lips as she remembered those times.

Flop ran off to investigate the wonders of the park grass, so Jori sank onto the old rope swing and pushed herself back and forth. At last Jori admitted to herself what she had known for weeks.

She was in love with Chris. The knowledge had hung there, suspended in her unconscious until she could deny it no more. It wasn't just his good looks or his handsome physique. It had more to do with the sad, mischievous little boy that hid behind those deep blue eyes, waiting to be freed whenever propriety got lost.

It had a lot to do with the way Chris's big strong arms made her feel secure and the way his very nearness comforted her.

Jori admitted that her love also had a lot to do with the effort he had made to fit in with the community. Chris was a good sport. He had tried hard to get to know his patients and their life-style while clearly acknowledging his deficits in the area of agriculture.

Finally, Jori conceded the impossibility of that love. Chris would return, sooner or later, to his big-city hospital and his wealthy friends. He would resume the cold, impersonal medical practice he'd had before. It was inevitable.

And he should, she told herself vehemently. It was what he loved to do, the reason he had spent years in training and then working in residencies that offered little in monetary recompense and a lot in stress and worry.

Abruptly, the reason for Chris's choice in the field of medicine dawned on Jori. She had heard only a little of his childhood, but it was enough to leave Jori with the impression of a cold, sterile atmosphere. Chris was a person who liked to touch people—a handshake, a pat on the shoulder, ruffling a child's hair. He was always touching her—brushing a hand over her hair, or pressing his long finger against her chin. Jori could only imagine the impact such a frigid childhood would have on a man as sensitive as he.

But Chris had risen above it. In his own way, he had eventually let himself come to care for the people of Mossbank. And in such an atmosphere, he seemed not to need the immunity a large city hospital would have given. For so long Chris had taken care of others while he ignored his own needs. He'd found this place where he could relax, be himself, be accepted. But Jori wondered if his newfound peace would last in the impersonality of the city hospital.

Jori stared at the sodden grass beneath her feet. "I know how much he loves his work." The words came heavily but she said them, nonetheless.

"I know that he's not mine. He never was. He's committed to his life and I to mine here in Mossbank. So, Lord," she sighed heavily, "what am I going to do? I still want to be part of a happy loving family. I want to have children and enjoy them while I'm still young. Do you have another plan for me?

"I love him, God. I never thought it would happen again, but it has. And it's all so hopeless." The heaving sobs finally ebbed away, leaving her drained and lifeless. "What am I going to do now?"

"What's a pretty girl like you doing out on an awful night like this?" The voice was low and filled with laughter.

Jori wheeled around to stare up into a face she barely recalled from high school.

"David? David Andrews?" Jori whispered at the tall lanky man in front of her. "What in the world are you doing back in Mossbank?"

"I could ask the same of you." He grinned, bending to grasp both of her hands in his. "Last I heard you had made it. Big-time."

"I live here now," she told him quietly. "What about

you? You were doing something political, as I recall. And married, too!''

His craggy face fell.

''Yes, I was but we split up about three years ago. Marilee wanted to stay on and move up the fast track but I got downsized and decided to change directions. I'm setting up an office in town and I'm going to practice here. Nothing earth-shattering. Just small-town basic law.''

They chatted for several moments before the clouds opened again.

''I'd better get back home. Davey's with a sitter but I don't like to leave him too long. He's my five-year-old son,'' David explained. ''And the pride and joy of my life. Hey, maybe we can go for coffee or lunch sometime.''

''I'd like that,'' Jori murmured, thinking of the woman who had left little Davey with his father. It didn't seem fair somehow. She wanted a child to love and take care of so badly and other women abandoned theirs.

''Good. How about lunch tomorrow?'' David's face crinkled in a huge grin. ''No sense wasting time.''

Jori agreed with a smile, and they arranged a time and place. As she whistled to Flop and headed for home, Jori considered this new turn of events. Maybe this was what God had in mind for her. No doubt Chris with his fathomless blue eyes and big grinning smile was meant for someone else and God had sent David along for her to be with.

''I can be the best darn stepmother going!'' A few seconds later she was giggling merrily. She'd only just met David again and suddenly she was a stepmother? ''Come on, Flop. The rain's seeped into my brain.''

Thankfully, Chris and his mother seemed to have left, and although Jori supposed she should have felt guilty for abandoning them, she relished the opportunity to sink into the hot, bubbling bathwater and soak away her frustrations.

For her, there was no future outside of Mossbank. There

couldn't be. If there was one lesson she had learned, it was that she belonged right here. The people who cared about her were here and she couldn't abandon them. She would stay and pay off her debt to them, and lead whatever life God gave her.

"I'll learn how to be satisfied with that," she told herself. "Just like Paul says in the New Testament—I have learned to be content in whatever state I'm in." It wasn't a cheering thought but Jori knew there was nothing else to do.

"Not unless a minor miracle comes along," she whispered to Flop. The phone rang as she was emptying the tub.

"Miss Jessop? This is Lara Mandon. I'm sorry to call you so late, but I knew you'd want to know our decision immediately."

"Yes, I do." Jori crossed her fingers as the woman from the agency cleared her voice. "Am I going to be allowed to adopt?"

"I'm sorry, but no. The board feels that with the shortage of babies and the surplus of couples willing to adopt them, it would be remiss of us to put you on our list. I hope you understand."

"No," Jori said trying to keep the bitterness from her voice. "I don't understand at all. I'm more than willing to give a child a home and you're telling me that I can't. That you don't want to let me have a baby."

"There are several other avenues open to you, Miss Jessop. You could try fostering for the state, although they generally prefer two-parent families. Or perhaps some medical intervention...artificial insemination, maybe?"

"I don't think so, but thanks anyway, Miss Mandon. It was good of you to call."

As she replaced the phone, Jori steeled herself against the tears. Her dream of a family had turned to ashes.

Stoically she stood and began straightening the room,

pretending that life went on when she felt dead inside. The phone rang again and Jori picked it up listlessly. It was Jessica.

"Hi, Jori. We have a daughter, Liza Jean!"

Jori swallowed her pain and congratulated her friend before demanding all the particulars.

"Well, she was born early this morning. She weighs five pounds, two ounces." There was a long pause and Jori knew something not quite as wonderful would follow. Finally Jessica's tearful voice told her the rest.

"They are going to operate in the morning, Jori. Her heart is defective. The doctors are going to try to repair it right away. Dan and I are sitting here, just waiting." Her friend's soft, tearful voice faded away.

"Jessica, little Liza is going to be fine. You have to believe that. I'll be praying and so will the rest of the town." Jori made her voice firm and convincing. "You and Dan just rest and know that we'll all be here, waiting for you three to come home."

They chatted for a few moments more until Jessica turned the phone over to Dan.

"How's my best nurse?" Jori thought he sounded tired, deflated.

"Oh, I'm just fine, Dr. Gordon, sir. Congratulations, I hear you are a father. Poor little girl to end up with a bossy fellow like you." The banter continued for several moments. Jori hid her own feelings as she fought depression off. Gradually it seeped away as Dan teased her.

"How's my stand-in doing?" he demanded. "I hope he's taken advantage of the good advice I gave him."

"What advice?" Jori asked absentmindedly, pulling a brush through her long hair.

"About you, of course. I told him my nurse was ready for love and he would fill the bill nicely."

Jori groaned, blushing furiously. The words lined up in

her head, ready to blast out at him when she heard Jessica's voice in the background.

"Stop lying, Dan. You only said Jori would keep him in line."

Jori breathed a sigh of thanks that she hadn't made a fool of herself. Still, Daniel Gordon, GP, had one coming. In a moment the answer came to her.

"It's okay, Dan. When you get home you will be far too busy changing diapers and eating Emma Simms's cheese-cakes. I'm sure you won't have time to worry about my love life." She grinned, satisfied, as she heard his groan in the background. She added the last bit of bait. "Chris's been filling your freezer with them for weeks."

"Jori, that's not fair. You know the woman can't bake…"

Jori cut him off midstream, smiling at Jessica's chuckles in the background.

"I have to go now, Dan. I have a hot date to plan and it's *not* with a doctor. Kiss Liza and Jess for me and thanks for phoning."

"Jori?" Dan's voice was soft and consoling. "I know how much you want your own child and that this must hurt you. But if God can look after Liza's medical problems, he can give you the desires of your heart."

"I know." Jori choked down the emotion that gripped her. "It's just that I'm having a little trouble on the when part." She straightened her backbone and tried for a light tone. "I'll be fine. You guys take care of each other and the baby. I love you, bye."

Happiness and sadness vied for uppermost position in her mind as she thought of the tiny baby that hung on to life so precariously. Another family looking toward the future with hope, she mused sadly. And she was still out in the cold.

"Stop feeling sorry for yourself and get on the phone," she ordered angrily.

Her mind breathed a prayer for the baby as she phoned Faith, Hope and Charity who would organize the members of the local ladies' group into a prayer chain. She had to believe that there would be a baby shower when the Gordons returned.

As she dialed, a question whisked across Jori's mind, leaving her shaken and wondering. Would she ever have a new little baby to hold and cuddle and call her own? Or a husband to share those wonderful moments with?

Chapter Ten

Dr. Chris Davis was not looking forward to leaving Moss-bank even given the cool, wet weather that had hampered the farmers this past week. The fact that it had also put a blight on his mother's now extended visit had something to do with that.

Not that she had been thrilled to be there anyway, for he knew she'd only stayed longer to insist he give up this work. And with the constant rain, there was little opportunity for him to point out the obvious natural beauties of the area. Not that she was interested.

Charlotte Davis was not accustomed to studying nature in the raw. She spent most of her time in her pristine, climate-controlled lab. Her trip west had been of necessity not for pleasure, she'd told him shortly. A duty she felt compelled to attend to.

"I did not come to this remote community to see the local sights. Your father and I agreed that one of us had to try to bring you to your senses." Her glance through the shabby hotel window had been disparaging. "I came to bring you back to where you belong."

"Well, I'm not ready to leave. Not just yet. Come on,

Mother. It's not that far to the city and you might enjoy it if you got to know the locals.''

Her straight, severe mouth had curled at that and Chris had known there was nothing to be gained by pursuing the matter. She would fulfill her *mission,* as she termed it, and then return to the work she considered more important than anything: research. Within minutes of entering the lab, Chris knew she would lose herself in the current project and forget about him until something or someone else reminded her of her motherly duty.

He didn't mind. Not anymore, he corrected himself. There had been a time when he had craved his parents' attention, some show of affection; had wished his mother knew how to bake cookies or hold birthday parties; that his father would come out to play catch once in a while.

But somehow, Chris acknowledged sadly, the impossibility of achieving that dream had finally been accepted internally. His parents were not like that. They could not show outward signs of affection with the spontaneity and uninhibited ease he had longed for. To compensate for the shortfall, they strove for excellence in their professional fields and taught him to search for it himself. It was just that work wasn't enough anymore.

Of course they loved him. Chris knew that. Both his parents were concerned about his career. He grimaced as he remembered his mother's caustically cynical remarks regarding Chris's current situation.

''I can't believe you're going to throw it all away,'' she'd muttered. ''And for what? There are lots of women who are just as pretty as your office nurse. And a lot more cosmopolitan in their outlook, I can tell you.''

''Mother, Jordanna Jessop was a world-famous, topnotch model. She is hardly small-town stuff!''

''Then why is she hiding herself in the boonies dispensing peace and goodwill? And if you two are so thick, why is she going out to lunch with that young man?'' his mother had countered. "She doesn't want you, Christopher. If she did and you decided to go back to Boston, I guarantee she'd follow. Don't sacrifice yourself here."

Chris didn't bother to explain that Jordanna couldn't and wouldn't leave the tiny community. Nor did he want to hear about some new man in her life. The bottom line was that Charlotte wanted him back in Boston. Now. She could not understand his growing affinity with his patients, let alone the unexpected pleasure he derived treating people who had become known entities. How did he expect her to understand someone like Jori? Charlotte couldn't even understand why he had consented to staying here for so long.

"You belong at the General, or somewhere like it," she had told him, mapping his future out in her usual organized style. "There is little call for your specialized skills here. You're wasting your talents."

That, it seemed, was the end of that.

"Mother, these are people with needs every bit as great as those I treated in the city. And if I screw up, or prescribe something that doesn't work, they come back and tell me. It's face-to-face here, personal. There are no huge bureaucratic paper trails to follow up."

Chris made no attempt to tell her that he had been enjoying himself. He knew her opinion very well. This wasn't *important* medicine. Not like the major surgeries he had performed within the hallowed confines of the major hospitals. To Charlotte, these were the little people, and as such, far removed from her milieu.

And in a way, Chris brooded, she was right. He had trained long and hard in order to be qualified to perform the specialized surgeries he had done. And he had enjoyed the work at first. He'd been proud of the success he'd become and the prestige he'd gained. But gradually, his life had become impersonal and cold.

In Mossbank, impersonal would never happen. Oh, some moved out and new folks arrived, but by and large, the majority of people were stable to the area. The baby you delivered last week would be back in periodically for the next eighteen years or so and you could monitor his progress as you stitched and casted and advised.

Chris liked that component of medicine more than anything. That sense of continuity was new and intriguing. And while he occasionally missed the high-tech, fast-paced operating room equipment, he relished the familiarity and friendliness with which his patients treated their doctor. He liked the way Jori treated him even better.

He loved her!

The realization hit him squarely in the stomach, driving away his breath. Chris didn't know why he was surprised. He'd been entranced by her ever since Dan had introduced them. She had only to stare at him with those melting chocolate-colored eyes, or tip her wide, generous lips into a smile and he could feel his knees buckle.

Jori was saucy and beautiful and bright. She glowed with a zest for living that refused to be dimmed by anyone. Her joy in life was as fresh and unspoiled as a child's. She bounded forward, embracing each day with her brisk, no-nonsense attitude that dared him to rain on her parade. And she refused to back down where her principles were concerned.

One of her most steadfast principles was to remain right here in Mossbank. Chris thought he had accepted her decision to bury herself here. Now, suddenly, he realized the personal implication her decision would have on him. Dan and Jessica would come back and he would leave. Alone.

It would be extremely difficult to build a surgical practice here and the travel involved in commuting to a city center didn't bear thinking about. Besides, there wasn't any teaching facility near by.

"It's all right, Mother. You can go back and tell Father I'll be returning to the fold. I've been offered a teaching position in the East. I start as soon as Dan and Jessica get back.''

It was amazing how quickly his mother had left after that. In less than half an hour she had packed her rental car, called the airline and taken off out of town like a cat chased by a dog.

''Nice seeing you, Mother,'' Chris muttered to himself as he strode back to the clinic. ''Don't worry about me. I'll be fine.''

Now he noticed Jori coming from the opposite direction. She was laughing and smiling at a tall skinny guy by her side. Every so often she leaned down and ruffled the hair of a little boy plodding along beside them, and Chris felt a fist of jealousy clench the muscles of his stomach. That should be him she was with, their child she spoke to. She waved at Chris then walked into the clinic.

But it can't be, Lord. I understand that. I can't ask her to leave everything she holds dear. He slowed up his pace, enjoying the ruffle of wind across his skin. *Her father's getting worse; day by day, week by week, he forgets a little more, and I can't, I won't ask her to abandon him. Maybe in the future...* The thought died away. There was no future. Not for the two of them. They would soon be separated by thousands of miles.

He sat on the park bench, lost in his thoughts, until an urgent voice broke through his musings. ''Chris, you've got to come right away. There's been an accident!''

He jolted to his feet, a surge of adrenalin racing through his bloodstream.

''It's Jonathan,'' he heard Jori gasp as she raced beside him to the clinic.

The little boy was whimpering as his mother held him, one hand pressing a spotless white tea towel against his scalp. His eyes were half-open, and Chris recognized the drowsiness of his patient.

''Hi, Jonathan,'' he called out cheerfully, patting the

boy's little hand. Carefully he peeled back the towel, wincing mentally at the gash that yawned open on the child's scalp. He replaced the towel and spoke sharply, hoping to rouse Jonathan enough to keep him awake.

"Jonathan, do you want to go for a car ride?" The child blinked slowly, his huge eyes regarding Christopher solemnly. "Keep him awake," he ordered Jori. "I don't want him nodding off just yet." He turned to Amy Grand, scratching notes on his pad as he spoke. "Did he fall?"

"Yes. About eight feet," she whispered, brushing her hand over the child's small body. "I was working in a flower bed and I'd left a shovel there. That's how he cut his head." Tears flowed down her white cheeks. "Bob's in the field so I piled both kids in the car and drove like crazy." She swatted away the tears and stared at Chris. "He's going to be okay, isn't he?"

"I'll know more after I've had a better look." She tried to stand and he pressed her down. "No, stay there. I want to move him as little as possible. Jori, bring a cart, will you?" He specified what he wanted on it and then left her to get it while he checked Jonathan's pupil reaction.

"You know that I'm a doctor, don't you, Jonathan?" The boy nodded imperceptibly, his eyes drooping. "And I want to help make you all better?" Again the child's head nodded. "Okay then. But I need you to help me out. And the first thing you have to do is stay awake."

"Too tired," Jonathan slurred.

"No, son. You can do it. You're strong." Carefully, Chris lifted away the towel and dabbed gently at the wound on the child's scalp, carefully removing the dried blood and dirt. As he took the swabs from Jori, Chris noticed that her hand was shaking. He checked swiftly, surprised to see how white she'd become.

"I'm fine," she told him grimly. "Go ahead."

One searching look was all he could afford but it told

him that Jordanna Jessop would stay the course. He turned back to his patient, all senses on alert.

The injury was a jagged cut from below Jonathan's ear to the back part of his head. There was some swelling, but Chris could not tell much beyond that.

"I want pictures," he instructed Jordanna. "And I'd like them before I suture him. Can you phone the hospital and tell them it's a rush?" She nodded and hurried away while Chris sat down to explain to Jonathan and his mother.

"At the hospital they have this machine that can take pictures of the inside of your head, Jonathan."

"Why?" The question was drowsy, and Chris sat the boy up more solidly in Amy's arms, checking the pulse as he did.

"The pictures tell me whether this is just a plain ordinary cut from a shovel or if you bumped your brain. I want to make sure your brain didn't get hurt."

"What if it did?" Jonathan demanded. "Do you have to cut it out? Auntie Jori said you're a cutting kind of doc-toh."

"Sometimes I do that," Chris grinned. "But usually I don't take out brains. Sometimes I sew people up so their insides can't fall out. I think that's what we'll have to do with you."

"Will it hurt?" Jonathan's voice was small and he bit on his lip bravely.

"The pictures won't hurt. But yes, when I sew you up it will hurt. A little bit. But it won't take long and then you'll be good as new. Will that be okay?" He waited while the child thought it over, head tilted to one side as Jonathan considered.

"Can Brit come, too?"

"No." Chris shook his head. "She's too small. Anyway, hospitals are really for people who need help. Did she fall, too?"

Jonathan giggled; it was muffled and short, to be sure, but it was a giggle.

"Brit didn't fall! She don't walk." His eyes were wide-open now as he grinned at his sister.

"What's wrong with her?" Chris pretended amazement. "Does she need her legs fixed?"

"A 'course not!" Jonathan sounded astonished. "Don't you know babies gotta learn to walk?"

"I'll have to study up," Chris promised gravely, lifting the child carefully from his mother's arms. "Shall we go now?"

He waited for Amy's nod of approval and then glanced back at Jori, assessing her state of mind with a clinical glance.

"Maybe Auntie Jori could hold you while your mommy holds Brit and I drive the car."

"Jon dwive?" The little boy's eyes twinkled up at him and Chris felt a stab of something deep within his heart at the trust he glimpsed there.

"Not today, pal," Chris said with a laugh, helping them into his car. "But when Jon's head is all better, I'll take him for a drive. Okay, buddy?"

Jon agreed happily, leaning against Jori's shoulder with a sigh and Chris let his eyes slide up to meet her brown ones, conscious of the woman in the back seat.

"Children suit you," he murmured, shifting into gear. "You should have lots of them." Mine, he whispered mentally and then stopped in disbelief as he saw the huge tears roll down her cheeks. "J.J.?"

"Drive," she whispered, staring straight ahead. "Just drive."

"Jordanna Jessop has a new boyfriend." Faith Johnson smiled triumphantly as she imparted this latest bit of news. When she noticed the skeptical looks on her friends' faces she frowned. "His name is David Andrews, he has a little boy called Davey and he used to live here, so there."

"The only Andrews I knew other than Clarence, was a family that had a shoe store in town. As I recall, their kids would have been much younger than Jordanna." Charity frowned.

"No, dear. That was Anderson. Andrews was the fellow at the seed plant, where they crush canola to make margarine." Hope smiled gently. "They moved when David graduated. He was such an intelligent boy—very good in the debate club, I recall."

"But why would Jori be going out with him? I'm sure she's in love with Dr. Chris." Charity glared accusingly at the other two. "Have you two been matchmaking?"

Faith grinned cheerfully.

"Only for you," she blurted out. "And that didn't seem to work out very well. Not now that you and Frank Bellows are together all the time."

"We're not together *all* the time," Charity muttered, face flushed a dark red. "And anyway, it was just for pretend—at first."

"What?" Hope stared. "Charity Flowerday, what have you been up to?"

With as little detail as possible, Charity tried to explain how it came about that she and the local undertaker spent a goodly portion of each day together.

"He's been very kind," she asserted. "I don't know what I would have done without him."

"You're in love with him!" Faith's faded eyes twinkled merrily. "At last!" She clapped her hands together. "I thought it would never happen."

"Hush, Faith!" Hope caught the glimmer of anger in Charity's brown focus. "Don't tease her. If and when Charity has something to say, I'm sure she'll tell us."

"I *have* something to say," Charity admitted softly. "Frank and I have decided to get married."

"I knew it!" Faith hugged and kissed her friend gleefully. "I just knew you were in love with him."

"I didn't. I thought you said you couldn't stand the man." Hope's perplexed face mirrored her confusion. "As I recall, you said he was boring."

"Well, as we got to know one another, we found we had a lot in common. But I thought we were going to decide about Jori and Dr. Chris?"

"Just one more thing," Faith begged, her face glowing. "When's the wedding?"

"We're having a very small one," Charity cautioned. "Close friends and family, but that's all. At my age you don't have a big celebration."

"Why not? It's a big occasion." Hope frowned.

"I'm not the kind of woman who looks good in satin and lace and I don't intend to wear it, Hope Conroy. I want something plain and simple but it will have to be soon because we want Dr. Chris there. After all, he was the reason we got together and he'll be leaving as soon as Dan and Jessica get back."

"But he can't leave without Jordanna." Hope's usually calm voice was raised. "I thought for sure they'd come to some arrangement, figure out some plan. Anyway, I wanted them to stay here."

"No, he's definitely going back...alone." Charity's voice was filled with sadness. "Dr. Chris has been offered a prestigious post in a teaching hospital. He says he's wanted it for a long time."

They sat, the three of them, pondering the situation.

"You say Jori's going out with someone new, Faith?" Charity frowned, scratching her nose.

"David Andrews," Hope murmured. A gentle smile tipped up the corners of her mouth. "He had quite a crush on Flossie Gerbrandt, if I recall. The two of them spent the last two years of school as steadies. I always thought she'd marry him."

"He did get married. But he's divorced now," Faith imparted knowledgeably.

"Is he? How nice." Faith and Hope stared at the strange sentiment coming from their friend's smiling lips. "I do believe I'd like to have some people over for dinner," she whispered with a wicked tilt of her eyebrows. "Flossie's already asked to help me with the wedding. What better time to discuss it than tonight! Now let's see…" She thumbed through the church directory, shifting her trifocals a little lower on her nose. "Ah, yes, here it is. New members—Andrews."

"She's doing it again," Faith whispered to Hope. "She's going to try and get them together."

"I know. And while she's busy with that, you and I need to plan a shower for her and Frank. I think a nice couples affair would be a rather pleasant shower."

"Piffle! She's already got her cupboards full," Faith exclaimed. "What in the world would we give them?"

"I think," Hope elaborated slowly, "we might consider a money tree with the funds to go toward a trip to that mineral springs. Remember? It's that spa that's supposed to be so helpful for arthritis. Frank has bad knees, you know. He'd enjoy it, too."

And they whispered and giggled merrily until Charity put down the phone. Her eyes studied them suspiciously.

"What have you two been talking about?"

"The future," Hope told her, jabbing an elbow in Faith's side as that woman started to speak. "And we think it might be a good idea if we have Dr. Chris over for dinner. In fact, we could make it a farewell evening. We've a lot to be grateful for."

Chapter Eleven

Jori knew she was in rough shape. It had been two weeks since little Jonathan's injury but she still couldn't erase the memory of Chris's wonderful skill as he'd soothed the boy. But hearing him say the same thing that was in her heart had made it so much worse. She would be good with kids, darn it! And she wanted to share them with Chris!

Christopher Davis was wonderful with children. He would make a wonderful father. But they wouldn't be her children; they couldn't be. He would leave and then she'd be all alone again.

She couldn't stop the awful message from whirling around in her brain regardless of how hard she drove herself. Alone. Alone.

"I declare, Jordanna Jessop, you look as skinny as a rail!" Jori heard Charity's voice as she got out of her car and walked toward her house. "What are you doing to yourself, child? Is your father worse?"

"A little." She pasted a smile on her lips. "But why are we talking about me? It's the day before your wedding—how are *you* doing? You're glowing!"

"I feel like that, too," Charity admitted. "Once I gave

up all my fears and inhibitions and explained to Frank why I was so hesitant to get married again, well, the burden just lifted.'' She giggled. ''Isn't it silly? I thought Frank had stayed away from me because I was all crippled up with this arthritis and now he tells me that he's been in love with me for years. He was just too shy to make the first move.'' She blushed. ''Thank goodness for Dr. Chris.''

''Yes, thank goodness,'' Jori agreed doubtfully.

''How are the two of you getting on now, dear? I know you were beginning to feel something for him. Hasn't it worked out?''

''No.'' Jori frowned. ''It hasn't. He's leaving, you see. And my place is here, in Mossbank. I've always known that.''

''Is that why you began going out with David Andrews?'' Charity asked waspishly. ''You feel Chris is unattainable?''

''Something like that.'' There was no point in prevaricating, Jori decided. Charity was her friend. It was time to tell her the truth. ''I want a home of my own, Charity. I want a family that I can share my life with. But I just can't let myself rely on someone and then have them abandon me.''

''And you think Chris Davis would do this?'' Charity demanded with a frown.

''He's leaving, Charity. As soon as Dan gets back. And I can't.'' She straightened her shoulders defensively. ''Besides, David is kind and funny. We share things from the past.''

''I think he's simply comfortable,'' Charity muttered, glaring at her knotted fingers. ''You're settling for less, Jori. And what's more, you're selling God short.''

''I don't think we should continue this,'' Jori murmured, not wanting to hurt the older woman.

''Yes, we should. And I'll tell you why. David is a nice man. *And,*'' she paused expectantly, ''he has a son. A cute little child that tugs on your heart strings, whose very look begs for some mothering.'' She waited for a moment. ''But David Andrews is a man, not a little boy. And he deserves a woman who can share his *life* not just his child. Someone like Flossie.''

''Flossie? Oh, but she's…''

''Been out with him several times,'' Charity confirmed with a nod of her white head. ''And he's been to dinner at her house. I think he really cares for her, or he could. If you'd let him.''

''But I haven't…'' Jori's voice died away at the intent look in Charity's discerning eyes.

''God has something special in mind for you, Jordanna. Something that He's planned since before you were conceived. And if you'll only let Him work in your life, you'll find more happiness than all the manipulation you can manage on your own.'' Charity wrapped one thin arm around Jori's shoulders and hugged her close.

''But you can't walk in fear, Jori. You can't duck out and take the easy way. You have to learn the lesson before you get the prize. Maybe it's time you stopped trying to control events and let God direct you the way He wants.'' Her voice dropped to a soft whisper. ''God has something He wants to teach you, my dear. Something so wonderful, you can't imagine. And when that day comes, today's trials will seem like nothing.''

''You sound like Dad,'' Jori murmured, glancing down at the gnarled old hands that held hers so lovingly. ''He quoted Psalms 30:5 today. *'Weeping may endure for the night, but joy comes in the morning.'*''

''James may have lost bits and pieces of his past but he has kept his wonderful memories of the scriptures.'' Charity smiled. ''And it's true, dear. You may not believe it now but take it from an old lady who's been through the valley. Cling to this—*'You will show me the path of life; Your presence is fullness of joy; At your right hand are pleasures forevermore.'"* Charity moved back a step, her face shining with happiness.

"Let Him show you the path to a full life, Jori."

The wedding of Charity Flowerday and Frank Bellows took place in the local church. It was a brief affair with the bride's best friends escorting her down the aisle, one on each arm. Charity had decided on a lovely cream woolen suit and she carried a small sheaf of deep pink roses.

"I, Charity, take you, Frank, to be my lawful wedded husband. To have and to hold, in sickness or in health, from this day forward, forever more."

The words rang through the tiny sanctuary with a sureness and clarity that brought tears to Jori's eyes. Frank's face was beaming with delight as he leaned down and pressed a hearty kiss against his new wife's lips in a way that made his devotion and great love that evident to the entire congregation.

Christopher had managed to seat himself beside Jori and now his fingers entwined with hers as his blue eyes noted the moisture on her cheeks.

"It's pretty special when it's someone like those two, isn't it?" he whispered softly. "But then," he added, staring at her, "I guess marriage is meant to be pretty special."

There was nothing she could say to that, so Jori contented herself with clapping as the happy couple strolled down the aisle, beaming as they accepted their friends' congratulations. She'd tried to keep him out of her life just as she'd wanted him out of her heart.

"Are you going to use all that confetti?" Chris whispered in her ear. Jori put half of it into his open hands and then eased her way to the front of the crowd surrounding the bride and groom on the cold, windswept sidewalk.

"Best wishes, Charity, and you, too, Frank. I know you'll be very happy together." Hugging the older woman,

Jori felt the constriction in her throat and hung on for an extra moment.

"You will be, too, my dear," Charity whispered. "Just keep trusting."

Jori stepped back and raised her arms, sprinkling the multicolored dots of paper over the white heads of her friends.

Just like God's blessings, Jori remembered from some wedding long past.

"All right, everyone!" Faith stood at the top of the steps clapping her hands to gain everyone's attention. "Don't stand around freezing. We have a lovely meal at the senior's hall. It's warm in there and you can visit all you like."

As a group, the townsfolk quickly moved to their cars to drive the short trip to the hall. Jori hugged her coat around her more snugly to shield out the wind and headed for her Jeep.

"Can I tag along?" Christopher stood beside her, his collar up around his ears. "I'd walk but it's too c-cold."

"That's North Dakota for you," Jori agreed, ordering her pulse to slow down. It didn't mean anything; he just needed a ride. "And this is only October!"

"You look very beautiful," he murmured when she pulled to a stop. "Red is certainly your color. Vibrant and full of life."

"Er, thank you," Jori murmured, unable to tear her gaze from his. "You look very nice, too."

"Jori," he whispered as she moved to open the door. His blue eyes were deep and intent as they studied her.

"Yes?" She tried to look away and found she couldn't. There was something so compelling in his eyes. Something that riveted her attention on him and denied her attempt to look away.

"I'll be leaving soon, J.J." he murmured. "Dan's on his way back and then I've got to go."

"I know. And I can't tell you how much we in Mossbank

appreciate this time you've given to us. I've enjoyed working with you, too." Deliberately, Jori kept the conversation on the same businesslike footing she'd used for weeks now. "But I think we'd better go in now. They'll be starting soon." She slid out of her seat and grabbed her purse before slamming the door and moving to the front of the vehicle. Her evasive tactics didn't work.

Chris caught up with her at the front door of the hall, his fingers closing about her elbow. His face was tight and controlled, his lips clamped together. Those vivid blue eyes were cool as they stared at her, but she caught the glint of understanding in his voice.

"We are going to talk, Jordanna. Maybe not here. Maybe not now. But before I leave, I intend to say what I have to say. And you will listen. It's too important to ignore." And then he leaned down and pressed a kiss against her surprised lips before yanking the door open. "After you, ladies."

Jori turned in time to see Faith and Hope sweep through the entry, their grins wide and understanding. With a grimace in Chris's direction, Jori tilted her head and walked through the door, somehow staving off her fury at his temerity.

Still, she mused, hanging her coat on top of another one in the cramped entry, he had kissed her as if he meant it. At least she had that to hold on to.

The reception was unlike anything the people of Mossbank had seen at a wedding before. Tables of food were scattered here and there throughout the hall inviting the guests to snack whenever they wished. There were plenty of chairs for anyone who wished to sit. No stack of presents waited to be opened. The bride and groom had requested no gifts in their invitation in the local newspaper. That didn't stop Harry Conroy and Arthur Johnson from collecting donations from anyone who cared to contribute and it didn't mean that there weren't a stack of cards and a few gag items displayed around the hall.

"The wedding cake is a train?" Chris sounded amazed as he stared at the seven-car confection that sat upon licorice tracks.

Jori grinned at him, catching the sense of fun that prevailed. "Yes, and I understand that it's all edible. Melanie said her mother insisted on it." As they stood staring, a group of small children ventured near, eyes wide as they stared at the masterpiece. Jonathan Grand was among them and it was he who reached out and stole a mint from the caboose.

"He looks good, doesn't he?" Chris murmured. "No aftereffects from his slight concussion, thank the Lord."

"They all look good," Jori told him sincerely. "Thanks to you. You've done a fine job here. I don't know how we could ever thank you."

"I don't need thanks," Chris told her gruffly. "I've gained more from being here than I could ever give. I'll be sorry to leave."

Jori was about to turn away when a sudden scuffling at the entry drew her attention.

"Hey!" A voice she knew and loved called out laughingly. "Can't a couple leave for a few weeks without you folks carrying on like this?"

Dr. Daniel Gordon, M.D., stood grinning in the doorway, his arm around the waist of his happy wife who carried a tiny baby in her arms.

As the rest of the crowd rushed forward to greet the prodigal and his family, Jori turned around, her eyes on Chris's bemused face.

"You knew, didn't you?" She felt her heart drop to her feet. If Dan was home, Chris wouldn't be staying long. There wasn't any point.

"Yes, I knew," he admitted softly. "But you anticipated

that from the beginning, didn't you, Jori? My coming to Mossbank was only ever a temporary thing.''

As the words stabbed through her heart, shattering all her dreams, Jori turned away, fumbling toward the ladies' room at the back.

No matter how much she'd hoped, how much she'd dreamed, the result was still the same. Chris was leaving.

Why? she begged, staring into the mirror. *Why couldn't he stay here?*

But there was no answer from heaven and other ladies were clustering into the bathroom now. Gathering composure like a cloak around her, Jordanna walked out of the room and toward the entrance. She would trust God with this; at least she would try.

''It's so good to have you guys home,'' she lied easily. ''And this is Liza! Hello, sweetheart.'' She ignored the pain in her heart and accepted the bundle of softly scented sleeping baby from her friend. ''She's a darling, Jess. Just a darling.''

Over the heads of the crowd, Jori's eyes locked with Chris's. She saw the need darken their depths and the way his eyes squeezed shut, as if to ward off the pain. Without a word he turned and walked through the door, completely forgetting his coat.

Chapter Twelve

Jori expected the days to drag, but in fact, she was kept busy as the three doctors spent the week catching up. Dr. Green wasn't affected by the transition much, except that he and Dan had grown close over the years, often covering for each other on a special weekend or holiday. The same connection had sprung up between Chris and Dr. Green, and Jori had noticed how frequently Chris had taken over some of the older man's workload. Now that was to be transferred back to Dan which meant checking and rechecking the files to make sure Dan saw the updates of those patients he'd been worried about.

If that wasn't enough to keep Jori hopping, there was a lot of after-hours community planning and organizing going on to welcome the new baby and shower Liza and her mother with an abundance of baby things.

"I'm so glad we had that house cleaned from top to bottom before they arrived," Charity rambled happily over the phone to Jori. "Jessica can have a bit of a rest. Speaking of that, it's my shift with the wee one soon, not that she needs monitoring. Her heart is better than ever. I'd better go." She stopped for a moment and then in a softer tone asked, "How are you doing, dear?"

"I'm praying a lot, Charity. That's all I can do now." Jori carried her dishes to the sink, dragging the phone cord behind her shoulder.

"My dear, that's the very best thing! When you can't see a way through, you have to pray and ask God to open one up."

They had just finished their conversation when the doorbell rang. It was Chris. A tired, pale Chris who stood on the doorstep shuffling from one foot to the other.

"Hi. Can I come in?"

Silently, she opened the door wider.

"I'm leaving tomorrow," he said bleakly.

Jori walked through to the living room dazedly and sank into the nearest chair, telling herself to breathe normally. The time had finally come, as she'd known it would. But now was not the time to be weak and give in to the tears that threatened to spill out at the thought of losing him.

"I'm sorry you have to go," she offered in a friendly but distant tone, her throat clogged. "We've enjoyed having you here."

"I've learned so much from you, Jori. I'm in love with you and I've been trying to tell you for days. But you've been so busy pushing me away, and there's been so much to do with Dan's return, that I let it go. I was afraid to hope, afraid to dream we even had a future."

His face clouded over, his eyes dark with the seriousness of his words. "But now I'm leaving and I've got to know for sure. Do you love me or do I have a bad case of wishful thinking?"

She stared at him. "Love? You really love me?"

He nodded.

"I love you. I've known it for ages. And I think you love me. I think we could have something wonderful together—if you'd give it a chance. Couldn't you come with me?'' The whispered words were soft and full of agony. ''We could get married right away.''

''Chris, I have a contract with this town that I won't renege on. My father is here and he needs the routine of seeing *me,* his one familiar face, every day.'' She sighed miserably, knowing that wasn't the only reason as the ugly thought of fear outside of this protected oasis gripped her. She could deal with life here.

Grimly she continued. ''Besides, I love this town. I've always wanted to raise a family here. I want to savor each moment of my days with people I like and respect. I guess that's the way God made me. This is the place He keeps bringing me back to.''

She stood before him and spoke the words as she watched his face tighten with that mask he so often hid behind.

''I've never pretended that I'm the big-city, sophisticated type. That's not me. I'm small-town, old-fashioned.'' She drew in a deep breath and continued in a whoosh of excuses.

''Besides all that, I don't think I could live your kind of life. The reason I know that is because for a period of my life, I pretended that I fit in, that I had something in common with people I neither knew nor cared about. And I paid the price for it.'' Jori cleared the tears from her voice and appealed to Chris to understand. ''But even if I *could* get past all that and leave my past behind, I still am not free to move.''

''Jori, I can't live here. I'm a surgeon. Boston is where I live, where I work.''

''I know,'' she agreed sadly.

He peered up at her in disbelief, a pained smile tugging at his lips. ''It's ironic really. I've always thought I was the type who couldn't be part of a family. But now, here, these past few weeks with you, I'm beginning to believe you and I could have the one thing that's always been beyond my reach—love, Jori. Real love. The kind that builds families.''

Jori stood staring at him, silently begging God for help.

''Say something. Doesn't it mean anything, that I want you to come with me? That I love you. Or are you too afraid?'' he demanded, eyes widening in his intensity. ''Too scared to leave your safe, cozy little town and take a chance on life in the real world?'' He was angry now.

''You'd better decide, Jori. Are you willing to throw away everything we could have together just because you're *afraid?*''

''I can't leave here, Chris. Not now, anyway.'' She hated saying it, but there was no other way out, no matter how badly she wanted one. ''I'm sorry. I've prayed and prayed but I just don't see a solution. We each have our own paths to travel.''

''But I'm in love with you! I want us to have a future. But not if you can't meet me at least halfway.'' His hands fell to his sides. ''I can deal with a lot of things, Jori. But I can't handle that. You're the only one who can find enough strength to let go of the past and embrace the future. I can't do it for you.''

Jori felt his words hit her like nails. She was trying! But he was asking her to give up everything!

''But Mossbank is my home,'' she muttered. ''These are my friends. I'm…''

''Safe here,'' he concluded for her flatly. ''You don't have to extend yourself one bit more than you want to. You can sit and wallow in the past as long as you want and no one will force you to see that life is passing by without you.'' His face was white as he gazed down at her.

''We could be there for one another to support and encourage when we needed it,'' he continued. ''We could move ahead with our lives, be somebodies, go somewhere.'' His voice dropped. ''We could have it all. But you have to let go of the past, of the fear that I'll hurt you like he did.''

She was shaking, Jori realized. His words and the pictures they'd painted made her long for such a life. But it was impossible. She couldn't give up her father, her town, her friends. Her security, a tiny voice whispered.

''What about my dad? And what do you give up?'' she demanded at last, unable to stem the doubts and fears. ''Even supposing I could get out of this contract and didn't have to worry about my father, you're still doing your parents' bidding. You're following their plan for your life. What is it that you want, Chris?''

He stood staring down at her for several long minutes. ''You,'' he whispered finally. ''And you know your father's not a problem. We can take him with us. But you won't even consider it.''

''I'm sorry,'' she said. ''So sorry. But this isn't God's time for us to be together.''

''There's a way,'' he said fiercely, drawing her into his arms. ''There is some way for us to be together. I just have to find it. And I will.''

Then his lips were on hers and Jori could do nothing but savor his kiss, his tender touch. For tomorrow it would all be gone and she would be alone again.

''You'll move on,'' she whispered brokenly, trying to hold back the sobs that raged inside. ''You'll be a wonderful teacher and your students will take what you know and pass it on to the world.'' She straightened and pulled away from him, watching his hands fall to his side.

''Go and do the work God's given you, Chris. You'll find someone who isn't afraid to give back your love and you'll be very happy.'' It hurt to say those words, but Jori knew there was no choice. She had to set him free; make him see that they both had to go on with their lives. Separately.

"I've already found her," he said stubbornly. "The woman I love is you. You just won't accept it."

"I wish I could." It was a prayer from the heart. "But I have to do what I think is right, even if it hurts. And my place is in Mossbank. We both know that you can't run a teaching hospital from here." She swallowed painfully. "Go and live your life, Chris. Be happy."

His fingers had brushed across her cheek, but he shook his head adamantly.

"We will be together," he insisted. "God didn't send me here, introduce me to a wonderful woman who is everything I've ever dreamed of, and let me see what my life could be like with her, just to snatch it all away. I'm going to believe that He has more planned for us." He brushed a quick hard kiss on her lips and then strode to the door.

Standing there, framed in her doorway, his blond head gleaming in the sunshine, Jori heard his low voice clearly across the expanse of the room.

"I'll be back, Jordanna Jessop. Somehow, some way, I'll be back. And we will be together. You just have to trust in that. And wait for me."

And with one last look, he left, leaving a finality and silence behind that tore at her heart. Alone. Again.

It hurt, but she had expected that, Jori told herself. And she had to get on with her life. And try to staunch the flow of pain that haunted her at what she'd given up.

"Medical clinic," she answered the phone several weeks later. A long drawn-out pause greeted her words.

Finally a cool, crisp voice inquired, "Is this Jordanna Jessop?"

"Dr. Davis." Her heart sank at the sound of Chris's mother's voice. "How are you?"

"I'm fine, thank you. I'm calling to extend my gratitude for your hospitality. I neglected to do that and Christopher has remonstrated with me several times."

"You're welcome," Jori told her, pain clutching at her heart. "H-how is he?"

"Christopher is very well, thank you. He has settled into a term position while another surgeon is on leave. It's just temporary, of course, but I can't tell you how happy they were to have him back."

"Oh." Jori couldn't think of anything else to say.

"He is very pleased to be back with his friends and is quite involved in several new projects." It was obvious that Chris's mother couldn't quite conceal the pride at her son's accomplishments.

"At the present he is negotiating with a team from another hospital to improve the surgical technology currently available there. In Australia, I believe. It's a lucrative position, and his father and I are hoping he will accept it. We're both very grateful for the kindness you extended toward our son."

Jori smiled sadly. Kindness, was that all they had shared? She could read clearly between the lines. Christopher Davis had moved far beyond her reach. He'd clearly put Mossbank and her behind him. Don't expect him back, his mother was saying. He doesn't belong there.

Unable to bear the pain of memory, Jori cut the call short, thanking the woman for her duty call and promising she would look them up if she ever traveled east.

Time dragged on. Months passed. Thanksgiving came and went.

"Good gracious," Glenda exclaimed one frosty December day. "Do you realize there are only tens days till Christmas? I've been putting off my Christmas shopping long enough."

"Maybe it's time for you to get away, Jori, even for a weekend," Dan gently advised her later that afternoon, noting the dark circles under her eyes. "You didn't take holidays this year, Jori. You need a break. Go and enjoy yourself for a change. Take Friday off."

Jori nodded her agreement. She took the day off and drove to the city to do some shopping, hoping to drown herself in the business of the holiday. But the busy mothers directing children through lines to see Santa ate at her like acid, and she turned away, unwilling to watch it any longer.

Listlessly, she drove to the old stone church her father had loved and sank into the worn pew as the famous choir began its yearly rendition of Handel's *Messiah*. The joyous message of peace and mercy swelled out, filling the arched building and resounding back to those in the audience. As one, they surged to their feet to the resounding "Hallelujah" chorus.

The wonderful old songs of joy filled her heart as she sang with all the others gathered for the festive celebration. Although there was no one she knew in the crowd, Jori felt her frozen heart melt with the joy of the season. And when several people wished her a merry Christmas, she cheerily did the same.

It wasn't strange or unusual. No one was unfriendly. In fact, she decided, gazing around, there was the same sense of community here that she'd always found in the church at Mossbank. She watched as the little old lady in front of her wrapped her arm through the elderly gentleman beside her. They exchanged a tender smile that tugged at Jori's heartstrings.

Was this what Chris had meant? she asked herself. That wherever they went, they would have each other. That other people and places could be home as long as Chris was there?

When she finally left, Jori carried away a sense of peace tucked within. She drove through the streets, gazing at the gaily decorated homes as a new emotion gripped her. It wasn't fear. It was longing; aching covetousness for a home with Chris and their family.

You'd have to move, her mind whispered.

"You wouldn't be moving away. These people will still be your friends. You'd be moving on *to* something."

Jori felt the aloneness close in on her when she steered back onto the highway. Tears coursed down her cheeks as the pain tore through her lonely heart. She had thrown away the best thing in her life. Tossed Chris away as if his love didn't matter.

"No more," she sobbed to herself in the darkened vehicle. "I can't live in the past anymore. Help me, Lord," she pleaded.

Perfect love casts out all fear. She heard the words through a fog of misery. Her father had said them many times; times when she had been so confused, afraid to venture out into the unknown. *Nothing is as bad as knowing you could have changed things and didn't.*

Her father had been right on the money. If she really and truly loved Chris and wanted to be with him, fear could have no part in it. She had to let him know that place or conditions didn't matter. She loved him; that's all that counted.

The next day she sat at home, wrapping the gift she had purchased for Chris. Jori brushed a finger over the leather-bound volume, a first issue of a Robert Louis Stevenson classic. Dated in the late 1800s, Jori had found it in a dingy bookstore. She remembered Chris's whispered admission from what seemed long ago.

"We never got to read fairy tales when I was a child," he had told her once.

She wanted to remind him to take the time. She wanted him to read them to his own son. She wanted to share those moments, to watch as he took the time his own parents never had. And when he did, Jori wanted to be there.

She wavered back and forth all day, but finally made her decision.

"Dan, it's Jori. I need to ask you something." She

waited a few moments and then blurted out her request. "Can I have next week off?"

"What? Why?" he demanded brusquely.

"There's something I need to do," she told him. "Someone I have to see." She waited, tensing as the silence stretched tautly between them.

"I'm sorry, Jori. Glenda has already asked for extra time off. Erma Stant will fill in for a bit but I can't really spare you. How about the week after New Year's? Would that suit you?"

"Are you sure?"

"I'm sorry, Jori. I just can't do it. Where were you going, anyway?"

"I'm not sure. Boston, I think. Maybe Australia." She refused to say any more and thankfully Dan didn't question her any further. "I guess I'll just have to work something else out," she muttered, deflated now that she had finally made the decision to go.

"See you tomorrow," he replied. Jori frowned at the sound of it. Why did he have to sound so darn happy about it?

She sat in her lonely living room, thinking everything out. The house was terribly quiet, the fire flickering softly in the fireplace and Flop snoring at her feet when the telephone rang. She picked it up absently, wondering who could be calling now.

"J.J.?" His voice sounded so dear, Jori's throat clogged up with joy. "Jori, are you there?"

"Y-y-yes," she whispered. "I'm here, Chris."

She heard his sigh, a whoosh of breath over the telephone line.

"How are you?" she asked softly, aching to hear the sound of his voice. "Where are you?"

"In New York. I'm at a conference. I'm presenting a paper." His words were clipped and short. "Jori, I don't want to talk about work. I want to talk about you. I need to know something, J.J."

His voice dropped to a whisper and she just caught the hint of unsureness in it. "I love you, Jori. It's not a temporary thing. It's not going to go away. You're buried deep in my heart." His voice stabbed pricks of pain at her heart while a swelling gladness filled her eyes with tears.

"I keep seeing your face when I go to work, your smile when my patient makes it. I went to church the other day and someone sang. They weren't half as good as you."

"I miss you, too," she whispered, half afraid to say so but overwhelmingly glad that she had when she heard his shout of joy.

"That's what I was waiting for," he bellowed.

"Chris? Are you okay?" She studied the receiver worriedly, wondering if everything was going as well as his mother had said.

"Tell me the truth, J.J. Do you love me?"

Jori could see his face in her mind's eye—his eyes sparkling with mischief, his mouth tilted up, his hair mussed, giving him that little boy look that tugged at her heartstrings.

"We've been all through this," she began.

"No, we haven't. I know all the problems. Believe me, I know!" Chris groaned, but there was a tingle of excitement in his tone that caused shivers to race up and down her arm. "Just answer the question, okay, sweetheart?"

"But…"

"Please?"

She couldn't deny that soft, cajoling dear voice any longer. On a sob of relief, she told him what was in her heart.

"Yes! I love you so much that I cry myself to sleep at night. And then I dream of you, and when I wake up I'm lonelier than ever."

There was a long space of silence before he rushed into speech. "J.J., if I can find a way for us to be together, will you marry me?"

The question stunned her and she stared at the black

instrument for a moment, wondering if she had made it up in her mind.

"Jordanna? Will you?" The sureness had dropped away now. She could hear the apprehension filling that smooth low tone.

"But, Chris, how?"

"Jordanna, I've been searching for you my whole life and I'm not going to accept that God dangled you in front of me, just to show me what I was missing. No, there's got to be a way. But I have to know that you feel the same way."

"Yes, Chris," she whispered, brushing tears away and straightening her shoulders. He was worth it, she told herself. Chris wasn't Trace; he wouldn't leave her in the lurch. "I love you," she told him plainly. "I would gladly marry you tomorrow if we could get something worked out." Silence dragged out between them until she heard the hiss of his breath against her ear. "I was coming to Boston to tell you that."

"I wish I was there." His voice was soft. "I'd hold you in my arms and never let you go."

Jori got lost in that vision and found herself abruptly jerked back to reality when his disgruntled voice chided her. "Jordanna! Are you listening?"

"Um, yes, I'm here." Her voice was dreamy. She tried to pay attention to what he was saying.

"Then listen. This is going to work out for us. I'm not letting you go. There's a way for us to have our dreams and I'm going to find it, so you'd better be ready, lady. Because when I do figure it all out, I'm coming for you and we're going to be married faster than you can say, 'Dr. and Mrs. Christopher Davis.'"

Jori tried to interrupt but he wouldn't let her.

"Never mind how or when. I don't know that yet." His voice was filled with jubilation. "But I'm going to knock on heaven's door until I get my answer. You get your wedding dress ordered and do whatever else needs doing, because when I come for you, I'm not waiting one day longer than necessary. It might take me days or weeks or months, but we are going to be together, Jordanna Jessop. And don't you forget it.''

Jori heard his words through a fog in her mind as happiness washed everything else away. She couldn't have misunderstood him; there was no doubt in Chris's voice.

''I'm giving it over to God, J.J. And you do the same. We can come through this.''

''I know we can,'' she whispered, taking the first tiny step of faith toward him. ''And when I get this contract finished, I'll live wherever you want, Chris. I can come back and visit with Dad and Mossbank will always be here.'' She swallowed hard, ignoring the warning voices in her head, trusting in the love that filled her heart. ''I want to marry you, Dr. Davis. As soon as you can work it out.''

''Thank you.'' His voice was barely audible above the clapping sound she could hear in the background, but the joy and relief in it couldn't be mistaken.

''Oh, no! It's my turn. I have to give my speech now! How am I going to talk about suctioning and sutures when all I can think about is you?'' he complained with a laugh.

''You can do it,'' she told him, a sureness ringing through her voice. ''You can give the best speech ever. Because when it's over, your mind will be free to start tackling our problem. I'll be thinking about you, Chris. And wishing you were here with me. Goodbye, my love.'' And gently, carefully, she hung up the phone.

''I will not be afraid,'' she whispered to herself with resolution. ''I will trust in the Lord for His perfect timing and I will wait.''

As she turned away, Jori caught a glimpse of herself in the mirror and tried to imagine what she'd look like in a wedding dress and veil.

''Please, God,'' she prayed softly, ''let it be soon.''

Chapter Thirteen

Jordanna Jessop was ready. She had her wedding dress; it hung in her father's bedroom, covered by a sheet, waiting for "that" day. She'd been given bridal showers by three local groups and the gifts sat in the basement, waiting for their new home. She'd chosen her bridesmaid, flowers, even the invitations. But although she had spoken to Chris almost every night on the phone, by March she still had no bridegroom and no wedding date.

"He'll be here, dearie." Faith breezed into the office with a smile. "The Lord works in mysterious ways, His wonders to perform."

"Uh, thank you." Jori stared at the woman assessingly. There was something different about her today. A light, she decided. Some inner joy that made her glow beautifully.

"You seem especially happy today, Mrs. Johnson. Is something special happening?"

"Just the spring," Hope Conroy interrupted, stepping into the waiting room with careful regard for the mud on her feet. "She always gets like this in the spring."

"In the spring a young girl's fancy turns to love," Faith misquoted, winking at Jori.

"Did you want to see Dr. Green or Dr. Dan today?" Jori decided to focus on her job. These days it was all that kept her sane.

"Oh, we're waiting for Charity," Faith informed her with a grin. "Then we're all going in together."

"Together? The three of you?" When Hope nodded her agreement, Jori shrugged and made a notation on the book before taking another stack of files from Dan's basket. By the time she returned, the three ladies had disappeared.

It was a relatively slow day so Jori began typing out the forms that lay waiting and tried not to think of Chris's phone call last night. He'd seemed distant, preoccupied. And when she'd pressed him about his location, he'd been vague.

"I'm hopping around a lot," he'd said. "Trying to get things organized. I'm hoping I can be with you soon."

Soon. It was an old line, and frankly Jori was growing tired of it. She'd managed to get through Christmas by spending time with her dad and having a long phone conversation with Chris. He'd spent all of January traveling with a group of medical men in Australia, which seemed hardly fair considering the winter she'd suffered through in Mossbank.

In February, Chris had suddenly decided to update himself on some medical thing that was happening in England and so she hadn't been able to write to him there, either. He wasn't going to be in one place, he said. Moving around a lot.

There had been flowers, lots of them, for Valentine's Day. And a monstrous box of Parisian chocolates that Jori dared not eat in case he came back and she didn't fit her dress. He'd even sent her a necklace, which was wonderful, and she'd thanked him for it. But she would rather have had him.

"If you'd tell me where you'll be, I could arrange to

take my holidays there," she had murmured sadly. "At least we could be together for a while. I miss you."

"Oh, Jori! You know I want to be there more than anything. And I will be. I think things are finally beginning to move forward."

But when she'd pressed him on how forward, he'd changed the subject.

"Just be patient. I am coming. Probably sooner than you expect."

"It couldn't be soon enough for me," she told him, stifling the sobs that tried to break through her iron control. "We can go anywhere, Chris. As soon as I'm finished here in September, I intend to find you. And you're not putting me off."

"I wouldn't dream of it!" He'd sounded amused, and Jori had petulantly said goodbye, wondering if he'd changed his mind about wanting her. It was the end of March, for goodness' sake, and nothing, to her knowledge, had changed.

"You can go home early today, Jori," Dan offered, emerging from a consulting room with a grin. "And I'm officially giving you next week off. You need a break."

"No, I don't," Jori protested, frustrated by everyone's good intent. She was alone, she wanted to be with Chris and she needed to keep busy. "I'll want extra time off when Chris comes, so I need to pile up the hours now."

"Well, you're piling up too many hours," Dan informed her sternly. "I know all about the extra shifts you've been putting in at the nursing home. But they won't be calling you this weekend. I've told them that you're to be off for a week." He smiled sadly. "Look at you, kiddo. You're skin and bones. Go home, have a bubble bath and order in some Chinese food. Relax and get some color back into those cheeks. And that's an order. Now, get out of here."

"Yes, sir, Doctor," she muttered gloomily, and shut down the computer dutifully.

"No, leave the filing. I want you to go home and relax. Understand? Liza can't use a baby-sitter who's burned out, you know."

"I'm going, I'm going," Jori muttered, grabbing her purse and heading out the door. "Boy, you've gotten really bossy lately. Must be fatherhood."

"You'll know all about it some day," Dan told her seriously. "Now, get going. And remember, go straight home."

"Yeah, okay." But as she headed down the street, Jori changed her mind and headed for the nursing home to see her father. Maybe he, at least, was having a good day.

James wasn't in his room so she checked in at the nursing station.

"I'm looking for my father," she said clearly. "James Jessop. Can you tell me where he is?"

"He was with the doctor a moment ago. In the television room, I think." The harried nurse turned away to remonstrate with a candy striper who had just knocked some medications on the floor.

"Okay, thanks." Jori strode down the hall, pleased to see her father standing by the window. "Hi, Dad!" She stood on tiptoe and pressed a kiss to his cheek. "What have you been up to?"

"I haven't been up to anything. I don't know why you say that." James looked in a bad humor and Jori took a deep breath for patience.

"I just meant, what have you been doing. The nurse said the doctor was here." She frowned. "I didn't see Dr. Green leave."

"Doctor? What doctor? Do you see any doctor? I was talking to a young fellow—what was his name?" He frowned, slapping his forehead with one hand. "Drat this memory."

"It's all right," she murmured hastily, and then stopped as James walked down the hall. "Where are you going?"

"It's supper time," he told her absently. "They always eat so early in this place. I get hungry at night." He kept going, walking down the hall, muttering to himself.

With a shrug and a deprecatory smile, Jori left the residence and moved toward home. It was a bad day when not even James wanted to talk to her!

She was almost through her front gate when a shrill, persistent voice stopped her.

"Jordanna!" Charity Bellows stood on the front steps of Hope Conroy's house, her face flushed and arms waving.

"Oh, good. I caught you." She scurried over and moments later had her hand on Jori's arm. "I've goofed, I'm afraid. Or rather, Faith has. She thought today was her turn to cook and she's made the most wonderful supper for my birthday."

"Oh, happy birthday," Jori said in confusion.

"Well, thank you, dear. But you see, the thing is, Frank is taking us all out for dinner and we have this food just waiting to be eaten. Might I bring some of it over for you? You've been working so hard lately and I'm sure you could use a good, hot meal."

"That would be very nice. Thank you, Charity."

"Oh, it's my pleasure, dear." She patted Jori's shoulder tenderly. "I know how awful it's been for you. All this dreadful waiting. It's a little bit like in the Bible, isn't it?"

"I'm sorry. I don't know what you mean." Jori frowned, trying to organize her thoughts.

"Yes, you do." Charity chuckled. "Where it talks about Jesus as the bridegroom coming back for us, his bride, and says that we don't know the day or the hour, but we must be ready at any time. That's just like you and Dr. Davis. It's so romantic."

"Isn't it, though?" Jori muttered dourly. "I'd appreciate anything you want to bring over, Charity. And thank you for thinking of me. I'm going to have a long soak in the tub, so just feel free to walk in and leave whatever you want in the kitchen. And thank you. Thanks a lot.''

''You're welcome. I know it's hard,'' she whispered. ''Please don't give up on him. Not yet.'' Then she turned and walked back to Hope's house.

''I won't,'' Jori murmured a long time later, drying herself off. ''But it's getting so hard to keep believing. Help me, Father.''

Jori pulled on a pale peach velour suit that was supposed to be part of her trousseau and started down the stairs, thinking of her dinner. Halfway down, the scent of flowers caught her nostrils and she glanced around, amazed to see huge vases of lilacs and lilies and pansies and daisies scattered around the room. And there, standing in the middle, holding the biggest bouquet of long-stemmed red roses was Christopher Davis.

''Hello, J.J.''

She stared at that dear face, soaking in every detail of it, from his blazing blue eyes to his dazzling white smile.

''Don't you remember who I am?'' he asked quizzically.

With a shriek of delight, Jori bounded down the stairs and across the room, throwing herself into his arms and hanging on for dear life. She sighed with delight as Chris's strong arms tightened around her and his mouth closed firmly over hers.

''I can't wait anymore,'' he breathed before his lips touched hers.

Jori knew exactly what he meant. She kissed him back with all the longing she had kept bottled inside for the past months.

''I love you, Jordanna Jessop,'' he said, his big hands tightening around her tenderly. ''I've missed you so much.'' One hand slipped through the silken length of her hair as he kissed her again and again.

Jori stroked her fingers over his golden head and tanned

face. Nothing seemed real, but if this was a dream, Jori was determined to enjoy it and let time stand still.

"Chris," she murmured, staring into his sleepy blue gaze. "Where did all these flowers come from?"

"I brought them. For you." Chris stared straight into her eyes as he spoke. One hand pressed a small package into her hand.

"So is this."

Jori stared at the package nestled in her hands and carefully opened the black velvet box. Glittering brightly, a wide gold band waited inside. It was a perfect match for the engagement ring Chris had sent her for Christmas.

Chris pulled it free and held it up for her to see. His blue eyes stared solemnly into hers. "I'm not waiting any longer, J.J." he said firmly. "I want us to get married. Right away. I love you," he told her steadily. "Please, say you'll marry me?"

"I—I…"

"Do you love me, Jori?"

Jori nodded. "Oh, yes. I love you more than anything, Christopher Davis. More than I thought I could ever love anyone."

He grinned that silly grin she had come to love.

"Then, darling Jori, does it really matter where we live as long as we're together? Isn't that the important thing?"

"Yes, darling," she told him firmly. "It doesn't matter where we live as long as we are together."

And as she wrapped her arms around his neck and returned his embrace, Jori vowed that she would never let anything come between them again.

As she pressed closer to him, she heard the crackle of papers against her ear.

"What *is* that?" she demanded curiously, thrusting her fingers into his jacket pocket. An envelope with Dan's office letterhead lay there and Jori stared at it curiously.

"Oh, that," Chris murmured, tightening his arms around

her. "Well, that envelope contains our future, my love."
He had a smug, self-satisfied look on his face that Jori
didn't understand.

"Go ahead, read it, my darling," he urged, as he sat
down on the sofa. "Read it."

Jori pulled out the single sheet of letterhead and at-
tempted to decipher the legalese covering it. She could
make out Chris's name at the top, the word *partner,* and
Dan's signature below. Hope billowed in her like a sail
catching a morning breeze.

"Chris?" she whispered, half afraid to believe.

He puffed out his chest before swinging her up in his
arms and dancing around the room.

"You are looking at the newest partner of the Community Health Clinic located in Mossbank, North Dakota," he
told her triumphantly. "I'm buying out Dr. Green's interest."

"But I thought…your mother said…Dr. Green is…"
Jori stumbled over all the questions running through her
mind. She was afraid to believe her fantasy had come true.

"Yes," he muttered, "my mother." He tipped her chin,
blue eyes meeting her soft brown ones. "My mother was
wrong about a lot of things. But especially about Mossbank
and my future. It's here, with you."

His kiss made Jori forget the questions that seemed so
important. Nothing was more significant than the fact that
Chris was here, holding her. She did allow one tiny doubt
to surface.

"Are you sure this is what you should do?" Jori peered
at him anxiously.

"Sweetheart, I've spent years doing what was expected
of me. My parents wanted me to go to medical school. I
went. They wanted me to choose a specialty. I did. They
wanted me to work in Boston and I did that, too, hoping it
would satisfy that need I had inside for their love, their

approval. But while I was here, I realized that my parents' dreams aren't mine. They never were.''

He kissed her nose and leaned back tiredly.

''I was wrong to let them superimpose their belief system on mine. I thought going back and teaching was what I wanted, but it was just another case of accepting other people's opinions over my own instinct.'' He glanced down tenderly, his hands closing around hers as one finger played with the brilliant solitaire on her left hand.

''By December, I realized that what I wanted was you and what I had right here. But I didn't know how to get it. Those months I spent here were the most satisfying medical moments I've experienced in a long time. I felt like I mattered and I knew that I wanted to keep you in my life. I just didn't know how God was going to work it all out. Now I know. And, yes, I'm sure.

''So, what do you say about marrying me tomorrow?'' he offered.

''I just happen to have a week off,'' she murmured. ''Thanks to Dan.'' She eyed Chris severely, a gleam of suspicion lighting the brown depths.

''Wait a minute,'' she demanded. ''Do you mean to tell me Dan was in on this?'' She was furious at the agony she had been through while her boss had known all along. Her fiancé nodded.

''You mean I sat here, alone, wishing, when he knew all along…'' Jori slapped at his shoulder in frustration.

''Don't be angry at Dan,'' he pleaded with her. ''It took me a while to realize what I had left behind.'' His hands tightened around her, hugging her close. ''When I did, I wanted to tell you myself. And then, of course, the ladies helped, too.''

''What ladies?'' she asked.

''Faith, Hope and Charity, of course. They remembered Dr. Green talking about retiring and when they questioned him, found that he hadn't because he'd never been able to find anyone to move here. He didn't want the townsfolk to suffer." Chris beamed at her. "When I phoned him and made an offer, he jumped at it like a trout after bait. Seems his wife wants him to travel and he's pretty keen on the idea himself."

"The Lord works in mysterious ways," Jori murmured, trying to understand it all, but losing the battle when Chris hugged her close.

"Amen," he murmured into her ear.

"Something's burning," she murmured at last, and whisked out of his arms to retrieve a smoking loaf of garlic bread from out of the oven. Fortunately, only the paper had been singed.

As she turned, Jori caught sight of a small hand-painted card on the counter.

"Chris, come and look at this," she called, and found him right behind her, his arms slipping around her waist.

"*'They that wait upon the Lord shall renew their faith. Teach me Lord to wait.'* We think you've waited long enough."

"It's signed Faith and Arthur Johnson, Hope and Harry Conroy, Charity and Frank Bellows."

"Angels of mercy," Chris agreed.

Epilogue

Jori panted through the tail end of the contraction and flopped back against her pillows tiredly.

"That's it," she huffed. "I can't do any more."

"Jordanna Jessop Davis! You've been bugging me about babies for as long as I can remember. And now that you're finally going to get your own, you're wimping out? I don't believe it." Daniel Gordon's stern look flashed above the white surgical mask. "Quitter!"

"Dan!" Chris's blue eyes were hard and cold. "Leave her alone. If she wants to stop—"

"Are you nuts?" Jori snorted at her husband in disgust. "There's no way I'm stopping this. Ooooh! Here comes another one." She grabbed his hand in her viselike grip and leaned forward, pushing with all her might.

"Push!" Dan ordered.

"I am pushing," she hissed through gritted teeth.

"Here comes another one. Push."

And so, summoning the last ounce of her strength from someplace deep within, Jori pushed with all her might.

"Congratulations! The Davis family now includes a son." Ignoring the squalling cry, Dan lifted the red-faced infant and placed him on his mother's chest. "Well done, Jori."

"A son, Chris! We have a son." Jori beamed up at her husband, towering above them. "He looks a lot like you."

"A boy." Christopher studied the baby, noting the perfect fingers and toes and the thatch of flaxen blond hair. He touched the tiny face carefully before patting his wife's shoulder awkwardly. His eyes were dazed as he gaped stupidly at Dan. "I'm a father."

"Yeah, pal, I know." Dan slapped him on the back, grinning like crazy. "Don't you have somebody to talk to now?" At Chris's puzzled look, he jerked a thumb toward the hallway. "Three nosy old ladies and a grandfather."

"Oh, James. Right." Chris leaned down and kissed his tired wife on the lips. "I'm going to tell your father, Jori. I'll be right back."

"Give her a bit of time to rest and get cleaned up," Dan advised softly. "You can stop by later."

It wasn't much later when Chris returned to his wife's hospital room. She was sleeping but woke immediately, glancing at the bouquet in his hands.

"Oh. Thank you," she murmured as she took the flowers from him.

"You don't like them?"

"Of course I like them. They're beautiful," she whispered, accepting his kiss. She hung on when he would have moved away. "I just somehow thought you'd bring roses."

"Roses?" He sounded scandalized. "You can have roses any day of the week, my darling. These are chrysanthe-*mums* for a mom—the mother of my son!" He stood proudly before her, his eyes glowing with love.

A beautiful smile lit up Jori's face as she laid the bouquet of flowers on the side of the bed and wrapped both arms around his neck, tugging his mouth nearer hers.

"Quite right, my dear husband. After all, how often does one get to be a mother?"

"I don't know." He grinned, brushing his lips against her while his fingers tangled in her hair. "But I'm willing to discuss it again whenever you wish."

Faith, Hope and Charity stood for a moment in front of the nursery, gazing at the lone occupant who slept happily unaware.

"This was by far the hardest case of all," Faith murmured, making silly faces into the glass.

"It took some special doing," Hope agreed, allowing her mouth to curve in a tiny cooing noise.

"That's the truth," Charity whispered, pointing toward the baby. "Sent right from heaven." She glanced at the two elderly ladies making foolish, nonsensical gestures at the sleeping child. "But for once I agree wholeheartedly with James."

"What did he say?" Faith demanded, knocking gently on the glass.

y *"Love bears all things, believes all things, hopes all things, endures all things. Love never fails."* Charity quoted the verse with a smile and threaded her arms through each of the other's.

"Come on girls, let's go home. We've done our job here."

And they toddled off into the night, content with all life offered.

* * * * *

In January 1999, look for Lois Richer's
next Love Inspired story,
A HOME, A HEART, A HUSBAND.

Dear Reader,

Isn't it hard to wait? I'm one of those people who shake Christmas gifts as soon as they arrive, trying to figure out what's inside. I detest long lines and delays in traffic because I want to get on with things. And I simply cannot understand people who dillydally, dithering between one choice or another. For me, the choice is quickly made. Did I mention I often make the *wrong* choice?

Perhaps that's why I empathize with Jori. She's so sure she's made the right decision. She's got things organized, her life is going along as it should, and she's ready for the next step—a baby. The trouble is, God seems to see things differently. And when God says "wait," no matter how hard we try to get around it, we have to wait until finally, His perfect will becomes clear to us mere mortals.

The Bible says that those who wait on God will renew their strength. And it further asks God to "teach" us to wait. You know, that's my prayer, too. But I hope He hurries!

I wish you persistent patience in knowing His will.

Available in
August 1998 from
Love Inspired™...

GOD'S GIFT

by

Dee Henderson

Everything changed for Rachel Ashcroft the moment missionary James Graham walked into her life. He touched her soul in ways she'd never thought possible, and she embraced this precious gift sent straight from heaven above. But as she helped James through his darkest hour, would faith's healing power lead them toward the light of love?

Watch for GOD'S GIFT in August 1998
from Love Inspired

Steeple
Hill™

Available at your favorite retail outlet.

IGG

Take 3 inspirational love stories FREE!

PLUS get a FREE surprise gift!

Special Limited-time Offer

Mail to Steeple Hill Reader Service™
3010 Walden Avenue
P.O. Box 1867
Buffalo, N.Y. 14240-1867

YES! Please send me 3 free Love Inspired™ novels and my free surprise gift. Then send me 3 brand-new novels every month, which I will receive months before they appear in bookstores. Bill me at the low price of $3.19 each plus 25¢ delivery and applicable sales tax, if any*. That's the complete price and a saving of over 10% off the cover prices—quite a bargain! I understand that accepting the books and gift places me under no obligation ever to buy any books. I can always return a shipment and cancel at any time. Even if I never buy another book from Steeple Hill, the 3 free books and the surprise gift are mine to keep forever.

103 IEN CFAG

Name	(PLEASE PRINT)	
Address		Apt. No.
City	State	Zip